The Hound of Music

Susan C. Daffron

An Alpine Grove Romantic Comedy

Book 11

Published by Magic Fur Press
An imprint of Logical Expressions, Inc.
P.O. Box 383
Ponderay, ID 83852

This is a work of fiction. All names, characters, places, and events are either the product of the author's imagination or are used fictitiously. Any resemblance to actual persons, living or dead, business organizations, events, or locales is purely coincidental.

The Hound of Music

ISBN: 978-1-61038-057-7 (paperback)
978-1-61038-058-4 (EPUB)

Like all of my books, *The Hound of Music* is dedicated to my husband James Byrd, my best friend and biggest supporter. Thanks for everything!

<u>Books by Susan C. Daffron</u>

The Alpine Grove Romantic Comedies

Chez Stinky

Fuzzy Logic

The Art of Wag

Snow Furries

Bark to the Future

Howl at the Loon

The Good, the Bad, and the Pugly

The Treasure of the Hairy Cadre

The Luck of the Paw

Daydream Retriever

The Hound of Music

The Jennings & O'Shea Mysteries

Sensing Trouble

Sensing Secrets

Sensing Truth

Chapter 1

Meeting Old Yeller

Tess Mitchell covered her mouth with her hand, stifling a yawn as she gazed across the cavernous paper-strewn room. Her ugly gunmetal gray desk sat in a row of equally ugly desks, steno-pool style. Almost daily, she mentally paraphrased the Bard: "My kingdom for a door."

The only person who had an office with a door was her boss, Geoff, with a G, Porter. He liked to say he had ink running through his veins, but Tess thought it was more likely gasoline. Although he'd been involved in his family's printing and publishing business since he could walk, the man was not much of a people person. Piddly issues would set him off on a fiery tirade, and this morning his ire was directed at Tess. Around the office, everyone knew Geoff never called employees into his inner sanctum to deliver *good* news.

With great reluctance, Tess ventured to his office and sank into the chair in front of his wooden desk. "Everything okay, Geoff?"

"You know it's not." He pushed his chair back, shoved some papers aside, and leaned forward to rest his elbows on the desk. "All this time off you've been taking is a problem. We've always let our sales people work flexible schedules, but you're abusing the privilege."

Tess made a conscious effort to tamp down the involuntary flash of anger. As an actress, she was trained in the art of pretending to feel something she didn't. At least no camera was around to reveal the telltale twitch in her jaw, and Geoff with a G was too self-absorbed to notice. She said evenly, "You know that I've been looking for a new place to live."

"How long does that take? Joey is complaining that you're not pulling your weight around here. He shouldn't have to be covering for you all the time. It's keeping him from tending to his own customers."

"This might be a bad time to mention this, but I need to take next Monday off."

If Geoff had been wearing his toupee, it might have shot off his head from the force of his raised eyebrows. "Are you kidding me?"

"I have an audition in Los Angeles."

"Again? I thought after so much time you'd given up on getting a callback."

"That movie didn't pan out. The producers decided to take the concept in a different direction, and the part I was trying out for was cut. This audition is for something else. It's a part in a commercial." Tess clenched her hands in her lap, mentally willing Geoff not to ask about the product.

"What kind of commercial?"

Crap. Her psychic powers obviously needed some work. "It's for a personal care product."

"What? Like toothpaste or something?"

"Something like that." She wasn't going to get into the specifics with him. "Anyway, I'll make sure that Anna gets her flyers before I head down the hill. She's supposed to give me her ideas for the ad layout as well."

"You'd better. She spends lots of money with us, you know."

"I know." Tess moved in her chair to indicate she was leaving. That commission money was vital to her ability to pay a pet deposit on a new apartment, so she needed to get going. "I have an appointment with Bea in a half hour, so I need to run."

"Fine. Go. Sell something. Sell a lot of somethings." He shook his head in resignation. "If you weren't so good at selling magazine ads and printing, I'd can your butt in a heartbeat."

"Probably." Tess grinned widely as she stood up. "But I *am* that good. And I promise I'm close to finding a new place to live. I can feel it."

"Would you try to feel it more quickly? Summer tourist season is coming up fast, which means lots of people need stuff printed. And ad sales close for the summer 1997 issue of the magazine in two weeks. We can't go past that date."

"I know. I know." Tess gave him a princess wave over her shoulder as she left the office. "Well, it's been nice chatting. Gotta run."

Having managed to successfully skate through another conversation with Geoff without getting fired, Tess got into her car and pointed it toward downtown Alpine Grove. Bea Sullivan owned the gift store in town, and Tess was looking forward to seeing her.

No one in the community was nicer than Bea, and the woman also purchased a lot of magazine advertising to promote her store, which made life better for Tess. Joey would kill to get the Bea Haven Gifts account because the commissions were sizable. Cash flow had been an issue lately and Tess wasn't sure how she'd be able to come up with first and last month's rent along with a pet deposit. Assuming she ever found a new place to live, of course.

Her fists tightened around the steering wheel. After stopping by the gift store, she needed to go drop off Anna's flyers and chat with her, then drive out to the toolies to dump a pile of forms at some new dog-boarding kennel. The owner had provided her own art for the order, so Tess wasn't going to get any commission money on layout, which was annoying. She'd still get credit for the print sale though, and Joey hadn't managed to sneak the account out from under her while she was out of town. That guy could be such a weasel.

If she turned on the charm, maybe she could upsell the boring forms into an order for brochures. The kennel was a fairly new business, after all. March was not looking too promising as far as commissions, so Tess needed to do something. The commission from Bea's ad was already earmarked for the trip to Los Angeles, and everyone else was wiggling around trying to avoid pulling the trigger and signing up for an ad. Sometimes Tess wanted to shake people and scream, "We go through this every single issue. Just sign the contract." But she smiled sweetly and listened to hours upon hours of stories about how the spring "shoulder season" was a challenging time for Alpine Grove businesses.

The good news was that, for a change, Tess had an audition to think about instead of the thrilling world of advertising and printing. Although being a pitch-person in a thirty-second television commercial wasn't perhaps her lifelong dream, it had been way too long since Tess had actually landed a role at all. When she was little, she'd daydreamed about being in musicals on Broadway, but as she got older, she realized L.A. was a lot closer. But now her agent was about to give up on her, and Tess was desperate to get a part playing almost anyone or anything.

The sad fact was that Tess had auditioned for every crummy B movie Hollywood had made in the last five years and received exactly zero offers. She'd tried out for parts as aliens, robots, robotic aliens, fourteen different screaming horror movie victims, and a chicken. As far as celebrity ratings go, not even getting a call-back for a part as a chicken drops you from the D-list down the scale to J, Q, or some other Scrabble letter nobody wants.

Although Tess was generally an optimistic person, failing as an actress in Los Angeles to the point that she had to give up and return to her hometown had been demoralizing. And years later, she was still wasn't any closer to living her dream of being an actress.

At what point did she need to face the fact that working in print sales wasn't just temporary? Was it time to accept the reality that she was doomed to have a job she was good at but didn't like? All those years of drama classes might have helped her become a great salesperson, but not a great, or even good, actress. Maybe that had to be enough.

~

After stopping by the gift store and chatting with Bea, Tess ran home to grab some lunch and scour the newspaper classifieds for any new rental listings. As usual, the paper revealed nothing promising. Many of the ads were for short-term seasonal rentals from a scummy property management company that was known for screwing people out of their deposits. She had enough financial problems without adding that into the mix.

Tess peered over the top of her newspaper and set down her sandwich. She had an audience. Nothing like food to attract her roommates, John, Paul, George, and Ringo. The feline Fab Four believed that human food only existed to be shared with them.

Ringo was a sleek blue gray cat who was inevitably the ringleader. The other cats deferred to his bossy, prissy nature. Although the other cats worshipped him, he was rather aloof toward Tess. Maybe it was because she'd gotten him first. The big gray cat had never quite recovered from the mortal insult of having three unruly kittens added to his world.

But when her neighbor rescued the tiny abandoned litter of kittens from under her front porch, Tess couldn't say no. Laura had begged and pleaded for her to take some of the kittens off her hands and foster them "just for a while until I can find them homes."

Tess should have known that "temporarily fostering" turned out to be code for "you're keeping these cats forever." And when you have a cat named Ringo already, it's pretty much inevitable that you name the three newcomers after the rest of the Beatles.

Technically, Paul was Paula. It's difficult to tell the sex of a tiny kitten and Paul was no exception. The brown and gray tabby was one of those cats who liked to get into everything. If a cat was doing something bad, it was likely to be Paul. While Paul was doing something rotten, George was probably running away.

Like Paul, George had some gender identity issues, and she was actually Georgette. If Tess had known more about cats, she would have realized that as a calico, there was a ninety-nine percent chance that George was female. Oh well.

Naming issues aside, George was a kitty lunatic. Her motto was run first, ask questions later. Tess thought she might be slightly insane or, at a minimum, at least a bit addled. Maybe her momma kitty had dropped poor Georgie on her head or something.

Although cat ladies aren't supposed to play favorites, John was one of those love-bug cats that everyone adored. The big orange tabby had round bulls-eye swirls on his sides and Tess thought of him as her "philosophical" cat because he would spend hours sitting in the windowsill contemplating the wildlife outside. And when he wasn't busy considering the fate of the universe, he was in her lap.

Tess leaned back and crossed one of her legs up on the chair, so John had a nice spot to settle in for a nap. He jumped up, curled into a ball in the crook of her leg, and began to purr as she stroked his rusty-colored stripes. Tess sighed, trying to let go of the stress of her conversation with Geoff. "So, Johnny-boy, you big orange galoot, what are we going to do about our housing situation, huh?"

John paused in his purring, raised his head, and gave her a blank stare. Tess smiled. "Yeah, I have no idea either. No one seems to want to rent a place to someone with four cats. It's unfair."

The term *cat lady* was so polarizing. At what point did a woman officially cross the line from a person who appreciated the unique qualities of felines to a true cat lady? When Tess had only one cat, people smiled and remarked that Ringo was a cute name. Now that she was a single woman living with four cats, the undertones of disapproval and tell-tale whispers were harder to ignore.

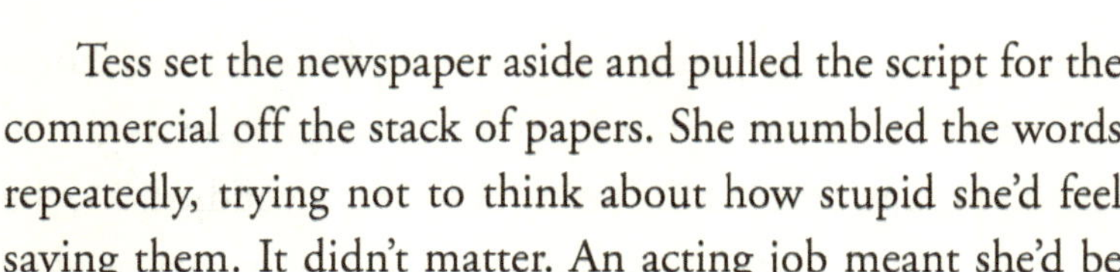

Tess set the newspaper aside and pulled the script for the commercial off the stack of papers. She mumbled the words repeatedly, trying not to think about how stupid she'd feel saying them. It didn't matter. An acting job meant she'd be acting. And getting paid.

The phone rang once and stopped, but once was enough for George, who leaped up and bolted from the kitchen. Paul yowled and ran after her in hot pursuit. Ringo glared at Tess briefly before sauntering out of the room.

Tess finished her sandwich and gently encouraged John to vacate her lap. "Okay, lunch is over. Time to find a new sleep spot."

The cat landed on the floor with a heavy thud and waddled out of the kitchen. It might be time to cut back on his food, but with four cats and a complicated schedule, trying to feed them separately was almost impossible.

Tess glanced at the clock. Was that the time? She looked at her watch. So much for getting out to the boarding kennel before two. The woman she'd talked to asked her not to come too late because she'd be busy walking dogs out on the forested trails near the kennel.

Tess dumped some cat food in the dish, grabbed her things, and ran out to the car, continuing to mumble her lines like a mantra. Memorizing lines was the worst part of acting. And in a short commercial, people weren't going to excuse even the slightest screw up.

As she got into the car, she reminded herself she had lots of acting experience. Years of it, in fact. Performing had been all Tess had wanted to do for as long as she could remember. When she was in high school, she'd been in every school play, taken every drama class, and been a member of choir, glee club, and even the debate team. If it involved using her voice, she was involved.

Of course, all those speaking roles also gave her a reputation for being unable to shut up. Hours in detention after school had given her lots of time to study her lines though. Sadly, in the strict social strata of high school, constantly talking to yourself in the hallways didn't tend to improve your popularity, so Tess had mostly hung out with the stage and band geeks.

As she rolled to a stop at the single light in Alpine Grove, the car made an un-car-like belching noise, which it tended to do when Tess was in a hurry. The Hyundai Excel had been the first brand new car Tess had bought for herself, mostly because it was almost the cheapest car in existence. Only a Yugo was less expensive, but those things were just too hideous. Tess did have a few—okay, very few—automotive standards. The boring, blue four-door sedan had about as much get up and go as a geriatric turtle with arthritis, but it usually was able to transport her from place to place. An old boyfriend once told her that the Excel sported a cool eighty-six horses under the hood, which Tess came to understand was a very small herd indeed.

The only good thing was that when Tess had purchased the car, she'd opted for a manual transmission because it was cheaper. Sometimes she could put the Excel in second gear and gun it, pretending it could roar up to twenty-five miles an hour. It squeaked and groaned all the way, but to its credit, it had hauled many boxes of printed materials in its trunk, keeping the businesses of Alpine Grove stocked with marketing necessities like brochures and flyers.

The dashboard clock had died a couple of years ago so Tess checked her watch. She was so incredibly late. Upselling these people on more printing was looking less promising with every passing minute.

~

Tess slowed the car to turn onto one of the long winding dirt roads north of town. She hadn't been this far out into the forest in quite some time. Although it was beautiful out here in the sticks, the roads were in terrible shape after a long winter of climatic abuse. Mud season was not the most appealing time of year in Alpine Grove, and it was easy to see why most of the vehicles owned by local residents sported a thick coating of grayish dirt. And all-wheel drive.

Maybe it was true of any place with dirt roads, but complaining about the holes, ruts, and washboards was a local pastime. People whined that their road was the "last one to be graded," as if the road department were plotting against their specific neighborhood.

Tess turned onto another dirt road that seemed to be in better shape, so she sped up a little. Being over an hour late was beyond the pale, and she pressed the accelerator, causing the car to rattle a little more as she navigated a bumpy section in the middle of the road.

The lump of dirt and rocks in the road became more pronounced, and when she skittered around a corner, Tess found out why. She yanked her steering wheel to the right to avoid ending up hitting the rear end of a gigantic yellow road grader that was moving at a snail's pace. The Hyundai's tires caught on some rocks, and the little car slid into the small ditch that ran alongside the road before promptly stalling out.

Momentarily stunned that she'd actually fallen off the road, Tess looked ahead of her. The grader had stopped. How completely embarrassing. With no ice or snow, Tess had no excuse other than speeding for landing in the ditch. She put the car in neutral, started the engine, and shifted it into reverse. Maybe she could get this crummy tin can back on the road before anyone noticed.

The dirt was loose and muddy, and the front tires spun ineffectually. Tess turned off the engine and opened the door to examine the situation. Now she would be even later dropping off these stupid forms.

She stood next to the car and placed one hand on the hood so she could lean over and check out the ruts the front tires had created. The situation was not looking good down there.

At the touch on her shoulder, Tess wheeled around and came face-to-face with someone she hadn't seen in more than a decade. She sputtered, "Luke, what are you doing here?"

He pointed at the grader. "Working on the road."

Tess had gone to high school with Luke Bennett although she'd had almost no contact with him because he'd been a jock and card-carrying members of the popular crowd like him rarely had any contact with stage geeks like her. Luke had been on the football team, and Tess had talked to him a couple of times when he was dating her friend Claire. That breakup had been legendary, and after the relationship had flamed out so spectacularly, Claire still had plenty of unkind words to say about the guy whenever the topic came up.

Somehow Luke looked different than Tess remembered. He was still tall with broad shoulders and the athletic build of someone who excelled in sports. His hair was still reddish and unruly, and obviously, he was older, but something about the shape of his face seemed different. His nose was narrower, and somehow the change made his sky blue eyes even more striking.

In high school, before she detested the ground he walked on, Claire had mooned about how cute Luke was, going on and on about his appearance to the point that Tess regularly had to tell her friend to shut up. Claire had been a cheerleader and liked to talk about the day Luke had lost a tooth in football practice senior year.

Because his teeth had obviously been fixed sometime in the last decade, Luke was now arguably considerably better looking, cruising the high road toward downright handsome. If Claire hadn't hated his guts, she might have swooned at the grown-up version of Luke.

Tess smiled weakly and gestured at the car. Why was it in a small town, you somehow managed to run into the last person you ever wanted to see? "I'm glad I didn't hit you."

"I promise that in an argument with Old Yeller, your car would have lost."

Tess tilted her head to gaze up at the massive machine, which was the golden yellow color typical of most heavy equipment. The machine appeared to be in remarkably good shape. "I think that's the cleanest road grader I've ever seen."

"Maintenance is important." He gestured toward the Hyundai. "Do you need help getting out?"

"I think I dug a hole in the side of your road."

"These things happen." He turned toward the grader. "Old Yeller has a winch. It'll take two minutes to yank out a lightweight car like that."

As it turned out, Luke wasn't wrong. Tess watched as he clambered back up into the grader, laboriously turned it onto a side road, and backed it up for an extremely large three-point turn. He drove past her car, so the back end of the grader was ten feet or so from the Hyundai.

When Luke opened the door to get out, a large German shepherd-like dog poked his head out, standing and panting in the cab with his big tongue hanging out. The dog had pointy ears, but short hair, so Tess guessed he might be mixed with some type of hunting dog like a coonhound. The way the corners of his mouth curved while he was panting made it look like he was smiling. Luke waved at the dog and said, "Get back, Barney," before slamming the door.

After hooking the winch to the car, he turned it on and with ten seconds of whirring, the tiny Hyundai was back on the road. Luke smiled at Tess. "Normally I do this kind of thing in the winter."

Tess shrugged. "I was in a hurry."

"Out here? Where were you going?"

"Some dog kennel out in the toolies called the Wag On Inn. I'm really, really late though." Tess didn't want to talk to this guy and made a point of looking at her watch. "Okay, now I'm even later."

"I think I know that place. I did some work for them a while ago when they set up the kennels."

Tess wasn't sure what to say. Claire hated this guy with a fiery vengeance, but it had been kind of him to pull her out of the ditch. "Well, thanks for your help. I should deliver these forms."

"Yeah, I gotta get this done so I can get back to town. I'm told my rental tenants are causing a neighborhood scandal, so I need to check on the place."

Tess repressed a giggle. "A scandal in Alpine Grove? Say it ain't so."

"One of my neighbors called after the tenants decided to try out a nudist lifestyle on the front lawn. People aren't too excited about seeing Willy's little willy when they're out walking the dog."

"I hate to ask this, but what's Willy doing on the front lawn?"

"Meditating or something. I don't know. Sounds like he sits there with his legs crossed and mumbles a lot." Luke grinned. "Kinda like you used to do in high school."

"I wasn't *mumbling*. I was practicing lines."

"Sounded like mumbling to everyone else. You do know everyone called you Mumbles, right?"

Tess tamped down her irritation. No one ever forgot *anything* in this town. "Yes, of course, I know. That's one of many reasons I didn't go to the ten-year reunion last year."

"I didn't either, but I heard Carl is now Carla. Oh, and Beth Connolly and Drew Emery got married."

"You're kidding! But they broke up. I know because I talked to him after she left for Arizona. The poor guy was a mess."

"Guess they made up sometime in the last decade." He raised his eyebrows. "I suppose you're still in contact with Claire, huh?"

"Yes."

"She still hates me, doesn't she?"

Tess nodded. "You might think ten or eleven years and moving thousands of miles away would have cooled her anger, but you'd be wrong."

"That figures. She'll never change." He shrugged. "What can you do?"

Tess pointed at her car. "Well, it's been nice catching up, but I need to get going. Thanks again."

"It was good to see you, Tess. Take care."

Tess waved as she got into the car and watched Luke walk back to the grader and climb up into the driver's seat. She giggled. Claire would flip out when she heard that Luke Bennett had a naked guy in his front yard. Tess couldn't wait to get home so she could pour a glass of wine, call her best friend, and share this bizarro trip down memory lane with her.

~

Tess drove much more slowly the rest of the way to the kennel. The place was located down a long driveway that wound through the forest. A log house sat beyond a gate and the dog kennels were located off to the left, nestled in a grove of huge cedars. Tess parked in the designated area and got out. The sound of many dogs barking filled the air. No one would be sneaking up on this place.

Tess stood and looked up at the enormous cedar trees that shaded the kennel buildings. There was a large fenced-in area behind the kennels, but no one seemed to be around. Maybe the woman was out walking dogs like she'd said.

As the canine cacophony subsided, Tess leaned on her car and recited the lines for her commercial audition to a squirrel sitting on a nearby rock. Apparently unimpressed, he ran off.

Oh well, it wasn't surprising that he had no interest in the product.

A thumping sound came from behind her, and when Tess turned to look, she found a gigantic dog thundering toward her. She leaned as close as possible to the Hyundai, plastering herself alongside the door as the great creature skidded to a stop. "Nice doggie."

The large brown shaggy dog wagged his tail and panted happily. Tess reached out to let him sniff her hand, and then petted his head. "Why are you just wandering through the trees without an owner?"

A female voice shouted, "Linus, where are you?" The dog spun around and galloped back the way he'd come.

A woman with her strawberry blonde hair pulled back into a ponytail came out of the trees with three dogs on leashes and the big brown dog trotting alongside her.

Tess started away from the car. This woman must be who she'd talked to earlier. With a sigh, Tess strolled past the kennel down the trail to meet her. Stopping in front of the woman and dog, Tess put out her hand, and said, "You must be Mia."

A flicker of an emotion flashed in the woman's eyes as she moved the leashes to one hand. Finally, she stammered, "Are you Test? I mean Tact, umm, *Tess*?"

"I'm sorry I'm late." Tess pulled her hand back since it looked like the leashes were complicated and rapidly forming into a knot.

"I tried to calm…*call*, you earlier, but the guy said you'd left. We had a problem and I don't have a check. The owner, Kat, left me a pile of signed checks before she went on her honeymoon, but…" Mia leaned over to disentangle a basset hound's leash from around her leg. She straightened and continued, "We had to call a plumber. It's been a bad day. A really long and really bad day. And I'm sorry, but I can't pay you. The plumber got the last check. Believe me, no stack of forms could be as important as getting that fixed."

Tess clenched her teeth. Geoff would have a fit if he found out about the lack of payment. "Since I'm already here, I'll just drop off the box of forms. When does Kat return?"

"This weekend they fly back from Hawaii." Mia waved her hands in a gesture of frustration and the three dogs looked up at her in surprise. "Two more days. I'm counting the hours. This has been an incredibly stressful two weeks. I'm going to need a vacation to recover from her vacation."

They arrived at the kennel door and Mia moved to go inside. "Let me get these guys settled, and I'll take the forms."

Tess stood outside with the huge dog. She looked down at him. "So you're Linus, huh?"

The dog wagged again and looked pleased that she knew his name. Tess stroked his head. "I guess you want your momma back too, don't you?"

Mia came back outside, and Tess got the forms out of the trunk. Mia refused to elaborate on what the plumbing problem was, and Tess asked her the same question she asked everyone she met. "Do you know of any rentals available in Alpine Grove?"

Mia didn't seem privy to any good intel on places to live, and the conversation stalled into awkward silence, so Tess gave up on small talk. Mia clearly wasn't in a chatty or even a good mood, and after saying their goodbyes, Tess made a mental note to call on Monday to get the money from the owner. What a huge pain. She'd have to drive all the way out here again if she wanted to sweet-talk them into more printing. At least the heavy boxes of paper were out of her trunk.

On the way back to town, Tess waved at Luke who was still grading the road. What an unbelievably tedious job that must be. This time she made a point of driving slowly and carefully avoided the big mound of dirt in the middle of the road. Seeing that guy once every ten years or so was plenty.

Back home, the Fab Four were adamant that it was dinnertime. Tess was late for the feeding program, and the feline team yowled their displeasure. After taking care of their needs, she checked her messages. Her agent hadn't returned her call about the upcoming audition, and not surprisingly, no one had magically come forward with a new place for her to live either.

She settled in with the classified ads again. There had to be something. Although finding a rental in the spring was difficult, nothing should be this hard. As Tess methodically went through each ad, she placed a check mark next to the people she'd already talked to and circled the ones that were left. A rustic off-grid cabin twenty-five miles out of town was not an appealing option.

In Alpine Grove real-estate speak, *off-grid* meant the electricity didn't work reliably, and *rustic* was a euphemism for falling-down shack. A place was available in Gleasonville, but the commute to work in Alpine Grove would be impossible with her unreliable vehicle. There was no getting around it: Tess needed a place to live in town. After asking everyone she knew and turning over every possible stone, it appeared absolutely nothing was available at all. Didn't anyone ever move out of this town? What was she going to do?

Weary of being alone with her thoughts, she got up and poured the glass of wine she'd promised herself earlier. Claire had grown up in Alpine Grove too, so she'd understand. What were best friends for if not to commiserate about the unfairness of life and having to live in a small town that didn't have enough rental properties?

Tess was all ready to settle in for a big gossip session, but it was not to be because she got Claire's answering machine instead of her friend. Tess patiently waited for the beep and said, "Hey, it's me. I have some great hometown dirt to share with you. Call me back when you get a chance."

John jumped into her lap, curled up, and began purring. Tess stroked the soft orange fur on his back. "At least you're always here for me, right Johnny-boy? How about you help me run some lines, okay?"

John continued to snore contentedly, which Tess took to mean, "Sure, I'd love to hear you recite that string of words for the ten thousandth time."

Chapter 2

Denials

Kat Stevens was curled up on the rattan sofa with a novel, sipping a piña colada and reveling in the last days of her honeymoon. Not working had a lot to recommend it. Not working in a tropical paradise was even better. Kauai in early April was a festival of greenery. Even the plants had plants growing on them. After almost two weeks on the island, she and Joel had explored every corner, checking it out from land, sea, and air.

The condo where they were staying was located right on the ocean with sliding glass doors that opened onto a balcony overlooking the beach. The night they'd arrived, the tropical breezes were so intoxicating, Joel had been unwilling to sleep in the back bedroom away from the sound of the ocean. They'd dragged the mattress into the living room and slept in front of the sliding glass door, letting the sound of the waves lull them to sleep.

Even now, Joel was sprawled out on the mattress reading. Or maybe sleeping. They'd taken a long hike on the Kalalau trail, which hugged the Na Pali coast. By the time they'd returned, both of them were sunburnt and exhausted. Kat had read the same paragraph three times, but she was on "island time" and so relaxed that she didn't care when her eyes closed again.

She lurched awake at the jarring sound of the phone ringing. After so much time away from clients calling wanting to board dogs, the noise was particularly alarming. Joel sat up, looking confused, and she said, "Got it" as she hustled by him into the kitchen.

Kat was surprised to find her house sitter, Mia, on the other end of the line. A flash of panic skimmed across her chest. "Are the dogs okay? What happened? Did the house burn down? Is someone sick?"

"Just your plumbing," Mia said. "I had to use the last check to pay the guy."

"Plumbing?" The last time Kat had a plumbing failure at the house, the shower had self-destructed, and Joel had fixed it. "Was there another flood?"

"It's the septic line. Things aren't draining, and things… well…there's gurgling. Um, you probably don't want the details, but it's not good."

"Wow." Kat put her palm over her eyes.

Joel placed his hand on Kat's shoulder and whispered, "What's going on?"

Kat made a face and mouthed, "Septic."

Mia said, "The plumber thinks tree roots are growing into the pipe or something. The pooper…I mean plumber wasn't clear about what's wrong exactly, except that he can't fix it. He said we should go next door and use the toilet in my trailer until you dig out the pipe that goes to the septic tank."

"Dig out?"

"I don't suppose you know anyone with a backhoe, do you?"

Kat paused. They'd met just about every person in the Alpine Grove construction industry when they'd put up the dog kennels. "Maybe. I'll ask Joel about it."

"What time are you going to be back here on Saturday?"

"Probably really late or even Sunday morning because we have to drive from the airport. It depends on how awful the traffic is getting out of L.A."

Mia said quietly, "You know how we talked about me maybe taking a few days off after you get back?"

"Yes."

"Chris is insisting that I take time off as soon as possible."

"Okay. I'll talk to you on Sunday." Kat hung up the phone and looked up at Joel. "I think Chez Stinky is returning to form. We have to dig up the septic line. Do you remember who did the excavation work for the kennels?"

"That was Luke Bennett."

"We need to call him. The trees are trying to invade the septic system."

Joel bent to kiss her. "I don't have his number here, so it will have to wait."

Kat looked at her watch. "It's three hours earlier here. I don't want to call Mia back because I think she might hate me a little right now."

"Then have some more piña colada. You'll feel better."

"No, we need to get him lined up as soon as possible. I'll call Maria and have her look up Luke's number in the phone book. She's probably just sitting on the couch watching *Friends* and eating a Twinkie."

"True."

"We have to return to real life in two days and I want indoor plumbing."

Joel shrugged and strolled back over to the mattress on the floor. "Say hi to Maria. I plan to continue with denial and relaxation for the time being."

Kat picked up the phone and dialed Maria's number, smiling at the sound of her friend's voice. "I need a favor."

Maria yelped, "You're not home already are you, girlfriend? No one cuts a honeymoon short. Well, unless you decided the engineer wasn't Mr. Right after all. What happened? Was there drama? Are you divorced already?"

"There's no drama. I'm still in Kauai and Joel is too. We're still married and having a good time here. No divorce is on the horizon, but it sounds like the plumbing at the house has a major problem. Chez Stinky is living up to its name again, so I need you to look in the phone book for the number for a guy named Luke Bennett. He's a heavy equipment operator."

"Is he hot? How about cute? I mean, the situation is pretty desperate, and I'm settling for cute."

"I suppose he's cute, but I think you're missing the point here. Our plumbing needs help."

"Maybe I should pay him a personal visit. How cute is he? Does he have all his teeth?"

"Let me call him first. If you want to watch him dig up our yard, you can. But I need his phone number."

"Oh yeah, one sec." The phone thumped, and Kat heard Maria yelling at her cat Scarlett to stop climbing the curtains. The tabby was a particularly acrobatic little feline.

Maria came back on the line and recited the number. "So are you going to tell me tales of tropical sexual exploits when you return? Because I got nothing here. It's a barren wasteland of love. Spring in Alpine Grove is nasty. Everyone's griping and whining about the mud. I can't wear my heels, and it's pissing me off."

"You couldn't wear them in the snow either."

"But then I could wear those furry boots and look like a ski bunny."

Kat glanced at Joel who had termed Maria's winter fashion attire "early Sasquatch," a fact that she'd never shared with her friend. "Yeah, well, the snow will be back before you know it."

"I miss you, girlfriend. It's dull without you here, and I'm bored. We need a wine and whine evening to help me recover. There are stories in the naked city that I need to share. There are even naked stories."

Kat laughed. "Naked stories?"

"Yeah, I guess there was a sit-in on someone's lawn the other day. The whole town was talking about it. I guess there was nudity and shriveling because hey, it's spring and it's still cold out there. These people really need to plan better."

"The smart nudist waits until summer to embark on his protests."

"Exactly, girlfriend. Timing is everything. Anyway, apparently they're protesting the fact that squirrels need more trees. These guys have been creating a better squirrel habitat by modifying their house."

"What do you mean modifying?"

"The back of the place looks funky. Maybe they own the house, but if they're renting, whoever owns that place might be a little upset. Unless he's a squirrel supporter too. There could be a whole squirrel movement happening for all I know."

"Alpine Grove is full of trees. How could the squirrels possibly need more?"

"I don't know the specific details of the political situation that caused the uprising. Or low rising because, you know, with the shriveling and all."

"You went to look, didn't you?"

"I confess I did. Some things you gotta see, and it's been a long time since I've seen a naked man. So I figured what the heck. It's like performance art. But smaller."

"I thought size wasn't supposed to matter."

"Well, that's a lie, girlfriend, and you know it. We've had that conversation."

"True. I should go, but I'll see you in a few days." Kat hung up the phone and crawled onto the mattress next to Joel. "I got the number, so I can call this guy tomorrow. But right now, I'm ready to share in your embracing of denial."

He wrapped his arms around her. "We've only got two more days. I suggest we make the most of it."

"This has been the best trip I've ever taken in my life."

"Mine too. And it's not over yet."

Kat kissed him enthusiastically. You could cram a whole lot of denial into two days if you set your mind to it.

~

The next morning, Tess did some packing and fretting about the fact that she still hadn't heard from her agent about the upcoming audition. Sure, she had the script, but the audition was on Monday. Shouldn't she have received more details by now? It was Friday for heaven's sake. Knowing where in Los Angeles she was supposed to meet these people would be helpful.

The cats were starting to realize that something was up with all the boxes in their environment. At first, they thought it was great. "Boxes are the *best* toys." But now they were starting to become suspicious that Tess was up to something. George had been hiding more than usual, which was a bad sign. One time, Tess misplaced George for a while. The cat was extremely skilled at hiding when she didn't want to be found. Tess was trying not to worry that the cat would opt to disappear on moving day. Of course, at this rate, they might all end up moving into the Hyundai.

Tess reflected wistfully about the house she'd grown up in. It was located right in the heart of Alpine Grove, but her parents had sold it when they retired to go play golf in Arizona. Dad had been a dentist who made good on his promise to get away from the snow one day and never look inside anyone's mouth again. They would have sold the house to her if it had been feasible, but there was no way she could have afforded it then or now. She'd been living in Los Angeles when Mom and Dad had decided to retire anyway, so it hadn't even been discussed.

Tess was dawdling with various packing and organizational tasks, so she'd have enough time to talk to her agent before heading into work. At precisely eight a.m., she planned to call her agent, Chloe Laramore, so her call would be the first one the woman received the moment she walked into her office.

When Tess had lived in Los Angeles, she'd gotten a few nonunion jobs and met Chloe, who had been impressed enough to represent her. After Tess was forced to return to Alpine Grove for financial reasons, she'd hoped Chloe would continue to help her get work, but that hadn't been the case. Tess was pretty sure Chloe had filed her stack of head shots in the circular bin and was preparing to drop Tess as a client entirely.

After dreaming about acting for years and struggling to work long-distance in a few plays, Tess had decided she would do it for real. She moved to Los Angeles and committed to pursuing a film-and-television career full-time. She needed acting credits and the only way to get them was to behave like a professional, get decent head shots, and make a demo reel. Armed with the goods, she could pound the pavement for auditions.

Tess had arrived in the big city during "pilot season," which runs from January through April. After countless auditions, she hadn't landed anything except a failed TV pilot, a few walk-on parts as an extra, and a couple of commercials. Although one of the commercials had led her to Chloe, Tess had never had enough money to pay the fees to join the union, so she still didn't have her SAG card, which limited the roles she could try out for. By the end of the summer, Tess was flat broke and unable to get even a crummy waitressing job that would pay for the rent on her dingy apartment in a scary neighborhood.

Depressed, demoralized, and more than a little afraid for her safety, she'd had a tearful conversation with her father and let him convince her that moving back to her hometown would be a good idea. Dad had told her about the job at the printing company and scored her an interview. Geoff was a golfing buddy of Dad's and had loved her enthusiasm when they chatted on the phone about the job. Of course, Geoff had no idea what a good actress she was, and when she returned to Alpine Grove for an in-person interview, she did such a good job of faking eagerness to have the job that he hired her on the spot. The sad fact was that since then, most of the time Tess had lived in Alpine Grove she'd wanted to return to L.A.

When the clock finally reached eight, Tess picked up the phone. Chloe answered on the first ring and said in a businesslike tone, "Laramore Agency."

"Chloe, hi. It's Tess."

After a short, yet significant pause, Chloe said in a syrupy voice, "Tess, it's so fabulous to hear from you, hon. How's life treating you in Cedar Cove?"

Tess tried not to grind her teeth. Chloe had a habit of calling people "hon" when she was blowing them off. "It's Alpine Grove, and I'm fine. Remember how you got me that commercial audition on Monday? I still don't know where it is being held. I'm taking off work, but I need to know the address and the time they want me there."

"Commercial?"

"You told me about it last month and sent me the script. I've been practicing my lines, and I'm absolutely positive I'll nail the audition this time."

"Mmm, yeah, let me look that up."

Tess tapped her fingers on the kitchen counter. Come on, how hard could this be? "Chloe, are you there?"

"Yes, yes, I've got it right here, hon. It's in Hollywood. Got a pencil handy?"

Tess scribbled down the address. "Thanks, Chloe. I'll be there and I know I'm going to get this one. Don't give up on me yet."

"I'd never do that, hon. We're a team."

Tess knew that Chloe was lying, but murmured a few kind words about what a great agent she was before closing the call. This commercial might be her last chance with Chloe, and she absolutely had to get the part or even this last remnant of her acting career would disappear along with the rest of her dreams of stardom.

Although Tess was usually a positive person, it was hard not to feel like a terrible failure. Acting was the only thing she'd ever wanted to do for her entire life. Performing dominated her thoughts throughout almost every day. She loved the process of stepping out of her humdrum small-town life and transforming into someone who wasn't a cat lady with a dead-end job living in the middle of nowhere.

She'd promised herself she'd return to Los Angeles if she could ever get enough money together. Although she missed the excitement of the city, if she were honest, she didn't miss the dirt, noise, traffic, creepy guys relieving themselves on the sidewalks, or any of the other "sights" that were to be found in her old neighborhood.

Alpine Grove might be boring, but at least she never worried about getting mugged or peed on when she walked down the sidewalk, which was a point in the little town's favor.

~

Tess tried not to dwell on the depressing call with Chloe as she went through the rest of her day. One thing that she liked about working in sales was that she moved around a lot and didn't have to sit at a desk for hours on end. Those times when she was trapped in the office writing up quotes were by far the worst moments of her job. But as Geoff had pointed out, today she needed to get out there and sell stuff. The magazine ad close date was coming up soon, and she was behind on her sales calls. It was past time to scare up some new advertisers and get some commissions.

The other nice thing about having a sales job was that she could do some of her work from home while still wearing her pajamas. Chloe wasn't the only one who received morning calls from Tess. While enjoying her first cup of coffee, Tess often made sales appointments, so she could visit people and do deliveries in the afternoons. Once Tess was satisfied that she'd called enough prospects to keep her busy for a few days, she was ready to go by the office, pick up some printed materials, and venture out into the world. It was time to get serious about those commissions.

After feeding the Fab Four, Tess stopped by the office to pick up her deliveries. The Italian restaurant needed their menus, the lawyer was getting his business cards, and an insurance office would receive their new claims forms. It was a big day in the world of printing.

Tess had already sold a magazine ad to the restaurant, and she'd given up on the lawyer who was way too cheap to ever cough up for an ad, so those appointments were simple drop offs. But the folks at the insurance company hadn't heard her marketing spiel yet, and she was ready to wow them with the merits of local advertising. Tess had always felt that sales was just another form of performing and she had her monologue for the Mountain Insurance Group all figured out. Their rival, the Sullivan Agency, had been around for years and was already a long-term advertiser. By comparison, Mountain was relatively new, so Tess needed to convince Brad that his company should sign up for a huge ad to outsell their more established competition.

Although it sounded like an easy peasy sale in her head, sometimes the reality didn't pan out the way she anticipated. Tess sometimes wondered if she had multiple personalities. When she was trying to make a sale, the calm, sensible professional side of herself was the persona she tried to project to the world. But sometimes it was like another person took over her mouth and blurted out comments she wished she hadn't. It was like the old cartoons with the little devil sitting on your shoulder whispering all the things you're thinking, but shouldn't say out loud. Those times when Crazy Tess came out to play, commissions tended to vanish into the ether.

She'd been having a nice conversation with Brad chatting about local happenings when he mentioned that the old theater in town had sold and they were going to tear it down.

Before she even had a conscious thought, Crazy Tess blurted out, "They *can't* tear down the Grove!"

Brad widened his eyes at her outburst. "Well, an out-of-town investment firm bought the building. They say it's going to cost too much to rehabilitate. If you examine it from a business and an insurance standpoint, there's no way it could be profitable as a theater again."

"But I performed there."

Brad stared at her blankly. "Uh, that's nice."

"You probably didn't live here then, but there used to be local performances. During Alpine Grove Days, there was a talent show. Everyone got involved, even little kids. It was a big deal. And then when I was in high school, I went on my first date at the Grove. It was a midnight showing of *Psycho*. My mom let me stay out late."

"Well, the place has been boarded up for years," Brad said. "I've never seen it, but from the sounds of it, the inside is in pretty rough shape."

"How could they do this? It's a part of Alpine Grove history. And it's old. Aren't there historical societies that care about old buildings?"

"I suppose." Brad squirmed in his chair. "Well, you know, I need to wrap this up. I have another appointment in a few minutes. Thanks for the brochures."

Tess paused, realizing her mistake. He was throwing her out. "Maybe we can talk about the ad next week."

"Yeah, well, I think I'll just wait until next year. Thanks."

Tess reluctantly left and crossed his name off her list in her day planner. So much for that whale of a commission. Brad's insurance agency wasn't even going to be a tiny minnow. Geoff wasn't going to be pleased about that development because he'd been convinced that Brad was eager to advertise and might even go for the back cover of the magazine. Oops. Perhaps it would be better not to mention this failed whale sale to her boss until after her audition on Monday.

The next appointment was with Bea Sullivan at Bea Haven Gifts who'd already signed up for an ad, so Tess was just dropping off a proof. Tess loved walking into the gift store, which was full of shiny, sparkly things she couldn't afford. It even smelled good inside.

Since Tess wasn't trying to sell anything, she had a good time chatting with Bea about changes to the design of her ad and various happenings around town. Bea was always in the know and had heard about the sale of the theater.

Now that the information about the Grove was old news to Crazy Tess, it was easier to maintain composure. Tess said,

"I can't believe someone would tear it down. It's a wonderful, beautiful old building."

"Well, a few people don't want that to happen. They're formulating a plan," Bea said.

"I heard some big-wig investment company bought it. What are these people going to do, buy it back?"

"They're looking at options," Bea said. "I don't want to get your hopes up, but if you're interested, I might have more information by the time you stop by to pick up the ad proof."

Tess crossed her arms. "I guess I'm interested. Right now, I'm mostly angry. I still can't believe the Cullins family sold it to some scummy out-of-town company."

In an obvious attempt to change the subject, Bea said, "Did you hear about the person staging a sit-in on Oak Street?"

Tess frowned. Was this Luke's naked renter? "Someone might have mentioned it. Was it a protest or something?"

"Apparently, two guys are roommates at the house and they've been feeding the squirrels. Now one of them is worried they don't have enough housing."

"So he staged a sit-in to demand a bigger house?" Tess shrugged. "I'm familiar with the shortage of rentals in this town, but that's a new twist."

"No, they think the *squirrels* don't have enough housing."

"The squirrels? But what about all the trees? Oak Street is totally shaded by those enormous maples. Isn't that enough for the wildlife?"

"Not according to Willy."

Tess smiled to herself. This *was* about Luke's renter. "Ah, I think I did hear about this from the landlord."

"You went to school with Luke, didn't you?"

"I don't know him well, but I ran into him the other day," Tess said, glad for the sake of her automobile that she hadn't *literally* run into him.

"He's such a nice person. I think Willy has been taking advantage of the situation."

"What situation?" Tess said. Bea liked everyone, so it shouldn't be a surprise she thought Luke was nice. Claire certainly wasn't as charitable.

"Willy is a cousin who had a few, well, problems, and Luke let him and a friend rent the house while they get their lives back together. I suspect Luke is regretting that decision now."

Tess smiled politely. "Where exactly is this house located on Oak?"

"Near Alder. You can't miss it. They've made a few, ah, *interesting* alterations to it."

Tess suspected that "interesting" was in the eye of the beholder, and Luke might not appreciate Willy's modifications.

~

After a long day of largely unsuccessful appointments, Tess wanted to get home, order a pizza, and crawl into bed surrounded by cuddly purring cats. Unfortunately, that dream wasn't realistic. What she actually needed to do was spend her evening continuing to pack up her belongings. On the way home, she'd stopped by the liquor store to get some more boxes to add to her collection. It didn't seem like she had much stuff, but putting it into boxes had changed her perspective.

As she opened the door, she was greeted by a yowl and a screech as George hauled kitty butt around a corner. Tess dropped her tote bag on the floor and silently scanned the room, which looked like it had been a victim of a houseplant bombing. Tess had adorned her place with a few pothos and spider plants. The cats had never seemed interested in the indoor vegetation, partly because they'd been in hanging planters. Not anymore.

Dirt and shattered pieces of flowerpots were everywhere, along with approximately ten thousand brown paw-prints. Tess moved into the living room, aghast at the destruction. What had gotten into them?

Tess crouched down to examine the prints, which were mud, not simply dry potting soil, and realized the sound she heard was running water. *Oh no.* She ran into the bathroom and found that the tap on the sink was open and water was running everywhere, mixing in with most of a roll of toilet paper, which was strewn throughout the small room.

Reaching to turn off the tap, she saw a gray furry form shoot through the hallway, stop, and make a horrible retching sound. After spewing the contents of his stomach on the rug in the hall, Ringo dashed toward the bedroom.

Tess jumped over the pile of cat barf and followed him. Pieces of shredded cardboard were scattered throughout the room and it was obvious that the cats had decided to consume some of the boxes that she'd set aside for packing. That would explain Ringo's gastric upheaval.

George shot out from under the bed as Tess surveyed the damage. More muddy paw prints adorned her bedspread, and one of the cats had hurled up another soggy mound of cardboard right in the center of the bed. Nice shot.

Tess closed her eyes, bowed her head, and put her face in her palms. Cleaning up feline devastation was not how she'd planned to spend her evening. She looked up at the sound of a knock at the front door.

As she walked by the bathroom, she noticed Paul sitting on the rim of the toilet seat and dropping something in. Uh oh. Ignoring the splashing noise, she hurried to answer the door.

When she opened the door, she found herself face-to-face with her landlord. With a feeble smile, she said, "Hi, Jim, what a surprise."

He leaned forward to peer into the living room. "What in God's name happened here?"

"I think the cats might have figured out we're moving." She gestured toward the room. "I think they might be acting out a little."

"A *little*? Are you blind? I got your message about having trouble finding a new place, and I was going to give you another couple weeks, but I changed my mind. I want you out this weekend."

"I can't. I have to be in Los Angeles on Monday."

"Then Tuesday. I want you out of here and everything cleaned."

"How about Wednesday? I need an extra day. I can do Wednesday. Please?"

"Everything needs to be out of this place. I mean it. I want you outta here. No more excuses. You were supposed to be out at the end of March. No more Mr. Nice Guy. I'm done with you and your cats." Jim turned and said over his shoulder, "And you can kiss your deposit goodbye."

Tess closed the door and leaned back on it, gazing forlornly at the ruin that had been her apartment. Jim had every right to be furious. What a disaster. The tan carpet was never going to be the same and was probably beyond saving. It had sported a few suspicious stains when she moved in, but nothing compared to the muddy mess that was strewn all over it now. Yuck. Of course, now that she was losing her deposit anyway, she wasn't going to get too hysterical about cleaning it either. Plus, they were going to gut the apartments anyway, so what difference did it make? This was so unfair.

Tess spent some time picking up pieces of cardboard, sweeping, packing, and feeling sorry for herself. What was she going to do with all her stuff and her cats? The situation was getting dire.

When her cleaning process circled back around to the bathroom, she uttered a tiny screech at the discovery that Paul's prize was a very, very dead headless mouse in the toilet. Leave it to Paul to find the most revolting thing to do and then do it. She should have known. Note to self: always, *always* put the toilet seat down from now on.

Tess grabbed the litter box scooper and gingerly fished out the decapitated rodent while reciting a lot of extremely foul language to express precisely what she was feeling about her feline roommates, their parentage, bodily functions, and mental capacities. After she disposed of Paul's little toilet bowl gift, she collected the cats from their various hiding places and locked them in the bathroom while she cleaned the rest of the apartment. She was too angry to even look at them. It was like they'd lost their collective kitty minds and staged a revolt about the impending move. As if that might help.

While she cleaned, she reflected on the Alpine Grove gossip about Luke's rental tenants. If he threw them out like he threatened, that meant he needed a new tenant. It was a long shot, and having Luke be her landlord wasn't appealing at all, but desperate times called for desperate measures. She wasn't sure she had the guts to call him, but she had no other options. If she were by herself, she could crash on a friend's sofa for a while, but none of her friends were willing to take in four cats. She knew because she'd asked.

Maybe she could put her things into a storage unit. But then what? The cats couldn't live in her car. It was April, and the nights were still getting cold. Maybe tomorrow, she'd take a little drive down Oak Street and see what everyone was talking about. She could relate to the squirrels. According to certain people, they needed housing as badly as she did.

~

After their time out in the bathroom, the cats seemed more subdued. When Tess released them from their confinement, all four pretended like nothing had happened. It was possible that they'd picked up on the fact that the woman who fed them was seriously pissed off. But with cats it was impossible to ever really know what they were thinking. When Tess finally went to bed, she was exhausted from all the cleaning. The cats did have the decency to lull her to sleep with their purring anyway.

The next morning, Tess packed more boxes and reserved a storage unit starting the following Wednesday. She also left a few messages with people she knew who had pickup trucks, begging them to help her move her stuff. Everyone seemed to be out enjoying the weekend. After making her calls, she wasn't sure what else she could do.

She picked up John and settled him in her lap. "I'm afraid to leave you guys alone in the house, but I need to run some errands. Can you behave?"

John uttered a plaintive meow, which probably wasn't a "yes." It was more likely a request for more food. Tess put him back on the floor. "Sorry, but you had your breakfast. I can't stand doing any more packing right now. I've got to get out of here for a while."

After a few more admonishments to the Fab Four about the need for civilized behavior in her absence, Tess closed the door behind her with a sigh of relief. She needed to clear her head, and nothing was better for that than going for a hike out in the forest. When she'd been in high school, sometimes it felt like she'd worn a path up the waterfall trail that was located outside of Alpine Grove. On her way out of town, she also could drive by Luke's rental house and take a look.

She got in the Hyundai and wound through a few side streets over to Oak. Luke's rental house was only a few blocks over from her apartment. The residential area of Alpine Grove was within walking distance of virtually everything. Her apartment was a beat-up old house that had been chopped up into small 600-square-foot apartments. Although Tess liked her place because it was convenient, it was tiny, and now that her landlord hated her, what she thought about it didn't matter.

She slowly drove down Oak Street and stopped across from a house that had a few people standing in front of it. They seemed to be chatting with a skinny man with stringy blond hair and a goatee who was sitting cross-legged on the front lawn. Given the guy's lack of clothes and the number of squirrels running around, Tess figured this must be the place.

She got out, walked over to the crowd, and stood next to a bald man who had a gray poodle on a leash. He said, "Willy, I think I speak for everyone here when I say it's time for you to go inside and put on some clothes."

A woman wearing a light blue cardigan added, "Aren't you cold? It's April, for heaven's sake. You'll catch your death."

Willy pulled his hands out of his lap and spread his arms wide. "I want to be with the spirit of the squirrels."

Tess frowned. That was a lot more of Willy than she needed to see. A squirrel ran over to Willy and scrounged around in the grass near his knee. Willy looked down. "See. They come to me. They know I understand."

The guy with the poodle said, "That's because you feed them all the time, you idiot."

Luke came around from the back of the house and stopped short at the sight of Willy. "I thought we agreed that you were leaving."

Willy looked up at him. "I need to say goodbye."

"Make it fast. And for God's sake, would you get dressed?" Luke gestured toward the crowd. "The neighborhood doesn't need another one of your nudie shows."

Luke walked to the curb where a blue one-ton pickup truck was parked and pulled some lumber from the long bed. He paused, turned toward Willy, and made a shooing motion with his hands. In response, Willy got up slowly, spread his arms and proclaimed his love for small furry creatures. Once the show was over, the neighbors lost interest and dispersed.

Luke lifted some more two by fours out of the bed, leaned them on the side of the truck, and smiled at Tess. "Looks like you missed all the fun."

Tess laughed. "I think I got the gist of it. Are you really throwing him out?"

"Trying to. He and his friend Stetson have trashed my house."

"You seem remarkably calm for someone with a trashed house."

"You didn't see me yesterday. Stetson drives me nuts, and I wanted to throttle him. I had to go for a seven-mile run to get over it." Luke set the lumber down and held it with his large gloved hands. "The neighbors have already had their daily dose of naked Willy. They don't need to hear me yelling at my lunatic cousin and his even more bizarre friend to boot."

"This person is actually named Stetson?"

"That's what he calls himself. Like the cologne. I don't know what his real name is, but the guy smells like a perfume counter at the mall and now the whole house reeks."

"When are they moving out?"

"As soon as I can get them out. It's going to take me months to get the house put back together. No one will rent it the way it is now."

Tess gave the house a quick once-over. He might be wrong about that. At this point, she'd rent pretty much anything with a roof. The place didn't seem particularly unusual, except for the addition of some squirrel-related yard art. It was a classic two-story bungalow with gray siding and two big picture windows. Three concrete steps led up to the front door, which had a tiny covering over it to keep the snow off the steps. "It looks okay to me."

"You haven't seen the back. Follow me, if you're curious." He picked up the boards, put the stack of wood on his shoulder, and started walking. "I can tell you for sure that this structure isn't water-tight anymore."

As she followed Luke, Tess recalled all of Claire's mooning about how hot he was, which with all the wood hoisting and muscle flexing was difficult to ignore. He was a large person who obviously was in incredible shape, probably because he spent so much time carrying wood and other heavy objects. The result of all that heavy lifting and running was impressive, and Tess found herself wondering what he'd look like hauling wood when he wasn't wearing the flannel shirt. Although it would be fun to witness, she wouldn't wish splinters on those fine shoulders either.

He stopped at the gate and opened it for her, interrupting Tess's fantasies about large shoulders and small running shorts. She walked through the gate and followed the stepping stones alongside the house. When she went around the corner into the back yard, she looked up and stopped short in surprise. The rear wall of the house was riddled with holes. "Oh my God, what happened? It's like Swiss cheese."

Luke set the boards down and looked up. "It turns out Stetson isn't good with saws."

"Can you fix it?"

"I hope so. He sawed through some kind of important boards. I'm going to try and shore it up, but the insulation is soaked, and the drywall is toast. The whole back side of the house needs to be rebuilt."

"Wow."

"It gets worse. Willy is an artist."

"I saw the squirrel sculptures next to the tree out front. Are those his?"

"Nope. He bought those somewhere instead of paying the rent." Luke walked up next to Tess. "Willy's preferred medium is spray paint."

"Like a graffiti artist?"

"Not really." Luke turned and leaned the wood against the weathered wooden privacy fence that surrounded the back yard. "More like a three-year-old who got his first box of Crayolas."

Tess smiled. "You know I've got to see this now."

He returned her smile. "Okay, since you're here, why not? I suppose it would be funny if it weren't costing me a fortune in repairs and lost rental income."

Tess followed him toward the back deck, which had steps leading to a set of French doors. If Luke was okay with cats, she had a suggestion for how he could recoup some of that rental income.

Chapter 3

Defining Moments

Tess followed Luke into the house. The French doors led to a dining area, which had an open archway over a bar that connected to the kitchen and an arched doorway that went to the living room. Sunlight streamed in through the collection of holes above the door and along the wall. The walls had been painted dark purple and sported spray-painted symbols and globs that presumably were Willy's version of art.

Tess said weakly, "It's, um, colorful."

Luke gestured toward the room. "This was painted off-white. It wasn't exciting, but it was fine. Once I cover up the seven hundred holes in the wall, it's going to be like a cave in here."

"Dark purple wouldn't have been my first choice." Tess got closer to the wall. "If it's any consolation, it seems to be peeling."

"That's the drywall disintegrating from all the water that's been pouring in every time it rains."

"Oh yeah." Tess shuffled through papers and clothes that were littered across every surface. "I see what you mean about the smell. I think the Stetson cologne might be to cover up… other smells."

Luke took a deep breath. "I know. I think I'm going to need some type of therapy or counseling after this nightmare."

A large German shepherd-hound mix bounded around the corner and almost crashed into Tess. She held out her hand for him to sniff. "Hey, you're the dog in the road grader."

"Barney was supposed to stay in the truck, but Willy must have let him out." Luke pointed at a potato chip bag on the floor. "Don't you even think about eating that."

Barney lowered his ears slightly, acknowledging the stern tone. Luke said, "Who can live like this? All this garbage everywhere is gross."

Tess surveyed the detritus on the floor, which would undoubtedly violate thirty or forty health-codes in a commercial establishment. "I noticed."

As she walked through the rooms, followed by Barney, Tess felt bad for the poor little house. It was a mess, and she wondered what on earth had possessed Willy to do what he'd done. Drugs? Massive mental health issues?

Luke didn't seem to want to talk about the current state of his rental, but he did point out some of the things he'd worked on in the past. In the kitchen, he gestured toward the cabinets. "Before they were chartreuse, I refinished them and stained them a cherry wood color. I put three coats of varnish on them and they would shine when the light came through that window."

Tess turned and leaned on the counter. It was the moment of truth. "I have a proposition for you."

Luke pulled his attention away from whatever Barney was trying to eat and looked at Tess in surprise. "*What?*"

"Get your mind out of the gutter. I'm not Claire."

He grinned. "Well, thank heavens for that."

"But I do have a problem. A big problem, which I think you could help with."

"*Me*? Haven't you been paying attention? I have enough problems of my own."

"You need a rental tenant and I very badly need a place to stay, or in three days, I'll be living in my car."

"Why? What happened?"

"My landlord is selling the apartment building where I live. It's a four-plex now, but the new owners are going to gut the inside, and remodel it so it's three apartments, none of which I'll be able to afford. I thought I had until the end of the month to find a new place, but I have to be out by Wednesday."

"What changed?"

Tess bit her lip, then dropped the bombshell. "I have cats. And they're not too excited about moving. I think all the packing tape tipped them off. And then they, well, acted out a little, and the landlord happened to stop by. He's angry and told me and the Fab Four to get out."

"Who are the Fab Four?"

"That's what I call my cats."

"You have *four* cats?"

"John, Paul, George and Ringo."

Luke laughed. "So you want me to let the British invasion into *my* house. Just when I thought things couldn't get any worse here, you want to throw destructive cats into the equation?"

"I could help you keep an eye on the place."

"What would anyone steal? Willy's underwear?" He raised his eyebrows. "I doubt anyone wants that. I'm sure I don't."

Tess mentally flailed for ideas. "Well, aren't you going to have to leave stuff here while you're fixing the wall? Tools, building supplies? Other stuff maybe?"

"I might, but a quiet residential neighborhood in Alpine Grove isn't exactly a high crime area. And more to the point, why would I want to let another person who is known to be a bad tenant live here?"

Tess waved her arms in exasperation. "Because I'm desperate. There are no rentals. *None.* I've been looking for almost a month. You know how tight the rental market is here, and it's worst in the springtime with all the tourists snapping up summer rentals. I'll pay you rent, and I don't care that this place has purple walls with holes and disturbing abstract images all over them. You can recoup some of that lost rental income."

Luke scratched the stubble on his chin. "I suppose that would be good. But when I'm here working on the house, Barney comes with me. I doubt the kitty Beatles would enjoy having him around here."

"I'll keep them locked in the bedroom upstairs or maybe in a bathroom. Please? I'm desperate. Before the cats lost their minds yesterday, we were awesome tenants."

He crossed his arms across his chest. "If I say yes, first you have to help me get Willy, Stetson, and their crap out of here."

"When?"

"Are you doing anything right now?"

"I was going to go for a hike."

"If you want to live here, help me drag all this garbage out of the house." He pointed at the doorway to the laundry room. "There are big black garbage bags in the cabinet above the washer. Put all the nasty dirty clothes in one bag and trash like those old pizza boxes in another one."

Tess walked to the room and grabbed the box of lawn and garden bags. "If doing this doesn't prove to you that I'm serious, nothing will."

With a sweeping gesture toward the dining room, he said, "After you. I'm going to go put Barney back in the truck and yell at Willy."

They spent the next three hours removing the detritus from the floor and dodging Willy and Stetson who were slowly wandering around making small efforts to pack their belongings. Stetson was a shorter, fatter version of Willy with dark brown stringy hair instead of blond hair. Neither of them smelled like they'd showered recently.

Luke directed Tess to put the bags that literally contained garbage in the back of his truck so he could take them to the dump on his way back home to Gleasonville.

Tess was surprised to find out that Luke didn't live in town. Gleasonville was a much larger community located south of Alpine Grove past the ski resort. "When did you move?"

"A few years ago."

"Do you miss the ole hometown?" Because Tess had left Alpine Grove for Los Angeles, albeit temporarily, she was curious.

"In some ways. But there's more excavation work in Gleasonville. Bigger population means more construction." He shrugged. "It looks like I'll be spending more time here again though. I have a job digging out a septic line at a house north of town. I've also got to fix this mess, so I can rent the house again."

"You have a lot of, um, crap to deal with," Tess said with a smile.

"Yeah, crap that means I'll be spending a lot of time in my truck driving all over Cedar County."

Tess picked up the garbage bag she'd been filling and put a twistie tie on it. "I think this is the last of it. Most of the garbage is now in your truck. Barney looks bored. He's drooling all over the passenger side window."

"I'm sure he is. Thanks for your help."

Tess put her palms together in a mock prayer move. "So will you let me move in? You've known me since we were in high school. I'm gainfully employed, and it's not like I've turned into an axe murderer in the last decade."

"All I knew was that you were Claire's friend. I think we spoke three words to each other in high school. Until the last couple days, I hadn't laid eyes on you in ten or twelve years."

Although he was correct that they'd traveled in wildly different social circles, Tess waved off the comment. "So what? You know who I am anyway. Like I said, I'll put the cats in a bedroom whenever you're working on the house. You won't even know they're here. *Please*?"

"I'm pretty sure Barney will know the cats are there, but if you're okay with that, I suppose it's better than letting this place sit empty ninety percent of the time." Luke pulled off a work glove and ran his fingers through his wavy hair. "Willy got a discount on the rent, but you'll be living in a construction zone. It will be a mess."

"I don't care."

He named a figure that was only ten dollars more than Tess had been paying for her apartment and she said "yes" almost before he got the words out.

Luke looked down at the work glove he was holding and then at her. "If I say yes, please don't make me regret this, okay?"

Tess gave him a military salute and grinned widely. "Absolutely. I promise. This will be great. You'll see."

Luke shook his head, but pulled a key out of the back pocket of his jeans. "Here's Willy's key. But part of this agreement is that you have to make sure he doesn't come back."

"I can do that." Tess took the key and stuffed it into her purse before he could change his mind. "It's a deal."

~

Tess stood awkwardly staring at Luke who looked mildly ill as if he'd just swallowed a cup of lemon juice. She said overly brightly, "I have a bunch of calls out to friends to help me move my stuff. My apartment is so tiny, I hardly have any furniture. All I need to do is switch my phone number."

"On Wednesday, I'll be around because of that septic job north of town. I've gotta get my trailer set up and haul the backhoe over there. I'll stop by after I'm done there."

"I'll be here taking care of your house for you," Tess said with enthusiasm. It didn't seem to have much of an effect on his morose expression, so she added, "Monday I have an audition in Los Angeles, but then I'm in full-on packing and moving mode."

"You mean acting? You still do that?"

"Of course. I'm an actress. And I have a good feeling about this commercial. I know I'm going to get it."

"You must have heard that they're going to tear down The Grove, huh?"

"I did." A horrible thought flashed through her mind. "Oh my God, you're not the one doing it, are you? How *could* you?"

"I'm not usually the guy tearing things down. I usually dig things up."

"Right. Like septic lines."

"Exactly. Clearing land for building. Leveling ground. Stuff like that."

"That's a relief." Tess put her hand to her chest. "I'm sick about the whole thing. I mean, didn't you go and see shows at the Grove?"

"Sure. Everybody did."

"I can't believe some evil developer wants to destroy it. They can't tear it down. They just *can't*."

"I suppose it's progress. Time marches on and all that."

Tess balled her fingers into fists. "I'm sorry, but it's just plain wrong. The Grove is a huge part of Alpine Grove's history. Tearing it down could damage the town."

"It's been closed for eight or nine years. Seems like we managed to cope."

"But I always thought it would reopen."

"Well, if you win the lottery, you can buy it." He gestured toward the house. "I gotta collect Willy and Stetson and take them to the Gleasonville bus station now."

"Where are they going?"

"Back to Nebraska. I called my uncle and told him I'm shipping them back."

Tess laughed. "If Willy is in Nebraska, keeping him away from here should be easy for me."

"Yeah, if he stays on the bus."

"He wouldn't get off, would he?" Tess had a little tremor of anxiety because she'd seen enough to know that Willy was weird enough to do pretty much anything.

"Guess we'll find out." Luke gave her a small wave as he turned back toward the house. "See you Wednesday."

Tess got in her car and sat for a moment, trying to decide what to do next. She'd originally been thinking of going for a hike, but that was hours ago. The idea of facing more packing at home after so much cleaning here was depressing, so she made herself a deal. Go for the hike to the waterfall tomorrow as a reward for good behavior today.

She drove the couple of blocks back to her apartment and was greeted by John and Paul. None of the Fab Four appeared to have committed any acts of badness, so Tess made herself something to eat and returned to the ever-so-tedious task of packing up her things.

Packing was one of those tasks that gave you lots of time to think. Claire hadn't called her back after she left a message telling her about her almost-crash into Luke's grader. That was odd.

She picked up the phone and left a message telling Claire that she was moving into Luke's house. If that didn't get a rise out of her friend, nothing would. Tess giggled when she hung up the phone. Claire would probably go into hysterics when she finally got around to listening to her voice mail.

Tess returned to the floor and her stacks of books. She had lots of screenplays and a giant tome of Shakespeare's complete works that she'd been carting around for years. She couldn't make herself part with those words that she'd spent so much time memorizing. It would be like giving away part of her soul.

She idly flipped through a screenplay for an indie-produced play. Sadly, the production had ended up folding before it ever got off the ground. But the rehearsals had been fun, and she'd loved the character. Meg was quirky and funny with a slew of great lines. Playing an enjoyable role and immersing herself in a character like that took Tess completely out of herself. It helped her forget all her problems and just live in the moment as another person. There was no other feeling like it in the world. And now some horrible developer was planning to raze the Grove Theater. What was the world coming to? Didn't anyone care about the arts anymore?

With a sigh, she set the screenplay into the box with the others. Packing and reminiscing about past failures was demoralizing. Why hadn't someone invented a device to scoop up all your crap and dump it in a new location? Or a transporter like they had on *Star Trek*? Those guys never had to dredge up boxes and pile things into them. What a pain. At this rate, packing could take the rest of her life.

Tess spent the remainder of the evening mentally railing against the reality of packing and fretting about the potential stupidity of moving into Luke's house. Over the years, Claire had called Luke every nasty horrible name under the sun. The woman had quite a vocabulary too. But what exactly had he done? Had Claire ever told her?

Luke had seemed fairly normal when Tess had talked to him, although he was understandably a little stressed about his house. That breakup in high school had been devastating for Claire. What had really happened with Luke? He must have done something truly horrible.

And now Tess was moving into the guy's house. Which thanks to his bizarro cousin was in such horrible disrepair that no one with half a brain would want to rent it. Except her. This was Crazy Tess taken to a new and even more insane level.

By the time she woke up the next morning, Tess had almost convinced herself that she needed to find Luke's number, call him, and back out of the deal. But she kept coming back to the fact that the cats needed a place to live too. Luke wouldn't be around much, and he obviously liked animals since he had a big goofy dog himself. And the sad fact was, she had no other options.

With her mind still swirling, after breakfast, Tess went off for her mental health hike at the waterfall. She'd been there so many times, it was almost like the car knew the way. She drove to an empty parking area, got out, and walked to the trail that led up to Lilly Falls. As she huffed her way to the top, the only sounds were the breeze through the trees and a few birds chirping at one another in the pine boughs above.

The falls were named after Lilly Miller, an Alpine Grove pioneer that Tess had played in one of the productions at the Grove Theater. That play was yet another piece of local history that might be lost. Who would want to put on a play about Alpine Grove anywhere other than Alpine Grove?

The trail ended at an overlook with a railing, so visitors could look down into a stone canyon below. The water was rushing madly from all the spring runoff, crashing over the cliff into the pool below. Something about being surrounded by the misty air and the noise of the rushing water never failed to relax Tess. She peered down over the railing and smiled at the rainbow that glittered across the pool below.

She walked back away from the overlook to a mossy clearing that was surrounded by trees. Settling into her favorite spot next to a massive cedar, she leaned back and closed her eyes. All of her tired muscles relaxed as the sounds of the waterfall and the birds serenaded her. Everything would be fine. She and the Fab Four had a place to live. According to Claire, Luke might be the devil's spawn, but Tess would hardly have to deal with him. Sure, the situation wasn't ideal, but nothing was forever. In the meantime, she'd muddle through and make it work.

~

Refreshed from her hike to the waterfall, Tess drove back to her apartment, ready to face the last of her packing. She also needed to get ready for her audition in Los Angeles the next day. Tess wasn't habitually an early riser, but she would have to leave at four in the morning to get to her audition on time. Although the journey would require many cups of coffee, she figured she could make it there, do the audition and then stay overnight at some cheapie motel before heading back Tuesday morning. Then she'd go to work that afternoon, move to a new place, and then be back in the office again on Wednesday. It was shaping up to be quite a week.

She sighed as she turned the key in the door. George scurried around a corner and ran into the bedroom. "Hi, George."

On the sofa, John stood up and stretched deeply with a mewly sleepy meow. Because so much stuff had been packed or thrown out, the cats didn't have much left to destroy. Maybe the Great Kitty Uprising of 1997 was a blessing in disguise. Now she had less stuff to drag over to the new place. Certainly fewer houseplants anyway.

The button on her answering machine was flashing wildly, so Tess pressed play. Without any preamble, Claire's voice blasted out, "Are you *insane*? First you leave a message telling me you had a nice little chat on the road with that loathsome piece of pond scum, and now you tell me you are moving in with him? Have you lost your mind? Taken leave of your senses? This is the worst mistake of your life and that's saying something because you've made some big ones. You know I say that with love though, right? But wait… where are you? Oh my God. You aren't moving in *already*, are you? You'd better not be. Call me back the instant you get this message."

Tess rolled her eyes at John. "I think she considers our relocation plan a bad idea. What do you think?"

John swished his tail and curled up in a ball, apparently unimpressed by the verbal rampage that had come from the answering machine. But he'd met Claire, so maybe he understood. She could be a teensy weensy bit melodramatic.

Not wanting to incur any more wrath, Tess dialed Claire's number and had a nice little chat with her answering machine to point out that she wasn't *moving in* with Luke, just renting a house he happened to own. And that she'd be in Los Angeles the next day.

Having taken care of her best friend duties, Tess returned to packing and making sure that everything in her apartment that could be nailed down was nailed down. The last thing she needed was more feline acts of destruction. She set up the kitty autofeeder as well, which was a popular decision. There was sure to be a lot of heavy eating in her absence, which might slow down any potential mayhem.

Ringo elected himself supervisor of the pre-trip suitcase packing process. If a cat could sneer, he would have. If Tess didn't know better, she'd think the sleek gray cat detested her entire wardrobe. Tess laid a dress out on the bed, picked it up, and scowled at it. No way. She pulled another dress out of the closet and went through the same routine.

Ringo sat near the stack of rejected dresses and licked a paw, as if he were pretending to ignore the proceedings. Tess laid out a purple dress and scrutinized it. Maybe this one would be okay. Ringo rolled over on his back and then onto the dress.

Tess reached down and shoved the cat off the fabric. "Ringo, stop that. I'm trying to decide, and you're getting fur all over everything."

Ringo moved into sphinx position and glared up at his owner. Tess said, "Fine. The purple doesn't work. I get it, okay?"

Apparently deciding that his fashion consulting task was complete, Ringo jumped off the bed and stalked off toward the kitchen.

For Tess, the trip to Los Angeles was a blur, partly because the first stage of the journey happened in the dark. Fortunately, anyone who had lived in Alpine Grove as long as she had knew every twisty turn in the roads that led down to Los Angeles, thanks to countless journeys to the airport. After the mountain road part, came the boring freeway part.

Then the action-packed, horrible traffic part. She knew every bit of the drive extremely well.

She managed to find a parking space in a grotesquely overpriced parking garage and hustled over to the address where Chloe said the auditions were being held. By the time Tess arrived, she was disheveled, anxious, and sweaty. She checked her watch. Was there enough time to hit the ladies room? It would be close. She hustled in, went for a minimal makeup adjustment, swished a comb through her hair, made a scrunchy face, and stuck her tongue out at the mirror. It was going to have to be good enough.

She entered Suite 232 and found herself in a room with about thirty-five other women who had long dark brown hair and brown eyes. As was typical, she was lumped in with a bunch of physical clones of herself. Tess tried not to fall into the comparison trap, but a lot of the women were a lot prettier than she was. Over the years, Tess had realized that she had one of those faces that was sort of cartoonish. Her mouth was disproportionately large and her eyes were almost buggy, so she wasn't a classic beauty by any stretch of the imagination. But when she put stage makeup on, her off-kilter features became striking. In person, she didn't stand out, but on camera or on stage under the lights, she did. Tess wouldn't have believed it if she hadn't seen the transformation in the mirror or on TV monitors before.

She sat down and tried to calm her nerves and collect her thoughts. The lines she was supposed to read whirred through her mind like an audio tape on repeat. As their names were called, women stood up, checked in with the receptionist, and slipped into the adjoining room. Moments later, they emerged. All the women waiting in the chairs looked up and watched as each aspiring actress left the room. After five or six women went through the process, finally the receptionist said, "Tess Mitchell," and Tess leaped up.

"That's me."

The sleek woman peered over the top of the heavy frames of her glasses and took the head shot photo and form Tess handed to her. "Is this information correct?"

Tess leaned over and pointed at the paper. "Well, I'm moving, so you'll see that I put dates next to the addresses. My phone number will be switched, but I'm not sure when that might happen, so I put my office number."

"Fine." With a sullen gaze, the woman pointed to the door. "You can go in there."

"Thank you." Tess hustled through the doorway and closed the door behind her. A bald man and an older woman sat at the table. The two looked as tired and bored as the receptionist.

Tess took a deep breath. "It's a pleasure to meet you. I'm Tess Mitchell. Would you like to hear my lines?"

The bald man behind the table shook his head and asked, "Are there any experiences you've had or accomplishments as an actress that have helped to define you as a person?"

Tess paused, momentarily taken aback by what he'd said. *What?* Why weren't they asking her to read her lines? She'd spent days memorizing them. "Um, I was told I'm reading for a commercial about toilet paper. I'm supposed to snuggle an animated teddy bear and cavort around a bathroom with a lot of pillows."

"Yes, we know. Answer the question."

"Okay, well, acting experiences that have defined me as a person? Wow, that's a tough one. I don't know. I've been in a lot of plays over the years. They were small productions. It's not like I was on Broadway or anything. Does that count? Maybe not. Hmm, okay. I know I don't have any arsenic or any old lace myself, but I do think Cary Grant is hot. I don't know if that defines me as an actress, although it might define me as a person I guess because I'm a movie nut. I've never found a corpse hidden in a window seat or solved a murder in real life, but I have had a midsummer night's dream. I don't know if Shakespeare was hot or not, but I do know he's dead. I'm sure I'm not a miracle worker, but I might be a member of the Conrad Birdie fan club. Oh, and I think things really sucked for Willy Loman. He got a bad rap, and I think grease is the word."

Tess stopped to gauge the reactions from her audience of two. It had happened *again*. Crazy Tess had taken over her brain, and the result was typical. The bald man's mouth was hanging open and the pinched expression on the face of the woman sitting next to him indicated Tess wasn't wowing them with her drama-oriented ramblings.

Tess took another deep breath, even though what she wanted to do was scream. This was so unfair. It was supposed to be an audition. No one ever said improv was required. It was a commercial for toilet paper, for heaven's sake.

The bald man seemed to awaken from his stunned stupor and said, "Thank you. We'll be in touch."

~

After she checked into her cheapie, noisy motel, Tess cried a little, ate some junk food, and generally wallowed in misery. Chloe was never, ever going to give her another chance. It was all over. Today was sure to be the last audition she'd ever get. Her acting career was as dead as a torched zombie in a slasher movie. Not just a little bit dead, but completely dead even beyond the point of becoming undead ever again. Her career, or lack of one, had taken a nose dive from pathetic to nonexistent.

The drive back to Alpine Grove the next morning was equally dreary, mostly because it involved so many hours of boring driving with nothing else to do but mentally berate herself for blowing yet another audition.

By the time Tess got back to town, she was exhausted from all the driving and lack of sleep at the crappy motel. The last thing she wanted to do was deal with work, but she had a lot of calls to make. Joey had covered her Monday deliveries, but she had to deal with the ones for today. Then get to her phone and set up some appointments for later in the week because apparently selling advertising and printing was all the career she was ever going to have. Tess wiped another tear off her cheek. Okay. Time to stop dwelling and moping about the unfairness of the universe. This was her life. She needed to be like the unsinkable Molly Brown. Time to suck it up and move on.

Tess successfully rushed in, grabbed her boxes of printing to be delivered, and got out before Geoff could corner her. Back in her car, she bolted out of the parking lot before anyone noticed. The last thing she wanted was to answer the inevitable question, "How did the audition go?" She'd probably burst into tears again.

Since she was having such a bad day, Tess decided to do the easiest delivery first. Deanna, the graphic artist for the magazine, had printed a new proof of Bea Sullivan's ad with the requested changes and Tess was going to drop it off at the gift store.

The cheery bells jingled as she opened the door to the shop. Bea smiled and waved at her from behind a display of wind chimes. "Hi, Tess. Geoff said you might be stopping by."

"Sorry I'm running late. It looks like Deanna put in the changes you wanted." Tess pulled a folder out of her bag. "Let me know what you think when you get a chance."

"Are you in a rush? You look upset."

"I'll be fine. I, ah, had a long drive this morning and I've been packing for a move. I'm just a little tired, that's all."

"That sounds exciting. Where are you moving?"

"A house on Oak Street."

Bea laughed. "Is it near the house we talked about the other day? I heard the squirrel guy is back this morning."

Tess tried to keep her expression neutral. *Crap. That loser.* "Interesting. I guess I'll be meeting my neighbors."

"Is something wrong, dear?"

"No, I just…I have to go. I remembered something I need to do. And I'm already behind on getting these deliveries done. I can stop by tomorrow to pick up your changes or the signed proof approval form. Just let me know." Tess hoisted her bag on her shoulder. "I'm sorry, but I need to run."

Bea gave her a hug. "I hope you feel better, dear."

Tess reluctantly pulled away. "Thanks, Bea. I'll see you tomorrow."

After racing back to her car, Tess pointed it toward Oak Street. She hadn't even moved in yet, and already she had to go chase Willy off the lawn. And why should this weirdo listen to her? She pulled up in front of the house and Willy was in his typical cross-legged yoga pose on the lawn with a group of people standing around, along with about fifteen squirrels, which were snacking on peanuts strewn across the lawn. It was almost exactly the same scene she'd witnessed the other day. Except this time, Luke wasn't around to provide an imposing and compelling reason for Willy to get lost. Luke had the size and presence of a nightclub bouncer. No one was likely to confuse Tess with someone like that, and it was unlikely that Willy would be impressed.

To mentally prepare herself, she ran through a few lines from a screenplay about Joan of Arc. Joan had led armies into battle, chatted with saints, and set entire cities on fire. That was a woman who didn't take any crap from anybody. Tess channeled her inner Joan, so she was ready to lay siege to Willy's latest live nude show on the lawn.

She marched up to Willy and pointed at his crotch. "I was hoping never to see that again. Why aren't you and your clothes in Nebraska?"

Willy looked up with wide, innocent eyes. "It's cold there. And the squirrels need me. I can't go back."

In her loudest, audible-in-the-nosebleed-seats stage voice, Tess boomed, "What part of *you don't live here anymore* do you not understand? You need to get off this lawn now."

Willy pulled his legs up and wrapped his arms around them. "I'm not inside the house, so what's the problem?"

"Your former landlord wants you gone. If you don't take your clothes and leave, I'm going inside and calling him." She pointed again. "Do you want me to do that? Because I will unless you leave this property right now."

"I'm cool being on the sidewalk."

"Nice try. That's not going to work. I'm walking inside now and calling." Tess reached into her purse, pulled out the house key and Luke's business card and held them in front of Willy's face. "Do you honestly want to piss off Luke any more than you already have? Angering extremely large people tends to be bad for your health."

The comment about Luke's physical size seemed to give Willy pause and he stood up. "Where am I supposed to go?"

"Nebraska."

He shook his head. "I can't do that."

"Fine. I'm calling." Tess held out the keys again. "Last chance. Get. Out. Now."

"But the bus is gone."

"Not my problem. Put on your pants."

Willy grumbled as he complied. "I can't believe how unfair you're being. I have rights, you know."

"I'm not the one who got off the bus." Tess pointed down the street toward town. "Go to the stoplight and wait. I'll go inside and call you a cab that will meet you there."

"I don't believe this." He buttoned his shirt. "Why should I do what you tell me to? Who *are* you anyway?"

"The new resident of this unfortunate house. One of the tasks I was assigned is to make sure you stay away from it." Tess made a shooing motion with both hands. "Go. Leave. Goodbye."

Willy's shoulders slumped, and he turned and began walking down the sidewalk toward town. The small group of neighbors that had witnessed the scene began applauding and cheering as he slowly strolled away. Tess took a deep bow and turned to walk up the short steps to the house.

She opened the door and gave her fans one final wave before going inside. Even though Willy was gone for the moment, she didn't believe for a second that he was gone for good.

Chapter 4

Time to Get Moving

The next morning, Tess focused on moving. Even though she wasn't sure how her new residence would work out, there was no turning back now. First, she needed to shuttle over approximately two thousand boxes of stuff, then pray someone who owned a truck would return her call begging for help. After that, she needed to settle the cats into their new environment. It was one more long day in a series of long days.

In addition to a tremendous lack of interest from anyone in helping her move on a Wednesday, she also hadn't heard from Claire since the blistering message on the answering machine. Maybe Claire was sulking. You never knew with her.

On the fourth trip to the Oak Street house, Tess found Luke's truck and a gigantic flatbed trailer parked out front. She pulled a box out of the Hyundai's trunk and squared her shoulders. Time to face the owner of this charming abode again. Barney stood up in the cab of the truck and wagged at her, and then disappeared below the window again to resume his nap.

She opened the front door and carried her box inside. The sound of hammering came from the back of the house. After setting the box next to the others near the door, she went to investigate. Luke was on an extension ladder doing something to one of the holes above the French doors, and Tess paused for a moment to admire the view.

She walked up alongside the ladder, tapped the metal rail, and said, "Hi. How come Barney is in the truck?"

Luke jerked and dropped a metal coffee can, which turned end over end, throwing nails throughout the room. Tess covered her head to avoid getting hit by fastener shrapnel.

Luke stomped down the ladder. "What are you doing here?"

"Moving in." Tess bent to pick up a nail next to her shoe. "Today is Wednesday, remember?"

"You shouldn't sneak up on people on ladders. It's not safe."

"I didn't *sneak up* on you. I saw your truck and figured I'd let you know I'm here and moving in my stuff."

Luke walked around the room picking up nails. "I heard you chased Willy away yesterday."

"I did. He hasn't come back, has he?"

"Not yet." Luke held up a nail and grinned before dropping it into the can. "Donald from down the street said you got a round of applause."

Tess walked over and dropped some nails in the can. "That was undoubtedly the most applause I've had in years."

"That reminds me. How was the trip to L.A. and the audition?"

Tess bit her lip, trying not to let her disappointment overwhelm her again. "Um, okay I guess. They said they'd be in touch."

"That's great. Congrats."

Tess threw some more nails into the can somewhat more forcefully than necessary. "No, it's not. Being in touch is Hollywood code for don't let the door hit you in the butt on the way out."

"Oh. Okay. Sorry, then. That's too bad."

"Well, it helped me get rid of Willy. I was already angry and in an extremely bad mood."

He laughed. "If he comes back, I'll sic you on him again, so you can let off some more steam."

Tess dropped some more nails in the coffee can and sat down on a wooden chair at the dining table. "I hate to ask this, but I saw you have that huge trailer out front."

"I took the backhoe out to that dog kennel today and did some digging. I had to break the news to them that I'll have to dig out the entire line."

"That sounds expensive."

"It is. They're depressed." He shrugged. "Running heavy equipment costs money. I gotta make a living."

"Don't we all. At this rate, I'll be selling ads until I die." Tess looked up at him. "Where do you keep all these huge machines?"

"When I sold the business, I kept the backhoe and a couple other things, but it's not like you can park them in your driveway, so I rent a warehouse in Gleasonville."

"You mean you sold Bennett Enterprises? I always wondered what happened to the company. Your dad was involved in building half the houses in Alpine Grove back in the day, wasn't he?"

Luke set the can on the table and sat down. "He was. I worked for him from the time I could hold a hammer."

"That's a little scary to think about."

He gave her a wan smile. "Dad was great with business, but not so great on safety. It's a miracle I didn't kill myself."

Tess pointed at the ladder. "I'm guessing that's why you yelled at me about ladder safety."

"I didn't yell at you."

"Spoke loudly and forcefully, then." Tess picked a nail out of the can and twirled it in her fingertips. "So you sold the business? How come? Did your dad retire?"

"Not voluntarily. He had a stroke, so I ran the business for a few years." He looked out the window. "It didn't go well, and I ended up selling the company."

"What do you mean it didn't go well?"

"It just didn't." Luke stood up. "Listen, I've got to finish patching these holes."

"Wait. I never asked my question because I got distracted by the idea of a little kid playing with hammers at construction sites." Tess dropped the nail back in the can as Luke picked it up off the table. "Could you help me move my couch and my bed? And maybe a bookshelf or two?"

He stopped and set the can back down. "You mean *all* of your furniture, don't you?"

"I hardly have any. You can't fit much in 600 square feet." Tess gestured toward the front door. "With that huge trailer, we could do it in one load. And it's only a couple blocks away. Please?"

"All right, but they're predicting rain tomorrow, so I'm going to have to stay here late patching the wall. Otherwise the dining room is going to look like a swimming pool by this weekend."

A chattering noise came from somewhere nearby, and Tess looked up at Luke. "Please tell me that squirrel isn't inside this house."

"That's what the holes are for. They make it easy for the squirrels to get in and out."

"Why do they need so many?"

Luke made a wry face. "I couldn't tell you. Willy and Stetson were a little vague on the details."

"If you help me get my stuff, I'll help you with the holes. If the cats meet a squirrel in here, I don't think it will end well."

"Let's go."

Tess rode with Luke and Barney in the truck to her apartment. Barney only drooled on her a little, but the cats were going to have a conniption fit when they discovered she'd been consorting with a canine.

Luke leaned against the wall with his hands in his pockets and watched while she chased down the Fab Four and stowed them in the bathroom. An open front door and her cats were a bad combination.

After depositing George on the sink and closing the bathroom door behind her, Tess walked into the living room and pushed a clump of sweaty hair off her forehead. "That cat is like greased lightning."

Luke laughed and pulled his hands out of his pockets. "Leave it to you to quote *Grease*."

"Don't you remember? In high school, I played Sandy."

Luke pointed at the sofa. "Grab the other end. Didn't that guy you went out with play Danny?"

"David and I went out for about five minutes." She grabbed the other end of the sofa and they started walking out the door. "Five terrible minutes. It was a huge mistake."

Luke looked behind him over his shoulder as he walked backwards down the steps. "You didn't tell me you lived on the second floor. Hey, slow down, would you?"

"I have to put my end down." She dropped the sofa on a step. "Ugh. This old ugly thing is heavy. Why do I keep moving it?"

"Why did I agree to help you?"

Tess picked up the sofa again. "Because I got Willy off your lawn and you didn't have to get involved."

He glanced at her with a reluctant half-smile as he moved down another step. "I'll admit that *was* a good way to score points with your new landlord."

~

After Luke and Tess got all the furniture strapped down to the trailer and moved to Oak Street, they went through the unloading process. The house didn't have much furniture and neither did Tess, so the random combination of household items might end up being serviceable, if not elegant.

For the time being, they dumped the incoming furniture near the front door. After Luke set down the last bookshelf, he said, "Are you ready to patch holes?"

"I have to do a couple of deliveries first. Then get the cats. They have to get out of my apartment too."

"Since we're done moving stuff, I'm going to bring Barney inside. Before you bring the British Invasion in, let me know, okay?"

"Sure. That reminds me. How come Barney was out in the truck before?"

"He was having a little time to himself so he could reflect on his bad behavior."

Tess laughed. "I'm glad my cats aren't the only ones who need time outs. See you later."

Zooming through her deliveries and appointments, Tess found that although she was physically tired, she was in a much better mood than she'd been in for a while. Maybe it was simply knowing that this awful move was almost over. It felt like she'd been freaked out forever about having no place to live.

When she was finally done with work, she returned to her apartment for the last time. She stood in the empty living room and surveyed the filthy carpet. Her rental deposits were already toast, and they were tearing out everything, so she'd expended zero energy in cleaning up. The little apartment seemed empty and forlorn.

A yowl came from the bathroom and she grabbed the kitty carriers and approached the door. "Okay, you guys. I hate to break it to you, but we're doing this thing."

Unfortunately, Tess had only two carriers and four cats. That meant she had to get two cats into each one. Getting a recalcitrant feline into a carrier at the same time another cat was frantically trying to leave was a tricky and involved task.

Fortunately the bathroom was small, so they couldn't get far. But the moment the Fab Four laid eyes on the evil carrier, they became wary. Tess had planned how to approach the problem in her mind on the way over. In theory, she'd pick up a cat, place him or her into the carrier, and close the gate.

It sounded good, but the reality of getting cats into plastic boxes rarely went as planned.

She got down on the tile and grabbed John first because he was the largest and easiest to snag. With both hands, she tried to ram his round orange body into the carrier. The problem was she only had two hands and he had four paws, which he used as anchors to keep his wide body outside of the door. When she pulled a paw off the door, before she could make a move to push him inside, the paw was outside the carrier again. John expressed his displeasure loudly as the other cats looked on with round eyes.

With a mighty shove, Tess said. "You're going in. I mean it." John lost purchase on the doorway and with a mighty yowl rolled inside. Tess slammed the door and exhaled the breath she'd been holding.

She went through a similar process with Ringo who dispensed with all sense of personal decorum and began flailing his razor-sharp claws in all directions while screaming bloody murder as if she were trying to rip off his skin. Good thing she was leaving the building.

Getting the two largest cats into the carriers was the most difficult part. After a considerable amount of wrangling, she got George into the carrier with John and Paul in with Ringo. When she was done, she leaned against the bathroom wall and rolled up her sleeves to examine the scratches on her arms. No one emerged from cat ownership unscathed. But at least the worst was over.

She collected all the kitty supplies from the bathroom and threw everything into her last box along with her phone and answering machine. She loaded the box and the carriers into her car, and then went back to lock the door. On her way out of the building, she threw the keys into her landlord's mail slot. At long last, she was out of here and this chapter of her life was officially over.

However, the Fab Four weren't going quietly, and they commenced a symphony of yowling as soon as she started up the Hyundai. The cats weren't fond of car travel and didn't care who knew it. Tess was pretty sure they weren't going to be too excited about their new home either, but there wasn't much she could do except suffer through their complaints.

When she got to the house, she went inside and Barney ran up to her. "Hey, where's your dad?"

Barney wagged his tail and cruised off toward the living room with Tess trailing behind him.

Luke was sitting on her old sofa eating a sandwich. He raised it in greeting. "Your couch is ugly, but it's comfortable."

"Maybe we could move it so it's not sitting right where we dropped it."

"Are the Beatles here?"

"They're in the car. I'm going to keep them in the master bedroom with me, so make sure you don't open the door once they're in there. The three younger ones haven't lived anywhere except my apartment and I think they're going to be freaked out for a while."

Luke took another bite. "Okay. After I finished nailing more patches, I moved most of your stuff in there."

"Really?" Tess paused for a second. "Thank you. That was nice of you."

"I didn't want to be tripping over all those boxes. I moved the other bed out and put yours in."

"That four-poster is pretty, but large. It looks like an antique. You moved it by yourself?"

"I took it apart. I got it at a huge yard sale out at the Hadley ranch a few years ago. The pieces are in the other bedroom and the mattress is on the floor. I'm ditching the single bed that was in there. I think Stetson slept on it and it stinks. That mattress can't be saved. I'll take it to the dump tomorrow."

"Eww." Tess pointed toward the door. "Is it okay if I bring in the Fab Four now?"

"Go for it."

"They're extremely unhappy. Could you maybe put Barney somewhere so they can't see him?"

"I'll feed him dinner. That will keep him amused." He stood up. "Let's go, Barn. It's dinner time."

Barney leaped up from his spot on the floor and charged toward the kitchen, followed by Luke.

Tess got the cats and their litter box and bowls set up in the bedroom, triple checked that the door was shut, and then let them out. She sat on the floor and watched while Paul and Ringo carefully sniffed around the new space.

George disappeared under the bed, and John came over to Tess and crawled into her lap, perhaps to show her that he'd forgiven her for heaving him into the evil plastic kitty carrier. She stroked the fur on his head. "Welcome to your new house, Johnny-boy. I apologize for the disturbing artwork on the walls. I don't like it either. This arrangement is only temporary until we find something better. I promise."

John put his head down, closed his eyes, and settled into a consistent purr. Tess could relate. It was a relief to have a home again even if it was only for a little while.

~

Tess sat on the floor petting John, thinking about Luke's sandwich while listening to her stomach growl. When was the last time she'd eaten anything? Once she felt like the cats were as comforted as they were going to get for the time being, she got up and tiptoed to the door. Managing to slip out without incident, she went to the kitchen to forage for dinner.

Compared to the one in her old apartment, the kitchen in the house was enormous. It had full-sized appliances, a double sink, and miles of counter space. Although Willy had done a terrible job painting the cabinets the hideous chartreuse color, there were a lot of them.

Tess had transported her food from her apartment along with everything else, so she went to the freezer, grabbed a frozen dinner, and threw it into the microwave. While the machine hummed and spun her food around, Tess idly scratched at a paint splatter on the countertop. Willy hadn't been a tidy artist.

The microwave beeped and she took her food out to the table in the dining room. Luke was up on the ladder again hammering. Tess did some admiring of the rear view of his Levi's while snarfing down her macaroni and cheese. He probably needed a haircut, but the way his hair curled around, hitting the collar of his shirt made her wonder what it felt like. Curly hair always looked so soft. Was it?

Luke descended the ladder, turned around, and his eyes widened. "How long have you been sitting there staring at me?"

"I'm not staring. I'm eating my dinner." She raised her fork and pointed it at the ladder. "You said I shouldn't startle you, and I don't want nails raining down on my head again."

"Are you ready to help patch holes now?"

"How? You only have one ladder."

"There's another one in the garage."

"Darn." Tess set down her fork and moved to get up.

Luke waved his hands in a downward motion. "Forget about it. Finish your dinner. I'm almost done anyway. I need to cut six more squares of wood, nail them up, and call it good. With patches on the outside and inside of the wall, the squirrels and water should stay out for the time being, unless the whole wall collapses."

"There's a distressing thought. On a related note, is there still a squirrel in the house somewhere?"

"Maybe." Luke looked up at the ceiling "I heard some scrabbling earlier, but it could have been from the roof."

"I don't suppose you saw any squirrels exiting stage left through the holes in the wall, did you?"

"Nope. Some could be here somewhere, I guess," Luke said over his shoulder as he left the room. "I saw other evidence that they're still inside."

Other evidence? Yuck. When she and Luke had cleaned up the Willy garbage, she'd vacuumed up quite a bit of squirrel excrement. Tess speared a piece of macaroni. Maybe Willy thought squirrels made great roommates, but she wasn't convinced. At least cats used litter boxes. Squirrels clearly did not.

She looked at the last box she'd brought in that contained her answering machine and a bunch of kitty toys. Her phone number wasn't supposed to be switched over to the house until the next morning, but she was curious to see if anyone had belatedly called to help her move. The silence had been deafening.

She set up the answering machine on the pass-through bar that went between the kitchen and dining room. It was close to a wall phone, so Tess plugged everything in and pressed the Play button.

The first message was from Joey who called from work saying, "Gosh, time sure flies. How did it get to be Wednesday already?" The bottom line after all the hemming and hawing was that he was busy. Tess did a mental eye roll. What a shocker. The next message was from Claire, who as usual didn't hesitate to launch into what she wanted to say. She squawked, "Aren't you *ever* at home? You haven't moved into that house, have you? You'd better not have done that without talking to me. Do you have any idea what you're doing?"

Tess stared at the answering machine waiting for Claire to finish her tirade related to Luke. It took a while for Claire to get through exactly what she thought of him, which was punctuated by quite a few colorful, graphic phrases that were physically and anatomically improbable. Finally, Tess pressed the button to erase the message.

When she looked up, Luke was standing in the kitchen holding squares of wood, gazing at her through the pass through. He held up the wood and tilted it toward the machine. "Sounds like Claire hasn't changed."

Tess frowned. "Not really. We've been playing voice mail tag for days, and she has some, uh, strong opinions about me living here."

"I got that." He turned and walked out of the kitchen and returned to the ladder in the dining room.

Tess walked to the French doors near the ladder and stood next to Barney, who was curled up for a nap. He raised his head, tipped his tail a few times and went back to sleep.

She looked up at Luke. "I'm sorry. Claire gets melodramatic sometimes."

"You don't need to apologize. It was kinda startling to hear her voice, that's all." He whacked a few nails into a board. "She's entitled to her opinion. Obviously, it hasn't changed."

Tess threw up her hands in exasperation. "I don't know what happened, even after all this time. I mean what's her big problem with you? You broke up. So what? Couples break up all the time, particularly in high school. You were what seventeen? Eighteen?"

Luke descended the ladder and bent to collect some more nails from a box on the floor. He threw the nails into the can, stood, and smiled at Tess. "Hey, if Claire hasn't told you, I'm certainly not going into it."

"You two broke up after that awful homecoming dance. I went with David, you went with Claire, and your friend Jim and his girlfriend were at the restaurant too. What was her name?"

"Joanne, I think."

"Right. Joanne. They were J and J and thought it was so cute. Ugh. That was the worst evening."

Luke chuckled as he climbed back up the ladder. "You're right about that."

"David complained about having to get dressed up the whole time. Then he spilled marinara sauce all over me."

"Oh yeah, I remember that. You freaked out."

"I did not *freak out.* Talking with your hands is one thing. I'm okay with being expressive, but don't use your breadstick as a baton when it's covered with tomato sauce. My dress was ruined."

Luke came back down the ladder. "That guy could really talk."

"Tell me about it. He never shut up."

"So I guess that's why you dated for five minutes."

"We were in all those plays together, so everyone assumed we were a couple. If I was ever going to have a date, it would have to be with him."

"You said it was a mistake."

"We had no chemistry. The first time we kissed, it was horrible."

Luke scratched at the stubble on his jaw. "I probably shouldn't ask this, but why? Or how?"

"It was slobbery and gross and a massive turn off. Like I had a jellyfish stuck to my face."

"Ouch."

"Well, maybe not a jellyfish, since it didn't sting. But something with tentacles. Maybe a squid or an octopus." Tess shuddered. "Yuck."

"Guess it wasn't all happy like *Octopus's Garden* then."

"Why are you fixated on this Beatles thing? Now *that* will be stuck in my head for the rest of the night."

"Don't blame me. I didn't name your cats. You did." Luke picked up the box of nails. "Okay, I'm done. Barney and I have gotta get home."

"Already? Are you hungry?" Tess was just getting into the conversation and the idea of being alone with her boxes unpacking was unappealing. "I know you had a sandwich earlier, but I have lots of frozen dinners."

"That sounds tasty, but we should get going. It's a long drive."

"You don't want to do it hungry. Barney got his dinner and I got mine. It's only fair." Tess smiled innocently. She was dying of curiosity and the only way she'd get the real scoop about what happened with Claire was to hear it from Luke.

Luke glanced at the dog, who was flat on his side snoring loudly. "I suppose I can let him sleep a while longer."

Tess walked to the refrigerator and opened the freezer with a flourish. "You have a wide selection of gourmet options."

Luke peered in and grabbed a box. "This works."

"Now you can tell me what happened in high school."

"Nope."

"Oh, come on."

Luke pressed buttons on the microwave. "If you're trying to bribe me with frozen food, it's not going to work."

Tess returned to the table. Foiled again. She'd worm it out of him eventually. "Okay then, tell me about this house. Did you live here before you moved to Gleasonville?"

"For a while." He pulled the food out of the microwave and sat down at the table. "It was a fixer-upper. Built in 1930 and kinda falling apart. I restored it."

"It must have been nice."

"I should have never let Dad talk me into renting to Willy."

"Why did you?"

Luke set down his fork. "Long story."

"I've got time."

"Shouldn't you be unpacking, calling Claire back, or checking on the kitty Beatles?"

"Probably. But I don't want to do any of those things. Why did you rent to Willy?"

"Why do you want to know?"

"I love stories and I'm sure there's a story there." Tess went for her sweetest, most innocent smile. "So tell me."

Luke poked at his dinner with the fork. "It was a stupid decision. I rented this place to Willy because my father asked me to. Dad and I don't have the greatest relationship anymore, and I was hoping to mend fences. It didn't work, so like I said, the whole thing ended up being a dumb mistake."

"What happened with your dad? I thought you said you worked for him since you were a little kid."

"I did, but after I took over the business, well, things didn't go so great. Having employees is complicated. There's all this record-keeping and banking you have to do, and I stink at accounting stuff. Construction is a seasonal business, and there was this revolving line of credit thing." He set down the fork again. "Dad's CPA was an…well, not a nice guy. We ran out of operating capital and he was yelling at me all the time about accounts and loans. It was bad."

"I'm not sure what operating capital is. Money, I guess?"

"Yeah, like money for making payroll. At the time, I didn't understand what the CPA was all pissed off about, which was a big problem." Luke looked down at the plate as he scraped the last of the pasta into a neat pile. "Selling the company was the right thing to do. But I still felt guilty—like I let down Dad."

"Not everyone is cut out to be a business mogul." Tess set her elbow on the table and rested her chin on her palm. "You have to accept who you are and who you aren't."

"I'm sure I'm not an accountant."

"Neither am I. And now I'm trying to accept that I'll never be an actress either."

~

After unburdening herself to Luke about her failed audition, Tess felt significantly better. Maybe she'd revealed more than she should have about the whole disaster, but it was a relief to share what happened. And at least her new landlord wouldn't expect that she'd be getting a sudden windfall from an acting job to help her pay the rent.

She and Luke chatted about Alpine Grove people and happenings over the last decade or so and shared family details. Luke's parents had gotten divorced a couple of years before his father had the stroke. After the split, his mom had moved out east and he hadn't seen her in a while. Luke's younger sister Rebecca, aka Becky, was living in Tokyo. She'd gone to Japan to teach English and met the man who was now her husband. Luke said that at the moment, they were on vacation in Thailand.

Tess vaguely remembered Luke's older brother because he was in the class ahead of them. Claire had mooned over him almost as much as she had Luke. As it turned out, Robert, who everyone used to call Robby, was now a big-wig investment banker in Los Angeles. Luke said, "He was always the smart one. Mr. Math Whiz should have taken over Bennett Enterprises, not me."

"It sounds like Robby had other plans."

"I suppose. But now he makes a big point that his name is Robert. If you call him Robby, he'll tackle you."

Tess grinned. "That might be okay if he's friendly about it. He was pretty cute."

"I guess he cleans up well. I'm sure you'd love all his tailored suits."

They continued chatting amiably until Luke glanced at his watch. "Sonofa…um…I had no idea it was this late. Barney and I need to get out of here. I've got that job at the dog boarding kennel tomorrow."

Tess jumped up and pulled her appointment book out of her purse. "Crap. I forgot. The owner of that place is supposed to give me a check. I never went out there again to pick it up. Geoff is going to kill me."

"I doubt that." Luke stood up and walked over to the dog who was crashed out on his dog bed. "C'mon, Barney. It's time to roll."

The dog raised his head and thumped his tail a few times. Luke said, "I mean it. Time to go home."

The dog stood up and stretched deeply as he uttered a long, squeaky yawn.

Tess looked at the clock on the stove. "It's two in the morning. Why don't you sleep on the mattress you threw on the floor in the downstairs bedroom?"

"No toothbrush."

"Live dangerously tonight and buy a toothbrush tomorrow morning."

"You don't care?"

"Well, tomorrow I'd appreciate it if you didn't talk to me until you brush your teeth. But it's your house. You don't have to leave on my account." Tess pointed at the ceiling. "I have my own space upstairs that's filled with vicious attack cats."

"I'll try not to upset the kitty Beatles." He chuckled as he picked up the dog bed. "Let's go, Barn. Looks like you don't have to sleep in the truck."

Tess waved at their retreating forms. "Sleep tight, you two."

By the time Tess staggered downstairs the next morning for her coffee, Luke and Barney had disappeared. Maybe he'd gone to find a toothbrush. As she scooped coffee into the coffeemaker, she reflected upon the conversation she'd had with Luke the night before. He was an incredibly good listener, which was handy because she was a good talker.

Even though she spent most of her days chatting with people in the process of selling advertising, she couldn't remember the last time she'd stayed up late talking to someone to the point that she'd completely lost track of time. When she was dealing with sales, a portion of her mind was usually busy calculating her commission or considering the approach she might take for her next appointment.

She set down her mug of coffee with conviction. As far as she could tell, Luke was a decent person. After hours of talking to him, she'd even go so far to say that he was nice. What was Claire's problem with him? Now that the phone bill was switched over to her name, it was time to rack up some long distance charges.

Tess picked up the phone and dialed Claire's work number. Her friend snapped, "Claire Collishaw," and Tess smiled at the uncharacteristic businesslike tone. "Hi, it's me."

Claire practically shrieked. "It's about time. Why haven't you returned my calls?"

"I tried, but I was in the process of moving. I've been busy, you know."

"You really did it?" Claire said in a softer voice. "You actually moved in with that weasel? Oh sweetie, why? *Why* would you do that?"

"Because I had no other options. And honestly, Luke has been nothing but pleasant to me."

"He might seem that way, but he's a lying snake. Lurking in the grass being sneaky, waiting to strike. Luring you into complacency until he stabs you in the back."

"So, about that. You need to tell me what on earth happened in high school. I can't figure out why you hate him so much."

Claire paused before answering. "It's embarrassing."

"More embarrassing than living in a house with squirrels?"

"Squirrels?"

"Never mind. What happened with Luke? I need to know what you have against my landlord."

"It's a long story."

Tess waved her hand in exasperation, even though no one could see it. "Why does everyone always say that? I'm not on a timetable here. Just *tell* me."

Claire sighed. "He cheated on me. And then I retaliated a little."

"A little? You mean sleeping with half of the football team after you broke up?" Tess knew Claire never did anything halfway.

"That too. But I also may have let his truck roll into the lake."

Tess muffled the laugh that wanted to burst out. This sounded like such a classic Claire move. "I'm not as surprised that you drove his truck into the lake as I am that Luke cheated on you. I mean, you guys were groping each other in the hallways at school. Everyone wanted you to go get a room."

"He won't admit it, but I know he did. Lying scum."

"How do you know?"

"I witnessed it. Over Christmas break, he was with some skanky girl from out of town."

"Where?"

"In his bedroom."

Tess paused to collect her thoughts. "Hold on. I'm lost. Did you walk in on them?"

"I was in the bathroom." Claire stopped for a moment before continuing. "This is the embarrassing part. I crawled up a tree and in through the bathroom window. The bathroom was connected to Luke's bedroom. I was going to surprise him."

"Did you catch him in the act?"

"I wasn't appropriately dressed for a confrontation."

Tess tried not to roll her eyes. "Were you wearing anything at all?"

"I was wearing my winter coat, but I lost it."

"How do you lose a coat in a bathroom?"

"I was trying to get the window open, and my coat got caught on a tree branch. The other times I sneaked into the house, Luke helped me inside. But the coat got caught, and either the coat was going to fall two stories down or I was, so I let the coat go."

"I guess you made it inside since you're still alive."

"After I ditched the coat, I sort of heaved myself through the window. It was complicated, and the tile was *freezing.* I was about to open the door and say 'surprise' when I heard Luke and the skank talking in the bedroom. They were busy in there."

Tess stopped scraping at the paint on the counter of the pass through. "Okay, don't keep me in suspense here. What did they say?"

"The skank said, 'Hold still. It's too big. I don't think it's going to fit.'"

Tess giggled. "Okay, I guess Luke is a big guy, but that might be more than I needed to know."

"Then Luke said something like, 'Ouch, you're pinching me.' And she says, 'This was your idea, you know.'"

"Well? Then what happened?" Tess practically shouted.

"The skank was giggling. Then I hear Luke say, 'It fell off. Can you find it? Well then, get another one.' The skank says, 'Is this how this is supposed to work?' Then Luke asks her something like, 'Should we stop? I don't want to do this if you don't.' And she says, 'No, it's fine. This is good, but it won't fit until you move it over here.'"

"So did he move it, uh, wherever he needed to?" Tess asked.

"I think so because the giggling stopped, but by then I was so upset, I went back out the window. I almost killed myself on that stupid tree. The bark was slippery from the rain and ice. And rough. I got about a million scratches all over me, and the worst part was I couldn't reach my coat.

When it fell, it caught on a branch half way down. So I had to find a way to get home naked."

Tess said, "I'm guessing this is the part where you drove the truck into the lake."

"I was angry, and I knew Luke had one of those magnetic boxes stuck underneath the truck with the key inside."

Tess knew that the house where Claire had grown up was near the boat launch at the lake, so the rest of the story was pretty clear. "Did you ever ask Luke about this?"

"He said nothing happened." Claire's voice raised a few octaves. "But I heard him. I heard *them.* The skank's giggling sounded just like me when I was with Luke. He used to whisper funny things when we made out. I thought it was cute, until I heard her."

"Are you sure they were doing what you think they were doing?"

"I could tell. And what *else* would they be doing in his bedroom?"

"I don't know. What was his excuse?"

"It was the most pathetic lie, *ever*. The lying scum said he was helping the daughter of some friend of his father's. *Helping*? Is that what he calls it? Was he helping her with an anatomy lesson? Or maybe helping her learn about the birds and the bees?"

"I'm guessing he wasn't too pleased about the truck either."

"His dad found out because the truck had to be towed out of the lake. Before vacation ended, we had a huge fight. There was a lot of yelling. After that, he avoided me for the rest of the year. I never spoke to him again."

Tess leaned against the counter. "That's quite a story. I can't believe you never told me this before."

"Your family went to visit your aunt that Christmas. Before break, you and I had spent so much time hanging out in my bedroom reading Mom's old issues of *Cosmo* and me going on and on about how I was finally going to lose my virginity over vacation. Then it didn't happen. I felt like my life was ruined, and the whole thing was totally humiliating. So when you asked, I just said we broke up."

"We were horny seventeen-year-olds, and sex was all we talked about. Heck, it was all we *thought* about. A lot of high school was humiliating. You shouldn't have been embarrassed to tell me."

"That's sweet of you to say and why we'll always be best friends."

Tess laughed. "Also because no one else would put up with either of us."

"That too."

Chapter 5

Pipe Dreams

After chatting for a while longer, Claire had to get back to work, so Tess wasn't able to extract any more information. Claire was a real estate agent in Connecticut, and she had a major sale on the line. The place sounded like a castle although it was referred to as a "summer home." Mansion or not, it was expensive, and Claire implied that she might have already spent most of her commission in anticipation of the big closing.

After she hung up, Tess got to work as well, setting up a few sales appointments for the afternoon. But her first task was to go out to the hinterlands and get the check from the dog boarding woman. Good thing Luke had reminded her before Geoff noticed the absence of any payment for all those forms. Yes, she'd been busy, but sheesh what kind of crummy salesperson forgets to collect the *money*? If Geoff found out, he'd have a coronary.

After dealing with her morning routine, and most importantly, feeding the Fab Four, Tess got in her car and headed north. It was a glorious spring day with bright green leaves and flowers popping out everywhere, as if all the vegetation was trying to forget about the long cold winter. If she had to drag herself all the way out to the sticks again, at least it was a beautiful drive.

She turned at the driveway and wound her way through the grove of cedar trees that led up to the kennel buildings. As she approached, she saw a group of people standing around with a few dogs. There was a guy wearing a red flannel shirt that she didn't know, but she recognized Luke and Barney. The short woman next to the guy in flannel was probably the owner of the place, Kat Stevens.

Barney was obviously having a great time playing with a nimble black and white dog that was running circles around him, darting back and forth in a complex game of keep away. Tess smiled at the scene. Poor Barney wasn't able to keep up with the speedy border collie, and he was panting at all the exertion. The gigantic brown dog Tess had seen before was looking on with interest, but not participating in the canine romp.

Tess parked the Hyundai and got out. Barney and the border collie ran over, but only Barney stopped to say hello. She reached out to pet his head while he drooled on her slacks for a moment. At least the pants were washable. And now she had access to a washing machine *inside* her house. If she never saw the inside of the Alpine Grove Laundromat again, it would be too soon.

Barney ran off after the border collie again, and Tess walked up to the group. She smiled at the woman who was surprisingly tan considering it was April. The house sitter had said the honeymoon trip was to Hawaii. The weather certainly must have been good. "You must be Kat. I'm Tess, and I think we spoke on the phone about your forms."

Kat held up a checkbook. "I guess I owe you money too. It's a theme we have going here today."

Tess glanced at Luke, who put his hands in his pockets but didn't say anything.

The man standing next to Kat also had a nice tan and scratched at his scruffy quasi-beard. "Please tell me the forms cost less than the plumber."

Tess handed a copy of the invoice to Kat. "The person who was here when I dropped off the forms said she ran out of checks because the plumber got the last one."

"I know. I'm sorry about that. We weren't expecting so many expenses." Kat gestured toward the man next to her with her pen. "This is my husband, Joel, and that's Luke. Feel free to talk among yourselves while I write out the check."

Tess smiled at Luke. "Actually, as of yesterday, Luke is my landlord. So we've met."

Kat paused in her scribbling to look at Luke and then at Tess. "I guess I shouldn't be surprised anymore. Everybody knows everybody here."

"Tess and I went to the same high school," Luke said.

"I was desperate for a place to rent," Tess added. "No one wants to rent to someone with four cats."

"I can relate to that type of problem," Kat replied. "People don't want to house sit for you either. They might once. But after the first time, they know what's involved. At this point, we may never be able to take another vacation again."

Joel shook his head. "Not to mention that we can't afford it."

Tess hadn't taken a vacation in more than a year. "Me neither."

"You just got back from L.A. the other day," Luke said.

"That was for an audition, which, as I told you, was definitely not a vacation," Tess said.

Kat handed Tess the check. "Here you go. I hate to spend money and run, but I have to walk dogs and get ready for a meeting."

Luke said, "Tess, it's about the Grove Theater. You should go too."

"What about it?" Tess said.

Kat handed Joel the pen. "I got roped into talking to people about starting a nonprofit because I helped with AGAA."

"What's AGAA?" Tess asked.

"Alpine Grove Animal Adoptions. It's a nonprofit a friend started to help homeless dogs. I don't know why I need to be there if Brigid is going. She founded AGAA. I'm just a lowly board member."

Joel said, "You're going because Brigid bribed you with food."

"I suppose that's true," Kat admitted. "It works every time."

Tess was a little lost as to who Brigid was, but she was sick about the fate of the Grove. "I'm confused. I thought some company bought the Grove Theater and is tearing it down."

"There's a group of locals who are organizing because they want to save it," Luke said. "They want to see if they can convince the investment firm not to demolish it."

"The insurance guy I talked to said it wouldn't be profitable as a theater," Tess said.

"The place was built in the twenties," Kat said. "A couple of women think they can convince the new owner it's a historic landmark, so it shouldn't be torn down."

Tess put her hands on her hips. "Well, they're right. It *is* a historic landmark. Luke and I both spent lots of time there when we were growing up."

"We did," Luke said. "Tess, you should go to this meeting with Kat."

"I have so much unpacking to do. You're the one who said my boxes were everywhere," Tess said.

"I don't live there, so it's a mess I don't have to see," Luke said. "Last night, you were telling me how much the Grove meant to you."

"I've got to get these dogs walked now, but the meeting is at the gift store at 7:30. They're desperate for people to help." Kat looked up at Joel. "I can't believe Tracy is blowing this off when her mom is the one organizing it."

"If Bea is involved, that makes a huge difference." Tess clapped her hands together. "She mentioned something about the Grove the last time I saw her, but I didn't realize anything was really happening. I'll be there. I need to run this check back to the office, but I'll see you later."

Luke pointed at the back of the house. "Since you agreed to the extra work, I should get back to it."

Tess waved goodbye to everyone and rushed off, her heart filled with joy. She wasn't the only one who loved the old theater, after all.

~

After walking five groups of dogs, Kat trudged back to the house. Since she and Joel had returned from their honeymoon, it seemed like half of the dog owners in Alpine Grove had suddenly decided they needed dog boarding. And Kat's dog walker, Mia, also needed a vacation after tending to the kennel for two weeks. So now Kat was on full-time dog duty and remembering why she hired a dog walker in the first place. Usually, Kat did the short dog walks in the morning and evening and Mia did the long tire-out-the-canines walks midday, so Kat could work on her other job writing freelance articles.

Kat was feeling Mia's absence, particularly in her feet. Time to invest in new hiking shoes. Or shoe inserts. Or something. All this walking was wearing her out and it had only been four days. She slowly slogged up the stairs to the front door and went inside.

Joel was in the kitchen making sandwiches for dinner since Kat was going to town for the meeting about the proposed nonprofit. He handed her a plate. "Bon appetit."

"Thanks." Kat walked to the table and sat down. She looked up at Joel as he sat down in the chair next to her. "Does it already feel like our honeymoon was a million years ago to you?"

"Pretty much." He put his arm around her and kissed her cheek. "But I still love you."

"I love you back." She set down her sandwich. "Um, I hate to cast aspersions on your truck, but it sounds worse than usual. I'm a little afraid to take it to town."

"You never have any problem casting aspersions on it, but I agree that noise it's making might not be good."

"It's not going to strand me in the middle of nowhere, is it?"

"I hope not."

"I think we should get another car. If you're gone, I can't go anywhere and vice versa."

He raised an eyebrow. "I'm not the one who sold my car."

"That's ancient history, and that poor little car couldn't cope with winter out here anyway." Kat took a bite of sandwich. Talking to Joel about spending money was always a delicate proposition. "We should get another vehicle, preferably one that's not twenty years old and unpleasant to drive."

"We can't afford it."

"We could make payments."

"That would add to our recurring monthly expenses."

"So what? We need a car. When you're using the truck, I hate feeling like I'm trapped here."

"What if we have a bad month with no dogs, no articles, and no programming work?"

Kat frowned and bit back what she wanted to say, making an extreme effort to sound reasonable. "As you just pointed out, we have three sources of income. Actually four because Jack and Becca pay their rent on the Shack on time every single month like clockwork. The odds of all of that income disappearing at once is minuscule."

"I wouldn't say that. You never know what could happen." Joel set down his sandwich. "Today, we're spending thousands of dollars on excavation work we weren't expecting. Between that and a trip to Hawaii, our budget is shot."

"But we need a car."

"We have the truck."

Kat was getting nowhere with this conversation and she didn't want to argue about it. They'd just returned from the most romantic honeymoon in history, so the last thing she wanted to do was get into a huge money fight. "I have to go. If I don't return, that means the truck died. Luke has a vehicle, so send him to find me."

"I'm sure he will have left here by then."

Kat stood up. "I noticed that he and Tess seem to know each other *awfully* well."

"He said they went to high school together."

"Is he just her landlord?" Kat gave Joel a salacious grin. "I mean the last two people we met who went to Cedar County High School together got married last year."

"You're being nosy."

"Just trying to lighten the mood." Kat walked to the hallway and put on her coat. "We need another vehicle."

"The truck is fine." Joel followed her and leaned on the doorway. "We can make do."

Kat put her arms around his neck, stood on tiptoes, and gave him another kiss. "We're not done talking about this."

"I figured we weren't. Drive carefully."

Kat went out to the old green truck and fought to get the evil hunk of metal to start. A primary reason she wanted a new car was because she hated the truck with a fierce passion. It was old and curmudgeonly, and she spent a lot of time saying bad words while driving it. Of course, Joel was well aware of her feelings toward his truck, which was probably why he was discounting her opinion about getting a new car.

Kat uttered a few unflattering phrases about the truck's mechanical failings as she ground the recalcitrant transmission into first gear. She'd been predicting the imminent demise of this stupid truck for so long that Joel would never agree to a new car until rusty pieces of the truck literally started falling off and clattering to the road. Plus, Joel was beyond frugal. She understood and sometimes even appreciated his conservative nature when it came to money, but it was still frustrating.

Before they'd gotten married, she and Joel had consolidated their finances. But now that the money was all in one account and it wasn't all her money, it felt weird like she was spending someone else's money. Was she allowed to? Did she have to ask permission to buy stuff now? The whole train of thought was stupid because some of what was in the account came from her freelance writing income and the dog boarding business.

Joel had everything organized into spreadsheets with categories for business and personal expenses. But every time they went over it together, Kat wanted to take a nap. For her, numbers were an outstanding sleep aid. Mostly she just nodded when he explained what they were looking at. Maybe Joel was right that they couldn't afford to buy another vehicle. How would she know?

Kat's thoughts continued to spin in a vortex of numerical confusion as she berated herself for not paying more attention to the last budget conversation. She drove to the large parking lot at her friend Maria's apartment building, got out of the truck, and walked to the gift shop.

When she entered the store, she waved at Brigid, who had founded Alpine Grove Animal Adoptions and convinced her to come to the meeting. Brigid also was a fantastic cook and Kat couldn't resist the spanakopita triangles that Brigid brought to almost every AGAA meeting. Kat was a sucker for tasty snackables and Brigid knew it.

Brigid gave her a hug. "How's my favorite blushing bride?"

"Trying to adjust to married life."

Brigid gave Kat a stern look as she held both her hands. "What does that mean? You look upset. Are you okay? You're not fighting, are you?"

Although Brigid was widowed, Kat knew that her life as a military spouse had been difficult. Although Brigid didn't mention it often, from the little she did say, it sounded like she and her husband had spent most of the time he wasn't overseas arguing with one another. Kat shook her head. "Joel and I have differing opinions about our current transportation options, that's all."

"Marriage is so hard." Brigid squeezed Kat's hands. "If you want to unload, I'm happy to lend a sympathetic ear anytime."

"I'm fine. Don't worry. We'll work it out." As a newlywed, it wasn't socially acceptable to say that life with your new spouse was anything other than rainbows and unicorns. If Kat mentioned any inkling of strife, within twenty minutes most of Alpine Grove would assume she and Joel were on the brink of divorce. They definitely weren't, but Brigid was probably right about marriage. The honeymoon was over, and sharing your life with another person wasn't always easy.

~

The festive bells on the door jingled as Tess walked into the gift store, which technically was closed for business. Instead of being filled with customers, a few women were standing around chatting near trays of munchies that had been placed on the counter. Bea was setting up folding chairs and smiled at Tess.

Tess grabbed a chair and unfolded it. "I'm glad to see people here."

Bea straightened. "Me too since it was a bit last minute. But word got out anyway."

"It's Alpine Grove. Word always gets out. I heard about it while I was out at the dog boarding kennel."

"I didn't know you'd met Kat." Bea pointed at Kat who was nibbling on an hors d'oeuvre and chatting with a red-haired woman who was as short as she was. "I left a message for you at work."

"I haven't been back to the office, but dog kennels need their forms," Tess said. "Everyone needs printing. Or, at least, it seems like it to me."

Bea gave her a hug. "I'm so glad you're here. You're the first person I thought of when we talked about having a meeting about the Grove."

"Me?"

"You're an actress."

"Not anymore. I'm giving up on that pipe dream."

"Oh for heaven's sake. Don't say that. You'll always be an actress. And when we talked the other day, you were so upset about the fate of the Grove." Bea checked her watch. "But I'm getting ahead of myself. We should get started."

Bea walked over to the food and spread her arms wide in an effort to herd the grazers toward the folding chairs. "I think everyone is here. Please take a seat."

Tess saw Kat grab some more munchies before sitting down. The food bribery program appeared to be working.

Bea pulled Margaret Connelly from her chair and waved for everyone else to be quiet. Margaret owned the bookstore in town. Over the years, Tess had spent a lot of time wandering through Twice Told Tales shopping for books, cards, and birthday gifts for friends and family.

Bea said, "Margaret and I have called you all together to talk about the Grove Theater. As I'm sure you know, the Cullins family that owned the theater for years recently sold it to a company out of state. After some research, we've found that this business invests in distressed properties. They look for the best way to make the investment profitable. Unfortunately, it sounds like at this point, they believe the most profitable option is to tear down the theater."

Everyone in the room grumbled at that comment, and Margaret shook her head so forcefully that her short gray curly hair swished against her chin. "Bea isn't finished. There might be another option."

"In a roundabout way, I was able to find out more information," Bea said. "Some of you might know my son-in-law, Drew. His father used to own various pieces of real estate around here. Because a person at the company that now owns the Grove knew his father, Drew was able convince him to tell him more about the company's plans."

"Drew says the person he talked to said they might be open to selling the theater because he hasn't figured out what to do with it yet," Margaret said, clapping her hands together. "So we have a great opportunity to save this historic building."

Tess raised her hand slowly to get Bea's attention. "How? I'd love to see that happen, but who has the money to buy it?"

Bea smiled. "Unfortunately, as we all know, since the Grove was boarded up years ago, no one has come forward with huge fistfuls of money to resurrect a failed business."

Margaret added, "But Bea and I have been talking, and we think that if the community bands together, collectively we could buy it."

Bea pointed at the red-haired woman next to Kat. "I invited Brigid because she has experience in setting up a nonprofit corporation."

"It's a lot of work," Brigid said. "But you could create an organization and make an offer to buy the building. The nonprofit could then run the theater as a business."

A woman in the back grumbled, "That's going to be a neat trick. Have you been inside the Grove in the last five or six years? There's a reason they boarded it up. After Floyd Cullins died, his daughter slapped a for sale sign on it and left it to fall apart. Nobody wanted to pay the outrageous price they wanted for that wreck."

Tess said, "But don't you remember what the theater used to be like? It was so beautiful—like something out of a fairy tale. The plaster on the walls had all those stencils and painted patterns around the archways. And remember the two balconies with the iron railings? There was one on each side of the stage. I remember looking out at them and at that high ceiling with all the dark wood and gold trim. Oh, and the lion head fountain in the lobby? Wasn't that amazing? I loved that place."

Brigid said, "You must have spent quite a bit of time at the theater."

Tess could feel her cheeks heat up. Oops. She needed to get Crazy Tess to crawl back under her rock. "I'm sorry to go on like that, but I have a lot of good memories of the Grove."

Bea said, "Tess was in a number of community shows. She was magic under those stage lights and simply mesmerized the audience."

Tess looked down and fidgeted with the buckle on her purse. "Oh, Bea, it wasn't like that at all."

"Don't sell yourself short. You were wonderful." Bea cleared her throat and held up a clipboard. "So it sounds like Tess is in. What about the rest of you? I need to find out who else is willing to support this effort. We have a lot of work to do. Please sign your name, and in the second column, write down any skills you have or suggestions for ways you might be able to help us raise money. We also need to do some research and figure out a viable business plan."

People quietly passed around the clipboard and murmured to each other. Tess felt oddly like an outsider. Even though she knew virtually every person in the room, at least by sight, she felt like the odd woman out because no one else was a performer.

Although there were a lot of things she didn't miss about her stint in Los Angeles, such as the city itself, Tess did long for the sense of camaraderie that she'd felt being around so many other struggling actors. On those sets and stages, she'd enjoyed being around other creative artists who understood the joy of performing. Maybe it was shared love for the craft or maybe it was just shared adversity. Every time she was in a production, the ensemble of actors had to endure various hardships like early call times, prop failures, lack of stand-ins, disgusting craft services food, and facilities failures such as makeshift or nonexistent dressing rooms and toilets.

But even with the various problems, it had been such a thrill to be around other actors, working with them and watching them perform. Over the years, acting had evolved from something that she did because it was fun and different to a huge part of her identity.

Until recently, Tess had never stopped to ask herself why she cared so much about acting. Now that she'd blown what was likely to be her last audition, if Bea and Margaret were successful in saving the old theater, maybe Tess could share what little she knew with the next generation.

Like the old adage went, those who can't do, teach.

~

After Tess signed up to help raise money and chatted with Bea for a couple of minutes, she drove the few blocks home. Bea was thinking they might be able to turn the Grove into a movie theater. The librarian was going to research it as a possible business idea and see what was involved.

When she pulled up in front of the house, Luke's truck was there. The Fab Four were undoubtedly beside themselves by now because their dinner was late, so she grabbed her bag and hustled to the door.

As she walked inside, Barney barked a couple of times until he realized he knew who she was. Then he ran up and enthusiastically greeted her. "Hi there, Barney."

Luke leaned on the kitchen counter at the pass through. "We're just dropping off some stuff I grabbed at the hardware store on my way home. I'll be painting this weekend. And maybe working on the wall if the rest of the stuff I ordered comes in tomorrow."

Tess sat down at the table. "Thanks for encouraging me to go to the meeting. Bea and Margaret have lots of ideas."

"That sounds good." He pointed at the stack of boxes near the door. "Could you move those before I paint?"

"Oh yeah. I'll do that after I feed the cats."

"Maybe you could put away some of your things. I don't want to be tripping on stuff tomorrow." He walked into the living room and gestured toward the dog. "Let's go, Barney. We're outta here. See you tomorrow."

After they walked out the door, Tess scowled at the boxes. Unpacking would have to wait until after the cats were fed. And what was Luke's problem anyway? She'd just moved in, and he was the one who said she should go to the meeting. He knew she'd been busy. What a grump. No wonder Claire still hated him all these years later. Men were always so unreasonable. Ugh.

The next morning, Tess went downstairs, had some coffee, and made her work-related phone calls for the day. Another meeting about the Grove was scheduled for Monday, and in between calls, she considered what she could do to help. Maybe she could make phone calls and beg people for donations. When you got down to it, soliciting funds was just another type of sales. And she had lots of experience. She wasn't shy and had no problem picking up the phone and convincing cranky people to part with their money.

She reached to pick up the telephone handset to make her next sales call when the phone rang, and she jerked her hand away. This house was so quiet that a simple noise like the phone ringing practically made her jump out of her skin.

Her heartbeat accelerated even more at the sound of Dennis Gaylord's smooth talk-show-host voice. Even though it had been years, she still recognized it. Once upon a time, in what felt like three lifetimes ago, Tess had been hopelessly in love with him. That one shining moment in time was like a fairytale with sparkling dreams of a perfect future. That dream subsequently turned into a nightmare and their parting had been anything but amicable. Why in the world was he calling her?

"Tess, are you listening to me?" Dennis said sharply. "I asked you a question."

"Sorry, I'm surprised to hear from you, that's all." She put her hand on her chest. Having a heart attack while talking to Dennis would be awkward.

He continued, "I'm directing a play, and I think you'd be perfect for it. I want you to come read for me on Monday."

"Monday? I, well, I don't know what to say." Tess reached for the phone cord and twisted it around her finger. Back in the day, "read for me" had been code for "jump each other in the dressing room." Did he not remember that? What was he asking?

"Say you'll come here and read for the part."

"How's Jennifer?"

"Jennifer who?"

Tess looked at the ceiling, which had what looked like a deformed spider painted on it. But it was hard to tell. Willy's art defied classification. "Never mind. What's the play about?"

"It's a performance art piece that explores the division between the skepticism of ironic poetry themes and the epistemology of a sublime political aesthetic."

"What does that mean?"

"Didn't you hear me? Poetry and politics."

Tess tugged at her earring. Why on earth would he want her in a play like that? "Dennis, get real. You don't honestly think I'm a good fit for this, do you? I don't know what epistemology means, and the last audition I did was for a toilet paper commercial."

"It requires someone who is a little bit…well, creative."

Tess scowled. Now this call made sense. In Dennis World, "creative" was a euphemism for certifiably insane. Before they broke up, Dennis had made a big point that he thought she needed professional help. Sure, sometimes Crazy Tess came out to play and she blurted out off-the-wall comments without thinking, but Tess wasn't insane. Not clinically anyway. Most actors were a little nuts. But Dennis had constantly maintained that something was seriously wrong with Tess, not only to her face, but to other people as well.

The best thing Tess had ever done for herself was exit his orbit. Being one of his fawning fans had been exhausting and extremely bad for her self-esteem. On the other hand, she was older and wiser now. There's no way she'd get sucked in by his smarmy charm now. And the idea of acting *was* enticing, particularly since the odds of hearing from her agent again were slim to none.

She dropped the phone cord and placed her palm flat on it with a smack. "All right. I need to move some appointments around, but yes, I can get to L.A. on Monday. What time?"

Dennis gave her the details and when Tess hung up the phone, her heart finally returned to a normal rhythm. She slowly went up the stairs to get dressed for work. When she opened the door, the cats were sprawled out in various favorite sleep spots throughout the room. The poor little creatures were probably getting tired of being trapped in this bedroom. But Luke had said he might stop by later with Barney, and Tess didn't want to risk an interspecies altercation.

She sat on the bed and John crawled into her lap. As she stroked his fur, he commenced purring. "Sorry, guys. A little while longer and then I'll let you out of this room. Soon. I promise."

Ringo jumped up on the bed and sat looking expectantly at her. He raised a front paw and began fastidiously licking it. Tess reached out to pet him. "I know. Time to get dressed. Not to mention unpack. I need to put this stuff away."

She went to her suitcase and pulled out a dress. Ringo meowed plaintively, and she glanced at him. "You're right. This one makes me look fat. I should just give it away."

The cat resumed licking his paw, ignoring her. She laid a green blouse next to him. "How's this? Maybe with the gray skirt?"

Ringo seemed to approve of her choice and jumped off the bed. Tess smiled. "Okay, the green it is, then."

~

The next morning, Tess was determined to focus on unpacking boxes and putting stuff away, particularly in the bedroom. The cats were excited about all the new boxes, and the ten-by-ten space was startling to resemble a kitty obstacle course. The cats were also chewing on the flaps of some of the boxes, which was distressingly reminiscent of the Great Feline Uprising, an event Tess desperately hoped would never be repeated.

After feeding the Fab Four and admonishing them to consume the food and not corrugated cardboard, she staggered downstairs for coffee. Thanks to moving and other stresses, it had been a long, exhausting week. The idea of driving to Los Angeles again was looking less appealing. Not to mention seeing Dennis. Why did she agree to it?

She sat on a barstool at the pass through staring at the coffeemaker, watching it drip, drip, drip. This audition with Dennis was likely to turn out like a box of donuts: the anticipation was always better than the reality. Tess learned years ago that if you want to score points at a sales meeting, bring donuts. Everyone loves donuts because they're a sickly sweet and fattening guilty pleasure. Sitting in their pretty pink box, donuts look so tasty, who can resist? So you take one, eat it, but then realize you've made a horrible mistake because you feel sick for the rest of the day.

The audition was likely to end up being like the worst sugary bear claw, ever. Because Dennis had dangled the prospect of an acting job in front of her, she was sucked in by the idea. But this trip would probably be a huge mistake in the end.

Tess sipped her coffee slowly, savoring the stillness of the quiet Saturday morning. Not having to call anyone, go anywhere, or do anything outside of these four walls felt like an incredible luxury after so much running around.

The sound of the front door opening startled Tess from her ruminations. Barney bounded around the living room and stopped in front of her, wriggling and wagging happily. Tess wasn't that wired unless she'd had six cups of espresso. Clearly, the dog appreciated mornings far more than she did.

Luke walked through the door carrying cans of paint. He set them down in the living room and raised his eyebrows. "What happened to you?"

Tess looked down at her old pink terrycloth bathrobe. "Nothing. I always look like this at eight in the morning."

"I thought you'd be dressed by now." He gestured toward the room. "And maybe have cleaned up a little."

"Hey, I just moved. Work was a drag this week and I went to that meeting. I've been busy and I'm tired." She took a sip of coffee. "Why are you here so early? I mean jeez, what time did you get up this morning?"

"Four thirty."

"That's not morning. That's dark."

"I wanted to get an early start." He picked up a box. "How about you help me move these somewhere else? I need to start laying out drop cloths."

"Why are you painting when you're afraid the wall is going to fall down? Isn't the wall more important?"

"Because I can't work on this place full-time, I can't tear down the current wall. So I'm going to build a new one next to it and extend the back of the house into the back yard a little. That means I have to get a permit. Oh, and I need scaffolding, which I can't get until Monday."

"I guess you've put some thought into all this."

"I'm hoping that Willy and Stetson didn't drill enough holes for the wall to collapse."

"With you on that. I'll try not to breathe on it too hard." Tess encircled her coffee mug with both hands and pointed an index finger toward the kitchen. "Want some coffee? I made a whole pot."

Luke went into the kitchen and poured some coffee into a mug. He took a sip and peered over the rim at her. "Did something happen since I saw you the other day? You look depressed. I thought you said the meeting was good?"

"It was." Tess grinned. "Bea is on fire to save the Grove, and you know she knows *everyone*. I was doubtful at first, but I think with Bea involved, it could actually happen. They're getting organized."

"Are you going to help?"

"There's another meeting Monday to go over stuff, but I won't be able to go."

Luke walked out of the kitchen and sat on the other barstool in front of the pass through. "Why not?

"I have an audition in L.A."

"I thought you said that your agent was giving up on you after the last audition." Luke smiled. "It was a little more melodramatic than that though. I think you said you were doomed to sell printing until the Apocalypse takes us all out in a fiery inferno."

"Maybe not." Tess shrugged. "This opportunity isn't from my agent. A director called me."

"That sounds good. I'd think you'd be more excited."

"I would be if I didn't know the director." Tess set down her mug. "Dennis is a lying, cheating weasel with the moral character of slime floating on a pool of toxic waste."

"That sounds like something Claire would say."

Tess flopped her hands into her lap. "Probably. But you're nothing like Dennis. I mean, sure, you may have cheated on Claire, but not like him. He has one of those personalities that draw people to him. Like moths to a flame and all that. Then he makes them feel like garbage. It's hard to explain."

Luke looked down at his mug. "Setting aside whatever Claire told you about me for a second—which isn't true, by the way—why would you want to see this guy again if you hate him so much?"

"I might get to act again." There was a tightness in her throat, and Tess was afraid she might start to cry, which would be extra humiliating in front of Luke. "I know it sounds ridiculous, but I miss performing so much. Acting is all I've ever wanted to do."

He put his palm on the back of her hand. "I know how it is to want something really badly that you can't have."

Tess looked up at him and somehow the sympathetic look in his blue eyes tore at her conflicted heart and she burst into ugly sobs. She put her palms over her face and squeezed her eyes shut but felt him put his arm around her and rub her back. She leaned on his chest, grabbing his flannel shirt and clutching the soft cloth in her hand. The warmth and scent of soap and sawdust was comforting.

Luke continued to hold her until she finally ran out of tears. She moved out of his embrace and stared at her feet on the rung of the barstool. "I'm so sorry. I don't know what happened. All of a sudden, it was all too much."

Luke rubbed her upper arm. She looked up and he smiled. "Are you sure you want to go on this trip?"

Tess took a deep breath, trying to behave like a grownup again. "No, but I told Dennis I would, and I can't give him the satisfaction of backing out now. But I feel like a huge failure as an actress. I mean, how could *this* be my best option?"

"Well, don't let him know you feel that way or you'll never get the part." He grabbed the cup off the counter. "Oh, and you should call Bea and let her know that you won't make it to the meeting."

Tess sighed. "Yeah, I guess I should do that too."

"And then maybe put some of your stuff away."

"I'm working on it."

"Work harder," he said as he started toward the kitchen. "This place is still a mess."

"I know." Tess grabbed his hand to stop him. "So, um, thanks for listening. You're a lot nicer than Claire led me to believe."

"No problem." He squeezed her palm. "Claire doesn't know me as well as she thinks she does."

He might have a point. When was the last time Claire had even seen Luke? Ten years ago? Eleven? Tess put her coffee mug in the sink and went upstairs to get dressed. It was time to stop whining, get off her butt, and start moving.

Chapter 6

Feel the Force

Tess spent the rest of the weekend unpacking, watching Luke paint, and fretting about her trip to Los Angeles. The idea of seeing Dennis again made her feel sick to her stomach. Vomiting during the audition was a sure way to lose the part. Maybe it was for the best. Hadn't she already given up on acting once anyway?

Around noon on Sunday, Tess was tired of unpacking and walked over to the ladder in the living room. Luke was working on putting primer over the Willy art on the ceiling. She looked up and tapped his calf. "Hey, do you want lunch?"

"I was planning to pick up a sub at the cafe."

"How do you feel about sandwiches here? It's not exciting, but it's cheaper than the cafe."

"Okay." He stepped down the ladder. "Free is in my price range."

Tess assembled some sandwiches and set a plate down in front of Luke. "Enjoy."

He grabbed a napkin and looked across the table at her. "Are you feeling better?"

"Not really, and now I'm feeling a little self-conscious about crying all over your flannel shirt. Having a pre-midlife crisis isn't the best way to impress a new landlord. Sorry about that."

Luke set down his sandwich. "Don't worry about it. My shirts have seen worse."

Tess picked a piece of crust off the edge of her sandwich and nibbled at it. "I'm freaked out about this audition. Dennis said the play is about politics and poetry, which are two areas where I have zero experience or interest. He said I could bring a prepared monologue, but I might have to improvise too. And as you know, failing at improvisation is how I blew my last audition."

"Yeah, you said that didn't go well."

"It was a disaster. Dennis only wants me to read because he thinks I'm a lunatic."

"So don't go."

"I told you before. I *have* to go. Could you listen to my monologue?" At Luke's confused expression, she added, "It's a short speech from *The Sound of Music.*"

"That's not political, unless you count the whole 'Nazis are bad' aspect, I guess."

"I know, but it's either that or Shakespeare. I was thinking Maria might be easier to relate to than Lady Macbeth. And then, if they want me to sing, I can do that too."

Luke shrugged. "Go for it."

Tess launched into the scene at the convent where Maria confesses to the Reverend Mother that she was out singing in the mountains without permission.

"Sounded good to me. I'm no expert, but I think you'd be a great Maria." Luke leaned forward and folded his hands on the table. "But what happens if you actually get a role in this political play? Would you move back to Los Angeles? How long would the play last?"

"I haven't thought about that because I know I won't get the part."

"If you're convinced you're not going to get the part, why go? You seemed excited after the meeting about the Grove. Why not focus on that? Maybe they'll do plays there again and you could act. Hey, you could even get them to do *The Sound of Music.*"

"Even if they manage to keep the theater from being torn down, it sounds like they'll show movies. That's great for Julie Andrews, but not me. And let's face it, how many actors could there be in Alpine Grove? I doubt we could even round up enough people to play the Von Trapp kids. We'd have to ditch a couple of the little ones. And then what do they sing? 'Do, re, mi…oops, never mind'?"

"You were in shows when you were young. Who else was? I think I remember Bea was in something I saw."

"She was the lead in *Hello, Dolly.* The guy who owns Lowell's Hardware was in that too. I think his wife, Natalie, and a couple of their kids might have been in some plays too. A few people I remember performing have since died. There was a theater troupe, but I'm not sure how many people who were involved back then are still around."

"I sure don't know, but this is Alpine Grove. Everyone knows everything about everyone's business. It would be easy enough to find out."

"I could ask Bea. She'd know."

Luke stood up and walked to the ladder. "Sounds like a good idea."

"Will you think I'm weird if I sing while you're painting?"

He laughed. "Musical accompaniment might be nice."

Tess sang about the hills being alive, a few of her favorite things, problems like Maria, and a few other choice selections from *The Sound of Music* as she packed. Occasionally, Barney would be moved enough to offer up some howling, yipping, and baying noises. Maybe it was the canine way of showing musical appreciation. Or sing along. Tess wasn't sure, but he seemed to enjoy himself. It also was liberating not having to worry about neighbors pounding on the wall because she was making too much noise. There was something to be said for living in a free-standing dwelling with no shared walls. Even if one of the walls might be in danger of collapsing. A girl can't have everything.

By the time Luke was wandering around the living room collecting his stuff, Tess had completely unpacked all the boxes downstairs and was in a much better mood. She hadn't spent time singing for the fun of it in an extremely long time.

Barney followed his owner around the room while Luke put away the painting paraphernalia. The dog sat patiently waiting while Luke washed the paintbrushes in the sink. Barney seemed to be quite familiar with the clean up routine.

Tess walked into the kitchen and leaned over to ruffle the dog's ears. "So where have you been all day?"

Luke said, "He was asleep on the back deck. I just let him in. While he was outside, he barked at a couple squirrels, but I don't think they take him seriously."

"How is he with cats? After I get back from Los Angeles, I'd like to introduce the Fab Four to the rest of the house. I think they're more than ready to leave my bedroom."

"Barney has been at job sites with cats, dogs, sheep, goats, llamas, alpacas, horses, and cows. Oh, there was a pot-bellied pig once too. I've worked on convincing him that he needs to behave himself, no matter what type of critter is around."

"I got the impression he stays in the truck. In the house, do you think he'll try and chase my cats?"

"Not unless he wants to get in really big trouble." Luke set down the paint brush he was holding. "I can't promise he won't ever do something dumb because he's a dog and you never know for sure. But he spent a lot of time at a friend's house who has a cat. Barney and the cat kinda got to be buddies. It was cute."

"I don't want the Fab Four to get hurt."

"Well, when you're ready to do the big introduction, I'll bring Barney's bed in from the truck and make him stay on it. Then you can let the kitty Beatles check him out first. He knows that when I tell him to go to his bed, he's gotta stay there."

"Okay, that sounds like it might work. I'm not sure how they'll react. George is the most likely to have a problem because she's so skittish. But if she hides under the sofa for a while, she'll probably be okay."

"Sounds good. Thanks for lunch and the serenade. I forgot what a good singer you are."

Tess laughed and shoved at his arm. "Aww, you flatterer."

"If I don't see you tomorrow, good luck with the audition." He leaned over to grab the paintbrushes from the sink, and his curly, longish, out of control red hair brushed close enough to Tess that she could smell his shampoo. And it smelled delicious.

She inhaled deeply and closed her eyes. When she opened them, Luke was looking at her with an inquisitive expression.

Tess smiled weakly and shrugged. "What can I say? Your shampoo, or soap, or something…it smells wonderful."

He bent down closer so their lips were practically touching and locked his gaze with hers. "Oh, really? You think so?"

Tess nodded and closed her eyes again. She felt his lips graze her cheek, which acted like a jolt of electricity that caused shivers to run down her spine. He whispered in her ear, "Your shampoo isn't bad either."

Tess didn't say anything, but his hair tickled her ear and she giggled. He brushed his lips along her neck and said, "You sure about this?"

As an answer, Tess threw her arms around his neck and pulled him to her. He moved his hands to her waist, pulling her up onto her tiptoes and pressing her against the counter. He started to mumble something, but whatever he might have said was lost to her kiss. His lips were so soft and warm. The scent of sawdust, shampoo, and the rest of him was intoxicating, and she tugged at his shirt, trying to pull him closer.

Breathless, Tess finally released her hold, and gasped, "Wow."

Luke groaned quietly, looked at her, and said, "I, uh, wasn't expecting that."

"Me neither." Tess smiled. "But, still. Wow."

"Yeah. No kidding. Wow."

~

Tess was so keyed up that it took more than an hour after Luke and Barney left the house for her blood pressure to return to normal. No wonder Claire had spent so much time groping Luke in high school hallways. Tess had practically jumped on top of him in the kitchen, which was not generally her style. But he had felt so good. Under all the work clothes and flannel was a lot of rather delectable male musculature. "Wow" didn't even begin to cover it.

The next morning, Tess left for L.A. and kept herself amused on the journey by thinking about the finer points of Luke's anatomy and reliving the "Wow Kiss" in her mind. There were worse things to think about than a fantastic kiss replaying on an infinite loop, and the boring drive down the hill passed more quickly than usual.

The building where the auditions were being held was located in a questionable area of Los Angeles, so Tess was glad her car wasn't particularly flashy or enticing. If some poor slob was dumb enough to steal the tin can, it wouldn't be the worst thing that might happen. She'd skip right over to her insurance company and happily take the cash.

After finally locating a legal parking space in a grotesquely expensive parking lot, Tess mentally collected her thoughts as she walked the two blocks to the building. She looked up at the gray brick structure, which might have once been a factory. Dennis wasn't spending a lot on niceties like office space. The edifice exuded a sense of dingy, urban blight, almost as if it retained the misery of the disgruntled sweatshop employees who had worked on some long-ago assembly line.

After discovering the elevator didn't work, she hiked up the stairs to Suite 504. Tess opened the door and entered a room with a beige metal desk and six dented and crooked metal office chairs that looked like thrift store rejects.

Where was everybody? She walked to a door on the other side of the room and knocked. "Dennis? Are you in there?"

The door opened quickly and Tess found herself facing someone she'd hoped never to see again. His black hair was slicked back using far, far too much hair gel, which with his long nose made him look like a cross between a Mafia Don and a mongoose. Tess was momentarily taken aback by his appearance. Dennis used to be handsome with the classic pretty features shared by many male actors and models. The mongoose thing wasn't working for him at all.

"Dennis." Tess put out her hand. "As we discussed, I'm here for the audition."

Dennis took her hand and brought it to his lips. Tess tried not to visibly cringe at the contact, but her mind was shrieking, "Ick!"

"I'm so glad to see you." He gave her his most ingratiating smile and gestured toward the metal chairs. "Pull up a chair and let's chat."

Tess did a quick visual inventory to determine which old chair was most likely to be able to support her weight and dragged it in front of the desk. Dennis settled in, apparently oblivious to the screeching noise the office chair made as he sat.

Tess carefully perched on her wobbly chair. "Do you want me to do a monologue?"

"No, just let me look at you for a moment. I want to absorb you."

More cries of "Ick!" careened through her mind, but Tess patiently sat and stared at Dennis while he gave her the once over.

Finally he said, "Let's start with facial expressions. First, do angry."

Tess made a fierce face, which was challenging because she had to simultaneously make a concerted effort not to roll her eyes in exasperation. This was stupid, even for Dennis. She returned her face to normal and asked, "Have you ever directed a play before?"

"No, this will be my first one. Acting wasn't fulfilling anymore and I'm moving in a different direction." He made a swirling gesture with his hand. "Now sadness."

Tess made a weepy face. Oh brother. This was so dumb. "How about I try speaking now? I have a short monologue from *The Sound of Music* I can do…it's when—"

"No, no, no." He waved his hands flamboyantly. "That's not what I need. I don't want anything prepared. I have to see your emotions. Stand up. Let's try some character studies."

Tess got up and moved the chair out of the way. "Okay, what's the character?"

"You're a pole dancer."

Tess put her hands on her hips. "You can't be serious. What does that have to do with poetry or politics?"

"Okay, no pole. Just dancing. But like a pole dancer." He waved at her with both hands. "Just do it."

Tess swayed a few times and stopped. "What is this play about? Am I auditioning for porn or something? Because if that's what this is about, I'm out of here."

"It's not porn, in fact the play was written by a highly regarded professor of literature. Let's try something else."

"Fine." Tess glared at him. "If you can't think of anything, I have a monologue from *Macbeth* too. Shakespeare is a little more highbrow than pole dancing."

"I've got it. Do a Shakespearean cheerleader. Spell out a cheer for me."

Tess did roll her eyes this time as she shook her hair, trying to quickly think up an idea of what she might cheer. She waved her arms and said, "Go, go. Out, damned spot. It's a sorry sight. Get out, I say. Out, damned, S-P-O-T!"

Dennis clapped his hands. "That was great."

Tess bowed. "Are we done?"

"One more. How about a substitute kindergarten teacher who has to read a Dr. Seuss book to the kids? But then she's possessed by Darth Vader."

"You can't be serious."

"I am. I want to see your range."

"Fine." She sat down in the chair and pretended to hold a picture book, casting around for ideas. *Star Wars*, not surprisingly, led her thoughts to Luke Skywalker, which circled her thoughts back to the real Luke in Alpine Grove. Her cheeks warmed at the visuals and she cleared her throat, trying to concentrate on the task at hand.

Dennis said, "Take your time."

Tess took a deep breath and began. "I sense his presence here. I sense his presence there. I sense his presence everywhere." She continued in a deeper voice, "In this one, strong is the force. Luke, I am your father, of course."

Dennis stood up and walked around the desk. "You're brilliant, Tess. I knew you'd be perfect for this role."

"Is there a script?" Tess was unmoved by his praise. The last time he'd called her brilliant, he'd been sleeping with her understudy who was apparently even more brilliant than Tess was, not to mention better endowed. "I'd like to see the script before I make any decisions on this."

"It's in development, but I know you'll love it." He reached for her hand and pulled her up out of the chair. "I think we should celebrate. You're here for the evening, right? Let's go out. We can paint the town red and you can see my new place. It's been so long. I've missed talking about craft with you."

Tess stepped back away from him. "I have a room booked already."

"Even better. You always were practical. We can celebrate, discuss the role, then go back to your place."

"Not if you were the last human male on the planet."

"Well, we'll need to collaborate, you know."

Tess scowled. "Define *collaborate.*"

"Work together closely. Very closely. Intense collaboration will be required for this role." He smiled. "You used to like it when we collaborated."

"So what you're saying is that I have to sleep with you to get this part?"

He dismissed her comment with a wave of his hand. "So? It's certainly not uncharted territory. In fact, you used to enjoy it."

"That's never going to happen, Dennis. It's one thing to sleep with your co-star because you're dumb and naive enough to fall in love with his character and think the character had anything to do with who *you* are." Tess picked up her bag from the floor and clutched it to her chest. "It's quite another thing to sleep with a director to get a part. Not in this or any other lifetime."

"Way to get up on your high horse. I know you haven't had an acting job in more than a year. And Chloe told me about your last audition. Good luck ever working in Hollywood again. You're not getting any younger, you know."

"That may be, Dennis, but it's okay. Better than okay, in fact. If this trip has taught me anything, it's that you are the worst form of Hollywood slime. May you die an agonizing death from the hundred thousand paper cuts you'll receive in the process of peddling this script around town." Tess thrust her bag over her shoulder and stormed toward the door. She opened it, turned and said, "Lose my phone number because I don't *ever* want to hear your voice again."

She slammed the door behind her and stomped down the stairs, the adrenaline draining from her muscles as she descended. By the time she got back to the Hyundai, tears were streaming down her face.

If she never set foot in Hollywood again, it would be too soon.

~

Tess stopped by the motel, told them she didn't need her reservation, and drove back to Alpine Grove. It would be extremely late by the time she got back, but at least she'd miss less work. Geoff was already pissed off at her for taking off on another audition trip. It might be a nice surprise for him to see her bright and early Tuesday morning.

The problem with driving for hours and hours all in one day is that you feel really strange when you're done. Tess got in so late, or technically so early in the morning, it almost wasn't worth going to bed, so she didn't. Instead, she fed the Fab Four, showered, drank four cups of coffee, and rolled into the office.

She was at her desk going through paperwork when Geoff came in at eight. He did a double take. "What are you doing here?"

"I work here," Tess said, and then took a sip of coffee with a grimace. Geoff bought cheap coffee that tasted like chalk. No wonder she came in late and made her sales calls from home. Freshly ground beans and a coffeemaker that had been cleaned in the last decade made a much tastier brew.

After a somewhat annoying conversation with Geoff to catch him up on the state of her sales, Tess went to work making calls and setting up appointments. By about ten o'clock, she was feeling strange. Her coffee jitters had turned into a raging headache, yet she felt like she was lost in a fog. Even though she was awake and still sort of wired, she was exhausted. Perhaps pulling an all-nighter hadn't been the best idea.

By the time she went home, Tess was so tired she could barely think straight. Bypassing dinner, she went upstairs, fed the cats, and crawled into bed, eager for possibly the worst Monday in her personal history to finally *be* history.

The next day at work, thanks to a decent night's sleep, Tess felt physically better. The furious seething anger at Dennis and disgust with herself for going to the stupid audition had also subsided. In its place, however, was a melancholy emptiness that she couldn't shake. Her acting career was really and truly over this time. Doing sales was okay, and she was good at it, but it was boring. Maybe she should think about taking classes to gain some new skills. But in what field? She had no idea what she wanted to do long-term. All she'd ever wanted to do was perform, so she'd never considered anything else as a career.

After work, she wandered around the house aimlessly putting away a few last things. She felt unsettled and desperate for something else to think about beyond her failure as an actress. The Fab Four had made it clear that they were tired of being confined to the bedroom, so with a flourish, she opened the door. "Behold! The world beyond this room awaits thee."

George screamed through the doorway, stopped, turned around, and charged back into the bedroom and under the bed. Tess laughed. So much for bravery. Ringo peeked his nose around the door jamb, and then sauntered through, sniffing at the hallway, slowly exploring the new frontier. Paul and John followed, patrolling the area in a zigzag pattern. Tess walked down the stairs and turned to watch the cats tentatively make progress behind her. It was a lot more space than they were used to accessing.

Tess sat on the bottom stair, waiting for them to catch up and offering a few words of encouragement. "It's okay. You've got a lot of exploring to do. This might take a while. Take your time."

The front door opened, startling Tess. She turned her head to look up the stairs at the cats, but they'd all turned tail and disappeared upstairs again. She smiled at Luke. "I'm glad Barney isn't with you. I let the cats out for a little exploration time."

"He's in the truck napping." Luke walked over and sat down next to her on the bottom step. "I was on my way home, but I wanted to find out how your audition went."

Tess grinned and said in a sing-song voice, "You wanted to *seeee* me, didn't you?"

He laughed. "Yeah, I did."

"I wanted to see you too." Tess looked up at him. "It's a long way to L.A. and I had a lot of time to think."

"Uh oh."

"Thoughts about you were positive."

"That's good."

"Thoughts about L.A. were negative. The audition was a disaster." She leaned her temple on his upper arm and gazed at the living room. "I need to find something else to do with my life."

He put his arm around her and pulled her closer. "You'll figure something out. There's got to be acting jobs outside of Hollywood, right?"

"Maybe. When I was little I thought I'd be on Broadway. That was a ridiculous fantasy. I've never even been to New York City, much less performed there."

"Hey, it's not like your life's over. You'll see the lights of Broadway someday."

"Not likely at this rate. I almost can't believe how awful the audition was. I had to do these dumb character sketches. One was about *Star Wars*. So I'm supposed to be thinking about Darth Vader, but I was thinking about you instead."

"I can't tell you how often I've been teased about feeling the Force."

Tess giggled. "I know. I remember. And I have come to the conclusion that Hollywood is a wretched hive filled with lots of scum and villainy."

"Was it really that bad?"

"Dennis assumed I'd have sex with him to get the part."

"What a total…uh, never mind." He wrapped his arm around her more tightly. "I'm sorry. Do you want me to beat him up?"

"Tempting, but no thanks. I doubt I'll hear from him again." She moved her head so she could look up at Luke's face. "All I wanted to do was get home, so I drove all night. Or into the morning. Anyway, it's been a strange couple of days."

"Sounds like it."

"Thanks for stopping by. I needed a hug."

A corner of his mouth turned up in a half smile. "I could give you a kiss too, if you think it might help."

With a grin, Tess turned so she could put her arms around his neck. "Why yes, I think it might."

Luke smoothed her hair back over her shoulders, then ran his hands up her neck and caressed her jaw with his fingertips. "Well then, I'm happy to oblige."

When his lips met hers, Tess closed her eyes and let the sensations wash over her. As the kiss became more intense, Luke wrapped his arms around her and pulled her against him onto the stairs. Her heart raced wildly, but one of the steps was poking into her back and she pushed him away. "You know, with a house this size, you'd think we could find more comfortable places to do this than in the kitchen and on the stairs."

"Someone invented cushions and mattresses for a reason." Luke pointed up the stairs where John, Ringo and Paul were sitting, each cat having claimed a step. "Plus, it looks like we have quite a few members of Sergeant Pepper's Lonely Hearts Club Band here with us."

Tess sat up and smoothed her shirt. "Hi, guys. You want dinner, don't you?"

Luke got up and extended his hand to pull her up. "I've gotta get home. I had to do a whole lot of hand digging today and I'm beat."

"I thought that's what the big machines are for."

"There are places I can't use the excavator, which means I had to take the old-fashioned approach with a pick. That dirt was full of rocks and it wiped me out."

"I saw a big pile of metal things in the back yard, so I'm guessing that's the scaffolding."

"Yeah. I dropped it off last night. It was kinda strange stopping by and not having you here."

"I was probably in my Hyundai swearing at other drivers."

"This weekend, I've gotta tear off the back deck, pull the French doors, block off the opening, and put up the scaffolding."

"So you won't be back here until Saturday?" Tess frowned. "I guess that makes sense, since it's not like you can work in the dark."

"I could paint inside at night after work." He reached out and took her hand. "I wouldn't turn down some help either."

Tess squeezed his hand. "This is like where Tom Sawyer convinces Huckleberry Finn that painting is fun, isn't it?"

"Maybe. But we might think of other things we could do that are more fun than covering Willy's artwork with industrial-strength primer."

"Like root canal?"

"Better." Luke pulled Tess to him and gave her a smoldering kiss. "I'm pretty sure we can come up with something way better, Huck."

Tess was pretty sure he was right.

~

Although Claire would have a fit when she found out, Tess had to admit that starting up a fling with your extremely sexy landlord was a great way to take your mind off your troubles.

She spent the rest of the evening thinking about how much fun she and Luke might have *not* painting when he showed up at the house the next day. It was certainly better than dwelling on the repercussions of refusing the disgusting advances from Dennis. Not that she had many contacts in the entertainment industry anymore, but if her name ever did come up, he'd undoubtedly now volunteer that she was "difficult" in addition to being nuts.

Hollywood was full of directors and other men who preyed on aspiring actresses. All those casting couch stories weren't a myth, and Tess should have known what Dennis would do once he finally got the chance to sit in the director's chair. Harassment and assault were rampant in Hollywood. Although she was lamenting the demise of her career, Tess wouldn't miss the catcalls, innuendo, and snide comments from Hollywood scum. Her little hometown might not be exciting or cosmopolitan, but at least she never was afraid to walk down the streets of Alpine Grove at night.

The next morning when she went into work, she had a message from Bea who had found a typo in her already-approved ad proof. Tess erased the message with a sigh. Deanna, the graphic designer, was fantastic at laying out ads, but a terrible typist and even worse speller. Technically, once a business had signed the form to approve an ad proof, the magazine was off the hook for typos, but there was no way Tess was going to let the word *golf* stay there when it was supposed to say *gift*.

Before she went out into the world to do her sales calls, Tess printed out the ad, circled the mistake and left it on Deanna's desk to fix. Later, she could drop a new proof with Bea, but it would mess up her afternoon schedule of sales calls. This type of thing *always* happened after the cut off for ad approvals. There was nothing like slapping a magazine on a printing press to suddenly improve everyone's proofreading skills.

Tess wasn't looking forward to facing Bea after ditching the meeting for her audition either. Bea Sullivan was the nicest person in the world, and letting her down made Tess feel as if she'd disappointed her own mom. In Alpine Grove, it was like Bea was everybody's mom.

When it comes to work, some days you're just not feeling it. For Tess, this was one of those days, and by the time she stopped by Bea Haven Gifts, Tess was tired and surly from sweet-talking her customers and carting boxes of printed paper all over the county.

The bells on the door jingled merrily as Tess walked inside the store. Bea looked up from the display of glassware she was arranging and offered a welcoming smile.

Tess held up the envelope with the corrected ad inside. "It's fixed. This time for sure. I stared at this ad for ten minutes to make sure there are no more goofs."

Bea took the envelope, pulled out the proof, and ran her finger across the page as she examined every word. "I think we've got it this time. Thank you for bringing it by so I could see."

"Anytime." Tess boosted her bag on her shoulder. "The magazine goes to press on Monday, so we should have copies for you late next week."

"We missed you at the meeting the other day."

Tess mentally cringed. She knew Bea was going to say something. "I'm sorry. I had an audition in Los Angeles. It was a last-minute thing."

"How exciting. What was it for?"

"A play, but I won't be in it." Tess gestured helplessly. "It will probably never see the light of day, and I'm giving up on acting anyway. I don't know why I drove all the way down there."

"Well, the meeting went extremely well. Did Luke tell you about it?"

"Luke was there? Uh, no, he didn't say anything." Tess recalled that they'd been busy, and he might have had something else on his mind.

"You know the librarian, right?"

"Margaret's friend, Jill?"

"No, the other one, Jan Carpenter. Well, she passed around some wonderful historical photos of the Grove that she dug up. She did all this research, and it's possible the Grove could qualify for inclusion on the National Register of Historic Places. That would be extremely helpful to our cause."

"Not if they tear it down."

"That's why we have to meet with the investor as soon as possible. Margaret and I set up a meeting, and we'd like you to go with us."

"*Me*? Why me? Shouldn't you bring the librarian who has all the facts?"

"Margaret and I can share her research. But you're passionate about the Grove. You performed there. No one else can explain that experience and what the Grove means to the community as well as you can."

Tess made a dubious face. "I don't know about that."

Bea put out her hand and touched her arm. "Please? We need you."

"Well, okay, if you think I can help."

"I absolutely do." Bea pressed her palms together. "This is wonderful. Margaret is going to be thrilled."

After getting the details about the meeting and putting it into her appointment book, Tess went home. She was tired of work and couldn't wait for the summer issue of the magazine to be over and done with. The last-minute desperate requests to add or fix ads always went down to the wire. If she heard, "Could you just do this one little thing for me?" one more time, she'd probably throttle someone.

After feeding the cats, Tess let them out of the bedroom so they could do some more exploring. It was fun to watch them poke their noses into boxes, sniff, and tentatively enter new spaces.

Tess was startled by the sound of the door opening and turned to watch the blur of felines bolting up the stairs.

Luke and Barney came inside, and Tess got up off the sofa with a smile. Luke was holding the dog bed, which he threw into the living room. Barney followed the bed and curled up on it.

Tess smiled. "He looks ready for a nap."

"Hanging out with all those dogs at the kennel tires him out." Luke held up a paintbrush. "I brought you a present."

"I'm touched." She raised her eyebrows. "You seriously want to paint?"

He threw the paintbrush onto the sofa, put his arms around her, and gave her a kiss. "Maybe later."

Chapter 7

Choices

A crashing noise came from upstairs, and Tess jerked away from Luke. "Uh, oh." She glanced at the dog bed, which no longer had a dog in it, and bolted for the stairs. In the bedroom, Barney was lying on the floor with his nose poked under the bed.

Luke came up behind her and said, "Barney! Go to your bed. *Now.*"

Totally busted, the dog leaped away from the bed and shot out of the room. The clattering of claws on the stairs dissipated as the dog presumably settled onto his bed.

Tess got down on the floor on her hands and knees and peered under the bed where she found four sets of eyes glinting in the darkness. "Are you all okay down there?"

A faint meow came from John, and Tess reached under the bed to stroke his head. "Sorry, Johnny-boy."

Luke crouched down next to Tess. "Are all the kitty Beatles accounted for?"

"Looks like it." She sat down. "I thought you said Barney was good with cats."

"He'd never hurt them, but I'm sure he's curious. I wasn't paying attention, and he decided to investigate." Luke stood up. "I suppose we should actually paint something, so I can keep an eye on him."

"I guess." Tess peered under the bed again. "I can leave the door open, if you're sure he won't hurt them."

"I'm sure. He got whapped on the snoot by a big ole Maine Coon when he was little, and I get the impression he finds cats confusing."

Tess stood up and headed back down the stairs. "He shouldn't feel bad. I'm a cat lady and I find them confusing sometimes too. Kind of like men."

Luke laughed as he followed her out of the bedroom. "Yeah, right. Men aren't complicated."

"Sure they are." She stopped next to the sofa, picked up the paintbrush, and then pointed it at Luke. "What are you thinking right now?"

"Nothing."

"Oh please. Every actor knows that people are always thinking something. That's part of what you have to convey. It's not just reading lines. You have to know what the character *isn't* saying too. So what are you thinking about?"

"My dumb dog really knows how to kill the mood. And you're hot." Luke grinned. "I told you men aren't complicated."

Tess smiled. "I guess that's not complicated, but it is surprising. Actors spend a lot of time having their appearance evaluated, and in my case, the word *hot* never comes up. Sometimes photogenic or quirky, but never hot."

Luke stepped closer to her and took the paintbrush from her hand. He slowly skimmed the bristles across her cheek. "Hotness isn't just what you look like."

"What?"

He leaned over so close that she could feel his breath on her neck. "It's also what you feel like. Smell like. Taste like."

Every hair on her neck was standing up, and Tess moved her head so he could kiss her lips. The paintbrush clattered to the floor.

A few moments later, Luke released his hold on her. "Here's what I'm thinking now. We have two choices. We either rip off each other's clothes or paint."

"Who says men have one-track minds?" Tess bent to pick up the paintbrush and give herself a moment to embrace rational thought again. She stood and looked into his eyes. "Although the first option appeals vastly more than the second, I'm still worried about the Fab Four, and I don't want to stress them out more than they already are. So I think we have to paint."

"Whatever you say, Huck. I'll get the drop cloths."

Tess went upstairs to change her clothes and check on the cats. Having a few minutes to settle her hormones back down was helpful too. She made a face and mouthed "Yowza" at herself in the mirror. Luke was more interested than she thought, and the feeling was definitely mutual.

Garbed in an old ripped pair of jeans and faded gray t-shirt with Bugs Bunny emblazoned on the front, Tess was ready to paint. She went back downstairs where Luke had thrown large canvas tarps over the sofa and the floor near the wall. He pointed at a paint can before climbing up a ladder. "That's the primer. The first step is to cover up the, uh, artwork."

"I know Willy thinks it's art, but it kind of freaks me out." Tess grabbed a paintbrush and slopped some paint on the wall to cover up a blob of wild colors. "It's like living with Rorschach tests all over the place. Sometimes I look at something and I think, 'Eww, giant, scary black widow spider.' Another time, I'll see a bat or a face."

"What about that one?" Luke pointed at the opposite wall. "I think it looks like a lobster climbing a mountain."

"If you turn your head sideways, it's like two people are… wow, that's complicated. Never mind."

Luke tilted his head. "Hmm, that would take some serious flexibility."

"Maybe they do yoga."

"Or they're acrobats. That thing on the left could be a trapeze."

"No way. That's physically impossible unless that blue thing is actually a close up of something else." Tess put down her paintbrush and squeezed her eyes shut. "Yuck. Now I can't see it any other way. Do you want some wine? I think I need to dull my senses."

"No thanks. I don't drink much, and I gotta drive home later."

At the abrupt change in tone, Tess looked up at him. "Really? Were those stories about the wild parties I didn't get invited to in high school all a big lie?"

"That was a long time ago." He glanced down at her. "But probably not an exaggeration either."

Tess went to the kitchen. "I missed all the good stuff. I had to live vicariously through Claire."

As she walked back into the room, Luke said, "Don't take this the wrong way, but why were you and Claire friends?"

"We still *are* friends." Tess set her wine glass on a bookshelf. "I mean yes, she moved away, but we still talk all the time."

"You just seem like different people, that's all."

Tess grabbed her paintbrush. "You mean because she was popular and I wasn't, right?"

"I suppose that's part of it."

"Claire moved to Alpine Grove in third grade, and we were best friends practically from the day we met. Over time, I got involved in theater and she found other things to do. But we were still friends."

"That must have been weird."

"Maybe for her, but not for me. Hanging out with a stage geek probably wasn't good for her social standing. But when you're head cheerleader and homecoming queen, who's going to argue with you?" Tess gestured with her paintbrush and splattered paint on the drop cloth. "Oops. And hey, you should know, Mr. Homecoming King."

"The whole homecoming thing was stupid."

"Give me a break. You and Claire were the dream couple. Everyone wanted to *be* you."

"It didn't seem so great at the time."

"What are you talking about? Until you lied about cheating on her, Claire thought you walked on water. She'd go on and on about you. It was nauseating."

"I didn't lie." Luke glared down at Tess. "And she drove my truck into the *lake*."

Tess giggled. "Yeah, I heard about that part."

"I don't know what was wrong with her. It was like she lost her mind."

"Well, you cheated on her, and in Claire's world, her life was over and she was humiliated."

"But I didn't."

"She said you'd say that."

"I *didn't*. Nothing happened." He stomped down the ladder and stood in front of her with his fists on his hips. "That was *years* ago. I can't believe we're talking about this. Why doesn't anyone believe me?"

Tess was taken aback by his reaction. Did he have some type of anger management problem? Maybe he said he didn't drink because he was a raging alcoholic. How would she know? Or a pathological liar like Dennis. "Bea told me you were at the meeting the other night."

"What?" He shook his head in confusion. "Yeah, I was. So what?"

"Why didn't you mention it?"

"I didn't think about it. The last time I saw you, we talked about your trip to L.A." He dropped his hands to his sides. "What does the meeting have to do with anything?"

"Just curious."

The phone rang and Tess ran to answer it before the machine picked it up. At the sound of Claire's voice, she glanced at Luke. "Hi. What's up?"

Luke looked around the room and started picking up the drop cloths. Tess watched him clean up while listening to Claire talk about her latest real estate deal.

Tess nodded, even though Claire couldn't see her. "That's interesting. Hey, um, can I call you back? The cats are up to something here, and I need to check on them."

As she hung up, Luke stopped in front of her. "I'll leave the paint here in case you want to cover up more art. This weekend, I'll come around sometime to work on the wall."

Tess reached out and grabbed his hand. "You could come by sooner."

"Yeah, we'll see." He let go of her hand and walked over to the dog bed. "Okay, Barney. You can get up now."

The dog leaped up and wagged his tail. Luke waved at Tess. "See ya."

With a weak smile, Tess raised her palm to return the wave, wondering how she'd managed to ruin a perfectly pleasant conversation so completely. The only thing she knew was that Luke was wrong. Men *were* confusing.

~

After work the next evening, Tess went to another meeting at the gift store about the Grove. It was a planning meeting for everyone to brainstorm ideas for the upcoming meeting Bea, Margaret, and Tess were going to have with the owner of the theater the following Monday.

Tess walked into the store secretly hoping Luke might show up, but he wasn't among the small group of people. She'd gone over their conversation in her mind many times and it was obvious she needed to hear Luke's side of the cheating with the skank story. Both times the topic had come up, he hadn't really explained himself. Maybe he didn't lie way back when. It wouldn't be the first time Claire had exaggerated, after all. And if Luke actually was a lying alcoholic with an anger management problem, it would be good to know sooner rather than later. Sure, they had unbelievable chemistry, but the last thing she needed was to be misled by another good-looking guy. Ugh. She had enough problems.

Bea came up to Tess and put her arm around her. "I'm thrilled you were able to come."

"No more trips to L.A. for me. I need to know what we're up against when we talk to this investor guy."

Bea asked everyone to sit down and Tess settled onto a folding chair. A number of the people in the room were familiar because they'd lived in Alpine Grove for years. Others she didn't know, except by sight. Maybe she'd seen them in line at the post office or something.

Bea introduced a property appraiser named Rebecca Mackenzie, Michael Lawson who owned the new advertising agency, and the research librarian, Jan they'd talked about previously.

Bea and Margaret reiterated that the investment company that owned the Grove might be open to an offer to buy it. When the company had purchased it, they got the property for a song, but didn't have any definite plans for the space. In fact, if the intel was correct, the people who owned the Grove now didn't seem to care what happened to the theater at all. The trick was figuring out what to offer and then how to raise the money.

Jan held up a sheet of paper. "I researched movie theaters as a potential business. The numbers are in this printout, but the real issue is the start-up costs. Restoring the Grove so it can be used again will be expensive."

"At the last meeting, Luke said he might be able to volunteer his time to help," Margaret said.

"We still have material costs. And as far as I know, no one has seen the interior for quite a while. Until someone with building expertise gets a look at it, we don't know what we're dealing with as far as restoration," Jan said.

Bea said, "Luke is going with us on Monday to look at the structure with the owner."

This was news to Tess. Yet another thing he hadn't mentioned. Did he know she was attending the meeting with the investor?

Brigid handed out information about starting a nonprofit corporation and said, "Assuming the building is salvageable and Bea and Margaret are successful in negotiating a deal, we'll need to get the nonprofit going. Here's some information I collected about next steps."

Rebecca Mackenzie raised her hand and waved a piece of paper.

Bea pointed at her and said, "Oops, I forgot. Becca has done a preliminary appraisal."

Becca added, "Technically, I'm not a commercial appraiser, but I found information about historic theaters around the country that could loosely be considered comparables. It's also challenging to assess historic value, but after Jan and I talked, I made a few calls. It's possible there may be grants available to help with restoration, particularly once the nonprofit is formed."

Tess did a double take, trying to assimilate what Becca had said. That woman was the fastest talker in the west. Grants sounded promising though. Becca had obviously done some serious research. Everyone else had been busy while Tess was off on her fool's errand to Hollywood.

A few more people passed out information, and then Bea said, "Okay, now we need to do some brainstorming on how we can raise money."

Someone piped up, "This is gonna take a whole lotta car washes."

"We put on a gala type event for AGAA, which did well, but we should do a different type of fundraiser for this project," Brigid said.

"Is the theater truly in terrible shape?" Tess asked. "I mean the obvious thing is to put on a performance to remind people what it used to be like."

"Has anyone been inside?" Bea asked. At the negative murmurings, she continued, "Well, we're about to go see it, so we'll consider that idea after we know what it looks like in there."

"Someone at the meeting last week said it was a wreck," Margaret said. "Who was that?"

Tess added, "If we do a play, I might be able to get a couple of friends to come up from L.A. to perform."

Becca asked, "Do you know anyone famous?"

"I was in a play with Danny O'Connor, although I doubt he'd remember me," Tess said. "Or I could talk to Leigh Miles. She was on a science fiction show in the eighties. We worked on a TV pilot together. It wasn't picked up, but I still talk to her sometimes."

"She played Harriet Plumb and wore the green jumpsuit. She traveled around the galaxy trying to save people whose brains were being attacked," Jan said. "I remember that. *The Prism Protectors*."

Tess shrugged. "I could ask her. Leigh is nice and it might help ticket sales to have a celebrity, even if she's sort of a D-list cult celebrity."

Bea clapped her hands together. "Okay, we're getting ahead of ourselves. It's time to get down to work. We need to think about numbers. Split up into groups of two or three and look over all the information from Becca on the appraisal and do some 'what-if' analysis and brainstorming."

Tess ended up sitting with Becca and Jan, which was fortunate given that she'd missed the last meeting. Plus, numbers were not her thing. Mostly she listened and took notes as the two women fired comments back and forth about grants and historical stuff Tess knew nothing about.

While she was scribbling notes, in the back of her mind Tess visualized the interior of old theater and what it felt like to stand on the stage. Just the idea of getting to look out across the audience made her heart do a little back flip of excitement in her chest. What if she actually got to perform at the Grove again?

Bea and these other women made it sound like saving the Grove might happen. They certainly were dedicated to trying. A lot of people were putting a lot of effort into researching options. It was inspiring, and a little part of her dared to hope that the beautiful old building and site of so many happy memories wasn't doomed to be smashed by a wrecking ball, after all.

~

Tess spent most of Friday muttering "TGIF" to herself. Even though she'd taken the prior Monday off and it had only been a four-day week, she was sick of magazine ads. The annoyances of the summer issue of the magazine needed to go away. Monday it was on the press for better or for worse, and people would have to get over themselves. At five thirteen p.m., Tess handed over the pile of proof pages she'd been scouring to Deanna. The ads were officially not her problem anymore. With a whoop, she drove out of the parking lot and headed for Oak Street.

She'd hoped Luke might be at the house, but no big blue truck was sitting out front. It wasn't much of a surprise, given that the last time she'd seen him, Luke was so clearly irritated. Yes, she'd sort of indirectly accused him of lying, but she kept wondering what he meant by "no one believes me." Someone other than Claire? Who else? She was determined to corner him and get the real story when he finally turned up over the weekend. Well, assuming he did turn up. Even if he was angry, he wouldn't want the wall of his house to fall down.

She released the Fab Four from their confinement in her bedroom so they could resume their daily exploration program. She still didn't entirely trust them or the holes in the wall, so it was safer to let them sleep away the day in her bedroom. It would be nice not to have to worry about these things once the house was fixed up and the cats were fully acclimated to their new home.

Tess went into the kitchen and rummaged around for food. The frozen food stash was looking thin, and she'd been so busy running around that she hadn't gone to the grocery store. Life had been unreasonably complicated lately.

On the pass-through counter, the red light was flashing on the answering machine. Tess reached over and pressed the Play button. Chloe's voice said, "Hi there, hon. I hope everything is good with you. Dennis said he saw you the other day and that reminded me that I need to give you a little bad news. I'm looking over my client list, and I need to trim the ranks, so I won't be able to represent you. I mailed the termination letter today. Take care, you hear."

Tess smacked the erase button. That was fast. That weasel Dennis undoubtedly called her agent the moment Tess stormed out of his office. Well, fine. She'd already decided she was done with Hollywood anyway.

Stomping to the refrigerator, she pulled out the bottle of wine and clutched it to her chest. As she reached up to grab a wine glass from the cabinet, something out the window caught her eye and she almost dropped the wine. Carefully setting it on the counter, she leaned over the sink to look outside.

The sun was low in the sky, so the light wasn't good, but she was pretty sure someone was out there in the back yard. Maybe it was Luke doing something with all the scaffolding parts. She went to the dining room, flipped the light switch for the outside light, and peered out the French doors.

Willy turned and gave her an open-mouthed look of surprise. Tess uttered an extremely unladylike phrase before opening the door. "What are you doing here? Don't you own *any* clothes?"

Willy crossed his hands to modestly cover a few delicate male parts and said, "I miss the squirrels."

"Maybe you've forgotten, but they have squirrels in Nebraska too."

"It's not the same."

"Get out of my back yard."

Willy put his fists on his hips. "It's not *your* back yard. You're not even related. So it's more mine than yours."

"Have you have heard of rent? I pay that. You didn't. Thus you were thrown out by your now-former landlord. Remember?"

"But Luke is family, and that's more important than money. Everyone knows that."

And people called *her* nuts. Sheesh. Tess was getting fed up with this guy. "Listen, Willy, Luke threw you out. I know because I watched him do it. Then I had to pick up the disgusting mess you made. *Go. Away.* Or I'm calling Luke, the police, and anyone else I can think of to make you get off my property."

Willy sat down and crossed his legs. "The squirrels need me."

"They're fine."

He closed his eyes, put his hands on his knees, and started humming. Tess spun around, slammed the door behind her, and turned off the outside light. The sun was going down and that fool could just sit in the dark and freeze his parts off for all she cared. Unfortunately, calling the police was more or less an idle threat because if she did, every single person in Alpine Grove would hear about Willy's latest escapade within ten minutes. The gossip mill would be on overdrive, and Luke didn't need that kind of publicity. But she needed Luke's help. Was he at home? Still at work? He could be anywhere in the county for all she knew.

She grabbed her bag and pulled out her appointment book. It was a little late, but maybe he was still at the kennel. When Joel answered the phone, Tess quickly explained the situation, trying her best to sound confident as opposed to mortified about the fact that she couldn't get one skinny naked dude to leave the premises. But it wasn't her house, so there was only so much she could do. Joel said Luke was still out front talking to Kat, but it might be possible to catch him before he drove off with his trailer of equipment.

After they hung up, Tess finally poured her glass of wine and settled onto the couch to wait. What an unbelievably stupid week. She set the glass on the coffee table, leaned back and let John jump up on her lap. "How's it going Johnny-boy? I'm sorry there's a weirdo in the back yard of our new house. I can't get him to leave." John purred sympathetically, and Tess closed her eyes. Maybe if she concentrated hard she could telepathically encourage Willy to return to Nebraska.

John jumped off her stomach, jolting Tess awake. She sat up and realized there was shouting coming from the back yard. She rushed to the back door where Luke was towering over Willy who was still sitting on the ground. There was a lot of yelling, but when Tess flipped the switch on the outside light they both stopped and looked at her.

She opened the French doors and pointed at Willy. "Hey, I warned you that I was calling the landlord."

"And the landlord wants you off his property," Luke added. "I don't know how I can make this any more clear to you."

"What's so wrong with Nebraska?" Tess said.

"I'm not going back there," Willy said with a determined frown. "I'm not."

"Have you been in Alpine Grove all this time?" Tess asked.

Willy nodded.

"Where have you been staying?" Luke said.

"The H12," Willy said. "But then they said the credit card I borrowed was declined and they threw me out."

Tess rolled her eyes. "Annabelle and Jon must have loved that."

"You ripped off my credit card?" Luke covered his eyes with his palm, then dropped his hand and glared at Willy.

"I thought I'd lost it somewhere and cancelled it. What did I ever do to deserve this?"

Willy sat up straighter. "Hey, my dad says you screwed over the whole family. This house should be mine, not yours."

Tess had no idea what Willy was talking about, but Luke looked like he might blow a gasket, which couldn't possibly end well for Willy. She walked down the steps quickly, grabbed Luke's hand, and said, "I need to talk to you."

"Tess, I can't…"

"Please." She dragged him into the house, slammed the door, and turned off the outside light again.

Luke shook his hand free. "What are you doing?"

Tess crooked her finger to encourage him to move into the kitchen away from the French doors so Willy couldn't see them. "I have an idea."

"Does it involve killing my cousin? Because I'm leaning toward that option right now."

"Better. And you won't go to jail."

"I'm listening."

~

After dinner, Kat was slumped down on the sofa reading a novel, but not really. Her mind kept drifting to how much money she was spending on having dirt dug. Obviously, she was in the wrong line of work. How did you learn how to drive a backhoe anyway? Was there a school? Backhoe U?

Joel nudged her in the ribs. "That must not be a page-turner because you're not turning any pages."

Kat giggled. "I'm thinking about learning how to drive large machines and dig up back yards. It pays better than writing or dog boarding."

"You might have trouble reaching the pedals."

"Everyone's a naysayer." She set down the book. "By the way, I need the truck tomorrow morning. I have to go to an AGAA meeting."

"I have a meeting at the bank about that report they want me to program into their system. I told you about it the other day. I have to do it on site. Maybe I can drop you off somewhere."

"I can't be gone for hours." Kat sat up straighter. "I have an article I have to finish."

"Is this you procrastinating again?"

"It's me allowing a certain amount of time to get things done."

"Maybe you should allow more buffer time."

"If we had another car, we wouldn't have these problems."

"But we would have a car payment." Joel raised an eyebrow in the classic Mr. Spock move. "I suppose you did warn me that we weren't done talking about this."

"We're not." Kat sighed. "I hate talking about money. And it's weird now that it's our money and not my money anymore. I want my own car, and I don't think there's anything wrong with that. I work hard."

"I know. But I don't think we should add another monthly expense right now."

"There has to be a way to work this out. We don't have to buy a new car. And anything we bought would be newer than your truck. Even another crappy truck would be better than nothing."

"I suppose we could think about that." Joel looked thoughtful for a moment before continuing. "Maybe we can look at something used but newer than the truck."

"That wouldn't be hard. As long as it has four-wheel drive and power steering, I'm good." Kat got up off the sofa and riffled through the newspapers that sat in the kindling box next to the fireplace. "Maybe there's something interesting in the classifieds."

"I've never wanted to buy a used car here because of the roads. After being thrashed on dirt roads, a used car wouldn't in any better shape than my truck."

Kat opened up the classified ads and said absently, "Again with the naysaying."

"Well, do you see anything good? We could go look at cars if you find something you like."

"Like new Cutlass Supreme. Rust on the engine. Zombie stickers on the windows. Slight urine smell from stray cats living in it." Kat peeked over the paper at Joel. "Eww. I guess he's honest anyway."

"Next. A Cutlass doesn't have four-wheel drive."

Kat scanned the entries, but it was not looking promising. "Nissan Pathfinder. Get this bad boy right here. Silver paint that will turn heads. Two hundred and ten thousand miles. No engine. But smokin' hot."

Joel laughed. "Turning heads is good, but I prefer vehicles with engines."

"Flatbed farm truck. Needs work. Parked in the pasture next to the old Garfield place. Ran it into a concrete pole. Not my fault."

"Everyone has an excuse."

Kat set down the paper. "You know the used car market is bad when the car that smells like cat pee is your best option. This is too depressing. I don't want someone else's derelict lemon. I want a new car."

"Maybe we can get a Gleasonville paper. They have more paved roads down there. And maybe fewer concrete poles."

"They also have car dealers. With new cars. Shiny, lovely new cars that aren't inhabited by stray cats or attacked by wily concrete poles."

"New cars also come with an enormous car payment I don't want to pay. A new car depreciates by about ten percent the second you drive it off the lot. If you purchase a twenty-thousand-dollar car, you lose two thousand dollars just by driving it home."

"I'm okay with that. I want to drive it home."

"You want to throw away two thousand dollars? Then let's look at it from the other direction. If you finance a twenty-thousand-dollar car, it's actually going to cost you a lot more than twenty thousand dollars because of all the interest you'll pay on a typical five-year car loan. Plus there are added expenses for maintenance, insurance, and gas."

"You're being cheap about this, even for you," Kat said. "I don't care if it costs more. I want a car. We *need* a car."

"Let's look at our financial picture again. If we decide it's impossible to find a decent used car, before we look at new cars, we need to know what we're willing to pay."

"I don't know what cars cost. Do you?"

"I haven't looked in a long time. Before we set foot on a dealer lot, we need to decide on the car we want that's in the price range we can afford."

"This is going to involve spreadsheets, isn't it?" Kat sighed. "You know how I hate that. Remember when we were talking about the loans for the kennels? My eyes glazed over."

"Let's go downstairs and we can go over the accounts on my computer. We can do some 'what-if' projections on different loan amounts."

"What if what?"

"What if we want our car payment to be three hundred dollars? How much car can we afford if we get a five-year loan? And how much down payment do we need to come up with to get the loan?"

"That's more than one if."

"A lot of car loans are sixty months." Joel leaned over and gave her a kiss. "So once we know how much money we have for the car, then we can look at which cars are in that price range. Then see if you like any."

"I already hate this process." Kat looked down at Linus who had placed his big brown head on her knee. "Even the dogs know I hate this. Can't we just go down to the dealer, point at a car, and say 'gimme this one'?"

"You could, but you'd probably get ripped off. That's what they want you to do. Did you buy your last car new?"

"No. I bought the Corolla from someone at work. My first car was a piece of junk I bought used. It didn't run in the rain."

"Buying a car from a dealer is different. They have a million ways to upsell you, mess around with the loan amounts, and tack on extras you might not even need or want."

"How do you know so much about buying new cars anyway? You have a twenty-year-old clunker truck."

"I've had other cars. New cars. I lived in Los Angeles, remember? All anyone thinks about is cars. I bought new ones every couple of years."

"*What*?" Kat shoved at his shoulder. "Then why are you giving me so much grief about getting a car?"

"I'm just trying to look out for us and everything we've built together." He put his arms around her. "Back then, it was just me, and I had what I thought was a steady job. Then as you know, I was unceremoniously laid off. My supposedly secure job and career wasn't secure at all. Now, I have a lot more to lose. Having lost everything before, I'm more cautious."

"I suppose that makes sense." Kat stood up and held out her hand. "All right, let's go downstairs so you can show me some smokin' hot spreadsheets, baby."

"Lead the way."

Chapter 8

Scared Straight

After Tess had succeeded in dragging Luke into the kitchen, he leaned on the kitchen counter with his arms crossed. "So you're saying you want to help Willy by scaring him?"

"Haven't you heard the term scared straight?"

"I guess."

"I've sold ads to a place that might be able to evaluate Willy tomorrow, if I ask nicely. Nancy loves me. But it's too late to call now, and I doubt Willy would go because he thinks he's fine out in the yard bonding with the squirrels. He sees absolutely nothing odd about sitting around naked talking to nobody."

"I noticed."

"You've shown that yelling at him doesn't work, so I think we need to take the Macbeth approach."

"You mean the play?"

"Yes, Shakespeare. Have you read it?"

"I think I slept through that English class." Luke smiled. "I suppose you memorized the entire thing."

"I played Lady Macbeth, but yes, I know the rest too. In the story, Macbeth gets freaked out by Banquo's ghost because no one else can see it. Macbeth thinks he might be going mad, and it's a turning point in the play. Willy isn't going to go anywhere as long as he thinks he doesn't have a problem. But if a ghost appears in the back yard and you say nothing is there, Willy might get worried. If you're the hero and save him from the scary apparition, I bet he'd go anywhere we ask tomorrow." Tess grinned. "I have the best costume, and Shakespearean English sounds intimidating if you do it right."

"I think you're a little too into this. But I don't have any other ideas, and I agree that the guy needs some serious help."

"Do you have one of those big flashlights that can stand by itself? I need the right lighting." Tess paced back and forth across the kitchen. "As for lines, I'll have to mix and match with the witches and steal some other stuff from Macbeth. This could be fun."

"Witches?" Luke scratched the stubble on his chin. "You aren't going to make me memorize stuff, are you? Because I'll never remember lines. I'm not the actor. You are."

"You get to play yourself, which shouldn't be much of a stretch. All you have to do is pretend I'm not there and save Willy from me. Don't look at me. Not even the slightest glance. Focus all your attention on Willy. Ignore absolutely everything I say. No matter what I say or how weird I get, you need to have no reaction."

"So I get to pretend you're not there and be a hero?" Luke said with a grin. "You're right. This *could* be fun."

"I hope so." Tess patted his forearm. "I need to get changed and think up some good lines while the sun sets. After it's dark and cold outside, I think Willy will be more receptive to my message."

"And maybe he'll consider putting on some clothes for a change."

"Don't go outside. I'll be back down in a minute."

Tess ran upstairs to her room and began rummaging through her box of costumes, running lines through her mind as she laid flowing robes out on the bed. When she was dressed and made up, she went back downstairs and crept around corners so she wasn't visible through the windows. Once she was in the kitchen, she peered through the pass through. Luke was sprawled out on the couch with one arm flopped over his eyes. With his other hand, he was petting Barney who was lying alongside the sofa.

Tess threw a kitchen sponge at him, which bounced off his head onto the floor. He jerked his arm away, grabbed the sponge before Barney could, and sat up.

She hissed, "Luke! Over here."

He got up and strolled into the kitchen, followed by the dog. In the doorway, he stopped short. "That's one heck of an outfit. You must take Halloween pretty seriously."

Barney sniffed at Tess and wagged his tail tentatively.

"With all the shadows, I should be able to scare the bejesus out of Willy." Tess pulled a frozen dinner from the freezer. "But first, I need something to eat."

"I've never eaten with a zombie or ghost…or whatever you're supposed to be."

"It's a bit of a hybrid." Tess fluffed out her dark robes and swirled them back and forth. "There's a bit of Hecate, a little apparition action, and some Banquo thrown into the mix. I think the wig pulls it together and makes it work."

"That and the makeup." Luke leaned over to examine her face. "That stuff around your eyes is creepy. How'd you do that?"

"A girl never reveals her makeup secrets." Tess pulled her dinner out of the microwave. "Are you hungry? There's only one frozen dinner left. I need to go to the grocery store."

Luke peered into the freezer. "Even the picture looks nasty. But I don't care. I'm starving, and I can't leave until you freak out my cousin."

"What's he doing out there?"

Luke casually walked out into the dining room by the French doors and returned to the kitchen. "Seems to be sleeping. Or maybe stoned. You never know with him. He put on pants and a sweatshirt too."

Tess raised her fists in a silent victory cheer. "Not seeing any more of Willy's little willy is great news."

Luke grabbed his frozen food from the microwave, sat down, and began eating. "How old is this?"

"I'm not sure. It was way in the back of the freezer in my apartment. I found it when I moved."

Luke gazed down at the plastic plate with a frown. "I think I'll make myself a sandwich." He got up, threw the dinner away, and turned back to look at Tess. "When was the last time you did the dishes?"

"I've been busy."

"This kitchen is disgusting." He gestured toward the sink. "I need a plate for my sandwich, and they're all piled up here."

"I know. It's convenient to have them right there. Just wash one. That's what I do."

"How about we do the dishes? *All* of them."

"I can't. Willy might see me."

Luke grumbled something under his breath, while he extracted a dish from the pile and washed it. After he ate, they played gin rummy to pass the time until it was dark enough for the big show.

After losing three hands, Tess said, "Okay, I give. You're some kind of oddly talented card shark. Let's go wake up Willy."

"What do you want me to do? Kick him or something?" Luke asked.

"Take a blanket out for him. Pretend to be nice."

"I don't have to pretend. I can be nice."

"Willy doesn't think so. He thinks you stole this house from him."

Luke mumbled something that sounded like, "What a load of spit," but Tess was pretty sure that wasn't what he'd actually said.

She pointed at the kitchen door. "I'm going to go around the side. While you give him the blanket, I'll set up my lighting."

"Sounds good. See you out there, Ms. Apparition."

Tess grinned and grabbed the flashlight. Even performing for an audience of two gave her a little thrill. She crept outside into the darkness and narrowly avoided smashing into the garbage cans, which would have ruined her big entrance. Ghosts didn't generally trip over piles of refuse.

She peeked around the corner of the house. Luke was standing over Willy. He dropped the blanket and said, "Hey, here's a blanket for you. It's going to get cold later."

Willy groaned and sat up. "Thanks, man."

Tess flipped on the flashlight and moved into the light, so it was shining from below up at her chin. She pointed her index finger at Willy and said in an eerie monotone, "By the pricking of my fingers, something insipid this way lingers."

Willy scooted backwards and looked up at Luke. "What the heck is that?"

Luke said evenly, "What is what?"

Tess boomed and waved her arms above her head. "Thrice the four cats hath mew'd and now the fire burns through faded bone. Would thou'st hear it from my mouth? Nature's creatures must be let alone."

Willy pointed at Tess and squeaked at Luke, "Who's the creepy chick?"

"I'm not a creepy chick. I'm your cousin, remember? I came out here to give you a blanket. I thought you might be cold," Luke said.

"Not you. *Her*." Willy jabbed his finger toward Tess. "She's talking about cats and creatures. Can't you hear her? She's right *there*."

"Nope. It's pretty quiet out here." Luke shrugged. "There aren't any cats or creatures either. Just me, giving you a blanket and wishing you'd leave my back yard and go home."

Tess spread her arms wide. "Come high or come low, you must hear this man's speech. You say thou nought, but you must depart. Fie! Do not dismiss him or consequences there shall be."

"Luke, you gotta help me, man. You need to do something about this chick. You're my cousin. We're family," Willy said as he continued crawling backwards. "Dismiss? I dunno what she's talking about."

"Who?" Luke said. "I'm the only one here."

Willy kept scuttling backwards. "The zombie chick. Can't you see her? Or it? I think it's *dead*, man!"

Tess went for her best Shakespearean stage voice and bellowed, "Thou has fear aright, but here's another more potent than the first. None shall harm the forest creatures. The power of man shan't keep them safe. They shall not vanquish'd be as they reign in the forested kingdom. The creatures art more powerful than thee."

Willy stopped crawling and stared at Tess. "Uh, so you're saying the squirrels will be okay?"

"Is that not what I hath proclaimed?" Tess waved her arms flamboyantly and swirled so her robes flew out around her. "Seek to know no more, but begone on morrow's day. Go back from whence you came."

Willy's eyes widened. "Okay. I'm gone. I'll leave tomorrow."

Luke said, "Do you mean that?"

"Yeah. I mean it. Cross my heart." Willy sat up straight and clasped his hands together. "Hey, man, I'm cold. Could I come inside? Just for tonight. I'm not liking the back yard so much anymore. And it would be cool if you could hang out here at the house, if that's okay. Alpine Grove is getting too freaky."

Luke held out his hand. "Sure."

Tess retreated into the shadows, flipped off the flashlight, and ran around the side of the house to wait for Luke to give her the "all clear" once Willy was settled into the second bedroom.

Mission accomplished.

~

Tess was in the master bathroom washing off her makeup when there was a light tapping on the bedroom door. She shooed the cats away and opened the door a crack.

Luke held out a daffodil. "Thank you. Willy is all tucked in downstairs. I hope you can get in touch with your friend tomorrow."

Tess smiled and took the flower from him. "I'm glad you're here. I want to talk to you."

Luke looked at her tank top and shorts. "Willy doesn't want me to leave. I'm not sure, but I'm wondering if he thinks I'm a ghost-buster or something."

Tess giggled. "Who ya gonna call?"

"You look like you're about to go to sleep. I'll be downstairs. I just need to boot Barney off, and then I can crash on the couch."

Glancing down at the calico cat near her feet, she pulled Luke into the room and closed the door before George could make a break for it. "I need to know your story first."

"What story?" Luke sat on the corner of the bed and clasped his hands together in his lap. "Didn't you ask me this before? I told you about selling my dad's business."

"I did." Tess went to the bathroom and put the daffodil in a glass of water. She came back into the bedroom and sat down next to him on the end of the bed. "But you didn't tell me the Claire story. And then I never let you finish, and then you got mad."

"I didn't get mad."

"You left, and it was pretty obvious you were upset." Tess raised her eyebrows. "So I need to hear the story. What really happened with Claire and the skank."

"Okay fine. First off, the skank was not a skank. Her name was Allana."

"Pretty name, but not familiar. She didn't go to high school with us, did she?"

Luke sighed. "Why is this so important?"

"Because Claire is convinced you cheated on her with Allana, and I want to hear the story from you."

"I didn't cheat. Allana was the daughter of a friend of my father's."

"What was she doing in your bedroom?"

"How do you know she was in my bedroom?"

Tess bent to pick up John and plopped the big orange cat in her lap. "Claire told me. She was there."

"No, she wasn't. I think I would have noticed."

"Okay, technically she was in your bathroom."

"What?"

"She climbed a tree." Tess turned to grin at him. "Naked, apparently. She lost her coat."

"You're kidding." Luke returned her smile. "That sounds dumb enough to be true. Only Claire could lose a coat in a tree."

"You also seem to have a real problem with naked people in your yard." Tess stopped petting John and turned her palms toward the ceiling. "So now you know Claire was in your bathroom. Why was Allana in your bedroom?"

"I was helping her."

"Claire thinks you were helping her have sex with you."

Luke leaned forward and scrubbed his face with his palms. "Jeez."

"She heard a whole conversation about condoms falling off. It was quite detailed."

"Nothing was falling off except parts."

"Eww."

"I mean *wooden* parts. From a bookshelf. We were in my room because I was helping Allana put together furniture. It was this desk and bookshelf combination thing she got for Christmas." Luke gestured helplessly. "It was like a puzzle with about four thousand screws and these little cam things and tiny dowels. But half of them were broken."

"I'm guessing some things didn't fit?"

"*Nothing* fit. It was a mess. Pieces of that thing were everywhere. Normally, I'm pretty good at building stuff. I mean I've been working construction for almost my whole life. But we spent hours trying to put that stupid thing together. I kept asking if this was how it was supposed to work."

"Claire heard you talking about things falling off, not fitting, and not working and made some assumptions."

"And then drove my truck in the lake."

"Yup." Tess moved John off her lap and patted Luke's shoulder as she stood up. "You might remember that Claire doesn't tend to do things halfway."

"I got in *so* much trouble. My dad was already furious because I couldn't put that stupid bookshelf together. He was trying to impress that guy for some reason." Luke stared at the ceiling. "And then…*and then*, dear ole Dad has to pay sixty-five dollars to get my truck towed. Do you know how long I heard about that sixty-five dollars? He *still* brings it up."

Tess grabbed her hairbrush from the dresser and sat back down next to Luke. She threaded her fingers through her hair and tugged on the tangles. Putting up her hair under a wig always made such a mess. She paused and set the brush in her lap. "Claire never told you she was in the bathroom?"

"She kept shrieking that she heard me." He shrugged. "I guess she did. After getting lectured by my father and grounded for all eternity, I wasn't in much of a mood to deal with her."

Tess stroked her hair with the brush slowly. "I guess you didn't lie. And you don't have anger management issues, do you?"

"It's not like I don't ever get mad. Sometimes I go running when I get pissed off." He looked at her. "What are you asking?"

"I'm wondering if you have a tragic flaw."

"Is this more Shakespeare?"

"Not exactly, although Macbeth had a tragic flaw. It was his ambition. He plots to murder the king and then is haunted by guilt."

"And ghosts like you from the sounds of it."

"I discovered late in the game that Dennis had a tragic flaw. He seemed perfect, but it turned out he was a manipulative liar." Tess set the brush in her lap and looked into Luke's blue eyes. "I'm hoping you're not. And not married, seriously involved, or otherwise entangled."

"Not entangled for a while because lately, all I do is work, drive, and sleep. I told you—I'm not that complicated."

"That's a relief." Tess fiddled with the brush in her hands and then looked up at him again. "The cats seem fine with you too."

Luke turned his head to look at the prone feline forms scattered around the room. "If fine means I make them fall asleep, then yeah, I think they're fine."

"Cats always do that. Sleeping means they're relaxed, not stressed."

Luke gave her a wry smile. "So I'm getting the impression that you might not be interested in painting right now."

"Nope." She reached over and tugged at a button on his flannel shirt. "Not painting. I think I'd prefer the other option you mentioned."

"Removing clothes does sound like more fun." He slowly pushed the strap of the tank top across her shoulder and leaned over to nuzzle her neck.

Tess tilted her head back and closed her eyes, enjoying the thrilling tremors that skittered down her spine. "Mmm, yes. A *lot* more fun."

~

The next morning when she woke up, Tess was surrounded by four cats and Luke. The cats weren't much of a novelty since one or more usually slept near her head. But being enveloped in Luke's strong arms and listening to his quiet breathing was definitely new. He looked so peaceful, and she studied his profile as he lay there sleeping. Again, she was struck by the fact that something about his face was different than it had been in high school.

She pulled her hand out from under the covers and ran her fingertips along his jawline.

A corner of Luke's mouth turned up, but he didn't open his eyes. "Is this your way of saying I have to get out of bed now?"

"Not necessarily. I was wondering what happened?"

"I think you know what happened." He opened his eyes and moved his head to smile at her. "You were there. Involved, even."

"Not that. Since we met on the road, it's bugged me that you don't look the same as you did in high school. What happened?"

"I got old."

"You're not old, but your nose looks different. Getting a nose job is such a Hollywood thing to do. It doesn't seem like your style."

Luke propped himself up on an elbow so he could look into her face. "You sure don't miss much, do you?"

"I spend a lot of time people-watching. It's an occupational hazard. Or it was for my former occupation anyway."

"Heavy equipment accidents are a hazard of my occupation. The nose job wasn't planned. The summer after my sophomore year in college, someone screwed up, and I ended up having a bunch of plastic surgery to put my face back together."

Tess traced his cheekbone. "Nicely done."

"It healed okay, but for a while I looked about as good as you did in that witchy ghost makeup. My left cheekbone was broken, and they took some cartilage from my ear to rebuild my nose. I also got six tooth implants. Plus, they fixed the one I busted in high school at the same time, so seven. I also trashed my shoulder, which ended my football scholarship."

"I didn't know that." Tess ran her hand across his shoulder. "Is that scar from the accident?"

"Yeah."

"Did you go back to college?"

"I went back to work."

"What did you study in school?"

"Mostly beer." Luke raised his eyebrows. "This may not come as a shock, but I wasn't much of a student."

"So you didn't select a major?"

"Never got that far." Luke rolled over flat on his back. "What is this? Twenty questions?"

She leaned over and gave him a kiss. "I'm just enjoying lying here with you in this bed, that's all."

"Me too, even though there's a cat next to my head."

Tess shooed John off the pillow. "I hate to leave all your sexy warmth, but we ought to check and see if Willy has run away while we weren't looking."

"I suppose." Luke sat up, ran his fingers through his hair, and leaned down to kiss Tess.

She smiled. "By the way, about last night? Wow."

"I might have to spend more time in Alpine Grove fixing this house."

"And checking in on your tenant."

After showering and getting dressed, Tess called her friend Nancy who worked at a rehab facility south of Alpine Grove toward Gleasonville. When she and Luke went downstairs, Willy was sitting on the sofa looking sleepy. Out in the back yard, Barney was lying on his side basking in the morning sunshine.

Luke said, "Thanks for letting the dog out."

"He jumped on the mattress and woke me up." Willy scratched at his goatee. "How come you don't put the bed together?"

"I haven't gotten around to it," Luke said.

Tess sat down next to Willy. Even though he was unwashed, stinky, and sleepy, his eyes no longer had the glazed look they'd had before. She said, "I have a friend named Nancy and I told her about you. She might have a place for you to stay, if you're interested."

"Any place is better than Nebraska. I hate it there," Willy said. "What's for breakfast?"

"How about we pick up something on the way there?" Luke said.

"Okay. I'll get my stuff."

Tess stood in the doorway and watched as Luke, Barney, and Willy got into the truck. Luke threw Willy's Hefty bag of belongings into the back and then paused. He leaned into the cab to tell Willy something then ran back up the sidewalk and the steps to the house. Tess grinned at him. "What did you forget?"

He grabbed her hand, pulled her through the doorway and closed the door behind them. Wrapping her in a massive bear hug, he kissed her to the point that she thought she might melt into a puddle of goo.

When he released her, Tess gasped. "Whoa. What was that about?"

"Driving to this place with Willy is going to take a while." He cupped her cheek and gave her another quick kiss. "I'll be back as soon as I can."

After he left for the second time, Tess flopped down on the sofa. All the excitement of performing and lack of sleep had left her exhausted. She closed her eyes and let herself sink into a little sofa snore time. When she woke up again, her mind was less addled from the presence of her sexy landlord and his weird cousin. But her stomach was less pleased, growling to express its annoyance that she hadn't eaten anything lately.

A cursory examination of the refrigerator and kitchen cabinets reminded her that she had no food, so she cruised off to the grocery store. If Luke would be spending more time here, she should stock up. Even worse, she was almost out of cat food. It just showed how busy and distracted she'd been lately. To the Fab Four, running out of cat food was an inexcusable offense.

When she returned to the house, she let the cats out of the bedroom and decided to cover up some more Willy art. A few of the monstrous blobs particularly bothered her, and it was way past time for them to go to the big Rorschach test in the sky.

Tess spread out the drop cloths and set up the ladder, so she could reach the swirly gob of spray paint that she thought of as Eskimo unicorn pornography. Ick. She poured some primer into an old coffee can and carried it up the ladder with her.

Although Tess would never argue that painting was as much fun as sex, it was relaxing in a methodical squishy, swishy way. She pondered the night with Luke as she slapped paint on the wall. To say they had chemistry was a massive understatement, but she liked hanging out with him too. Even though they'd spent a lot of time talking, she found herself wanting to know more. She was looking forward to catching up on the ten years of his history that she'd missed. Although Luke might think it was an odd quirk of her people-watching personality, she enjoyed simply listening to him speak. The timbre of his voice would be perfect for a truck commercial voice-over.

Tess was still painting when Luke walked in the door. He looked up and pointed at a spot on the wall that was covered with primer. "I'm glad to see the last of that one. Too much time here and I'd be having nightmares."

Tess gestured with her paintbrush. "That was one of my first targets. The walrus festooned with seaweed mating with a seahorse gave me the creeps."

"I didn't get seahorse from that one. I thought it looked like rhino drinking tequila shots."

Tess descended the ladder and set her paintbrush and can on the floor next to it. "A rhino? No way."

"Doesn't matter. Now it's just a nasty memory I can work to forget." Luke smiled and gave her a quick kiss. "I had an idea, and I stopped by the shop. Are the kitty Beatles around?"

"Somewhere. Is Barney in the truck?"

"Yeah. Do you think it will be okay for him to come inside?" He pointed toward the door. "I need to bring in some stuff too."

"I'll keep an eye out for the Fab Four, but it should be fine. None of them have ever been interested in visiting the great outdoors. It's chilly out there, and they're not fond of the cold."

While Luke went out to his truck, Tess walked around the house looking for the cats. Apparently worn out from exploring, they were all fast asleep on her bed so she quietly closed the door, just to be safe.

When she went downstairs, Barney was running around the room sniffing the paint and brushes. Tess laughed. "What's his problem?"

"Too much time in the truck. Checking in Willy took a long time. I know it's the right thing to do, but there's a lot of paperwork and we had to call his father." Luke shrugged. "That didn't go too well."

"Do you think he'll be okay?"

"I think so. Nancy is great. I can see why you like her." Luke held up a piece of wood. "I don't know if you spent much time listening to Willy, but it's hard to figure out what he's talking about. While I was driving, my mind kinda wandered and I had an idea. I brought parts for a kitty scratching post. Or I could make something taller with platforms too, if you want."

"What kind of parts?"

"Have you ever looked at those huge kitty climbing things in pet stores? They're a hundred bucks, and all they are is wood and sisal rope. I've got more wood than I know what to do with, and a big roll of sisal rope costs two dollars."

"This isn't going to be like the bookcase with scary assembly and things that don't fit, is it?"

"All you have to do is to wrap the rope around that piece of wood."

"It looks like a fence post."

"It's a cedar pole for post-and-dowel fencing. Not treated or anything, so it's safe. It's easier to wrap rope around something round. Then I just attach that to a base and voila, kitty scratching post. Or add another level and some more poles for legs, and it's a climbing tree."

Tess grinned. "What's the male version of cat lady? Cat guy?"

"Hey, I have a dog." Luke pointed at Barney who had collapsed on the sofa with his head hanging off the side, panting. "Kind of a goofy dog, but a dog."

Tess went over and sat next to Barney who plopped his head in her lap and drooled on her jeans. "You realize that making a cat lady a gigantic cat toy is a sure way to win her heart, don't you?"

"The thought had crossed my mind."

~

It didn't come as much of a surprise to Tess when Luke opted to stay in Alpine Grove so he could work on the house the next day. After another extremely pleasurable night, Tess did something highly unusual on Sunday morning. She prepared a meal using the stove. Cooking for herself was largely uninteresting, so she rarely did it, but cooking for two was more satisfying. After powering down a lot of pancakes and convincing her to help wash the towering pile of dishes in the sink, Luke went outside to set up the scaffolding.

When he returned, he brought in various pieces of wood and a toolbox and set them on the floor. Tess was assigned the task of wrapping sisal rope around the fence post. Luke worked on stapling pieces of old carpet onto the kitty platforms using a pneumatic staple gun that ran off an air compressor he'd set outside on the deck.

He stapled the end of the rope at one end of the post, and Tess carefully wrapped the sisal around and around, pulling it tight. The last time she'd helped build much of anything was when she'd worked on stage sets. It was fun sitting around chatting while constructing the kitty tree. She could easily imagine Ringo perched on the top platform lording over his kingdom.

Tess pointed at the dog who was curled up in a tight ball with an unhappy expression on his face. "What's wrong with Barney? Is he feeling okay?"

"He doesn't like the noise from staple guns or nail guns."

"That seems like it would be a big problem for a dog that spends so much time at construction sites."

"Most of the time he's in the truck. And a lot of the excavation work I do happens before anyone is working on any framing." Luke turned over the carpeted piece of wood and set it aside. "He doesn't care about the noise from the air compressor, saws or other power tools. But he hates nail and staple guns. Even though I think he knows the noise isn't going to hurt him, there's something about the sudden sharp sound he doesn't like. I've wondered if it's because it sounds kind of like a gun shot."

"Well, he looks like he has hound in him. Maybe he's a failed hunting dog? Aw, Barney, it's okay. I can relate to career failure." Tess reached over and stroked his head. "Only a little more carpet and he'll be done."

"Poor Barney isn't going to be too excited when I start rebuilding the wall either."

"The Fab Four will be able to supervise from the comfort of their new tree. This is going to be so cool."

"It's my gift to you for helping me get rid of Willy."

"It might be the last performance I ever do, so I'm glad you appreciated it."

"I'm sure you'll perform again." He leaned over and kissed her. "I'm looking forward to checking out the Grove with you tomorrow."

"I hope it's not as big of a mess as they say it is. This town needs the arts. Right now there's nothing except one bookstore. What if Alpine Grove turned into an 'arts town' with galleries and artists? Wouldn't that be cool? I mean, let's face it, three dive bars and a two-star motel aren't exactly cultural attractions." Tess set down the post. "Even better is that it means you don't have to leave tonight."

"My apartment has seemed a lot less appealing lately."

"I wish I didn't have to go to work tomorrow. At least the spring issue of the magazine will be on the press and out of my life. But now I have to start thinking about the fall issue." Tess pulled her knees to her chest and rested her forehead on them. "The ad sales cycle never ends."

"I know what you mean. I pushed back a job to Tuesday so I could go to the Grove meeting. Bea is really persuasive, but I'm not sure why she wants me to go. I'm not a commercial building inspector. Or residential or any type of professional."

Tess raised her head. "Of course, you're a professional. You've been paid to build stuff for years and years."

"That's not what I do now. I dig, level, and move dirt."

"And rehab old houses."

Luke pointed toward the French doors. "This is my house so if I screw it up, it doesn't affect anyone, except me."

"It might affect me too. But why would you screw it up?"

"Well, I wouldn't on purpose." Luke stood up. "I need to get more staples from the shed."

Tess straightened her legs out in front of her. It happened again. She'd touched on a sensitive subject without realizing it. Something was missing in his story, and she aimed to find out what.

When Luke returned with a box of staples, she stood up, and reached out to grab his forearm. "I need your help understanding something."

He grinned. "Is it something fun?"

"Probably not."

"Oh well." He sat down next to the carpet and wood scraps and loaded staples into the staple gun. "What is it?"

"I get the impression that you don't like what you do."

He took his attention from the staple gun and looked at her. "I never said that. I'm good at it and I earn a decent living."

Tess laughed. "You sound exactly like me. You wish you could do something else, don't you?"

"Not really. I didn't dream about doing something my whole life and study it in school like you did. I didn't even graduate from college."

"Do you like running road graders and backhoes and all that? Digging and leveling and whatever else you said?"

"It's okay." Luke picked up the wood, pulled the carpet over the edge, and fired some staples.

"What do you dream of doing?"

"Nothing."

"You mean you want to retire?"

He looked up. "I can't retire. I make a good living, but not that good."

"Bennett Enterprises built houses and buildings. How come you just do excavation?"

"It's easier."

"Do you miss building?"

Luke set the staple gun aside. "I told you. I wasn't cut out to run a big complicated company."

"Before that though. When your dad ran Bennett Enterprises, what did you do?"

"Everything. Framing. Plumbing. Electrical. Roofing. Metal work. Employees had a habit of quitting, so at one time or another, I ended up doing pretty much everything."

Tess pointed at him. "A-ha! I knew it. That's why you can build a whole wall by yourself. And why you're the right person to check out the Grove tomorrow. You'll be able to tell if it's so far gone that it's not worth saving."

"Almost any building that's still standing can be saved if you throw enough money at it." He shrugged. "But what if I'm wrong about the extent of the damage?"

Tess pointed at the kitty tree. "I know it doesn't seem like a big deal to you, but not everyone can just visualize something and put it together. I definitely can't."

"So what? I practically flunked out of school and destroyed the business my father built. Even Willy thinks I screwed up, and that's saying something."

Tess took his hand. "I think you're being way, way too hard on yourself. Don't you have dreams?"

"Says the woman who has given up on her own." Luke leaned forward and looked into her eyes. "You can't give up. Saving the Grove is the right thing to do for a whole lot of reasons. One of *your* reasons should be so you can perform there again."

"That's a little self-serving, don't you think?" Tess said with a smile.

"So what? If you can morph *Macbeth* into something that scares off Willy, you have talent that should be shared."

"Just like you should share yours."

Luke leaned over and gave her a kiss. "Okay, point taken."

Chapter 9

Climbing Mountains

Once the kitty tree was complete, Luke dragged it upstairs to the bedroom. Tess plopped John on the top platform. The big orange cat looked confused for a second, then spun around and settled into kitty sphinx position.

"Aww, look, he loves it. How cute is that?" Tess wrapped Luke in a hug and looked up at his face. "We could celebrate with a little afternoon delight."

"That sounds fun, but I have to clean up downstairs. Put my tools and all those carpet scraps away." He gave her a kiss and unwrapped her arms from him. "Maybe later."

Tess tried not to feel hugely rejected, but sheesh, it wasn't like the tools were going to run away and cause trouble. "I guess I can paint over some more Willy art. It's everywhere. I think the pornographic spiders, rhinos, and unicorns are reproducing."

"After I finish the wall, then we need to repaint the whole house."

"We?"

Luke smiled. "Well, only if you want to help."

"I could be convinced. But you'd have to ask *really* nicely."

"I can be nice."

Tess spent the rest of the afternoon and evening painting and puttering around the house while Luke did who knows what in the back yard. The farther Tess stayed away from the wall reconstruction project, the better. She'd already somehow managed to get herself roped into painting. But to be fair, covering up the Willy art benefited her too. Luke wasn't the only one worried about nightmares.

When Tess opened her eyes the next morning, she was less surprised to find herself curled up with Luke than she had been the day before. She could get used to waking up next to a large, warm sexy guy. Getting out of bed wasn't appealing, but it was Monday and she had to face the ugly reality of returning to the workforce.

She shoved Ringo off the pillow and gave Luke a kiss on the cheek before staggering downstairs to make coffee. After firing up a pot of go juice, she rummaged through her bag, which was hanging on one of the barstools in front of the pass through. She pulled out her day planner and settled into plotting out her attack for the day's sales calls.

Barney emerged from the downstairs bedroom, walked over, and planted his muzzle on her calf. Tess looked down at his eager expression. "I know you want breakfast, but I need coffee. How about you hit the back yard for some personal time?"

The dog wagged his tail and leaped around with unadulterated joy as Tess walked to the French doors and let him out. Dogs were a lot easier to please than cats.

Tess got to work making calls and drinking coffee. She was on her second cup when Luke finally came downstairs. She grinned at him. "What happened to Mr. I Get Up at Four Thirty?"

“I don’t get up that early when I don’t have to.” He leaned over the chair and kissed the back of her neck. “And it’s your fault I’m tired.”

“But worth it.” Tess turned and kissed him. “Because wow…*again*.”

“Hey, I said you were hot.”

After making her calls and dealing with the rest of her morning routine, Tess reluctantly said goodbye to Luke and went off to the office and her various appointments. The meeting to check out the Grove was at one, and while she was talking up the magic of printed materials, mostly she was thinking about seeing the old theater again. Ads for the fall issue didn’t close for months, so no one was too excited about discussing the next issue of the magazine. But Tess did manage to line up some new print jobs, so the morning wasn’t a total loss.

Promptly at one, Tess met everyone in front of the Grove. The outside had a Spanish Mission design with arched windows on the second floor. It looked more or less the same as it had for years with large pieces of plywood over the windows and big faded plastic letters on the marquee proclaiming that it was closed.

Tess gave Bea a hug. “It feels weird to be here and about to go inside.”

“It brings back a lot of memories, doesn’t it?” Bea squeezed her hand. “I know this is going to work. I can just feel it.”

Bea unlocked the door, and Tess walked into the old theater. She immediately sneezed from the dust. Built in 1927, the building had been a vaudeville and movie house, but fell into disrepair in the late seventies. Even though it was run down, the Grove had still been used for occasional shows until about 1986 or '87. As far as Tess knew, no one outside of the Cullins family—and maybe the grumpy woman at the first meeting—had been inside the building since it had been boarded up ten years earlier.

Tess turned her head and scanned the lobby. To look at the place, they'd been ten painfully unkind years. Maybe theater years were like dog years. She walked from the lobby to the main seating area of the theater and scanned the aisles. The old red seats sported approximately 3,267 tears and the ornate plaster symbols of two of the ancient Greek muses, Thalia and Melpomene, on the walls looked especially pained.

Tess came back out of the theater and met Bea and Margaret who were chatting in the lobby in hushed voices. Somehow it seemed blasphemous to speak in a normal voice.

Luke touched her shoulder and whispered, "Hey there."

Startled, Tess turned around. "I'm glad to see you."

"Sorry I'm late. I got a little too involved in shoring up the wall back at the house. It's a mess." He looked up at the ceiling. "Not like this though. I think that's water damage up there. Do you think they'll let us go up on the roof and take a look?"

"I have no idea. It's really dirty in here, but some things aren't too bad. I haven't asked Bea or Margaret what they think yet. We've just been looking around. It's so dirty and dark, it's hard to tell much."

Luke nodded but didn't say anything. He walked out of the lobby and into the theater area, strolling down the aisle toward the stage. Tess followed him and was overwhelmed by memories of what the theater used to be like with the lights on. Her thoughts leaped back and forth through time with flashbacks to the shows she'd acted in to the present time with sadness and despair at what the Grove had become.

Tess studied Luke's expression, wondering what he was thinking. He disappeared backstage for a while, and then moved stage left and examined a wall. What did he see when he looked at it? The expression on his face wasn't promising.

She went up the steps onto the stage and stood still, looking out at the rows and rows of red seats. Luke was poking at some of the plasterwork, and he dropped his hand as crumbles fell to the floor. In the silence of the cavernous empty space, the clattering of the pieces of plaster seemed excessively loud.

Tess recalled that the acoustics had been amazing in the Grove. She walked to the middle of the stage, clasped her hands in front of her, and sang, "Climb Every Mountain" from *The Sound of Music.* This dream was certainly going to require a whole lot of love. Not to mention money. Even though there was no orchestra, Bea, Margaret, and Luke applauded when Tess concluded her a capella version. She bowed and walked down the steps from the stage.

Bea walked to Tess and put out her arms for a hug. "That was beautiful, Tess. You made me cry."

Margaret swept a tear from her eyes and sniffled. "Me too."

Tess glanced at Luke who didn't say anything, but gave her a warm smile. She could tell by the shine in his blue eyes that he'd appreciated the impromptu performance too.

Bea said, "Luke, have you seen what you need to see?"

"It's impossible to evaluate the extent of the damage in an hour, and I'm not an expert. But I can tell you there's definitely been water damage. The roof leaks somewhere, and you can see the ceiling's got problems. It might have caused rot in the walls too, which is why the plaster is falling apart. And there's no way it's up to code."

"But can it be fixed?" Tess asked. "You said almost anything can be fixed."

"I did, but I also said it could be expensive. And finding someone who can work on old plaster could be tough." He shrugged. "Plastering like that is becoming a lost art. It takes training and special tools. It's not the type of thing I've ever done."

"But there have to be people who can do it, right?" Tess demanded.

"Sure. But not in Alpine Grove."

Bea's gaze moved from Tess to Luke. "I don't think we need to get into the details. Just whether or not it can be fixed."

Tess said, "Yes, it can."

Luke frowned. "You might need to raise a lot of money. I can't tell with just a walk-through like this what kind of costs you're dealing with. You ought to talk to a commercial building inspector with experience in historic building restoration."

Tess put her fists on her hips. "Is the Grove going to fall down or not?"

"Not yet." Luke looked at Bea helplessly. "I don't want to get your hopes up. This is a lot of work you're talking about here. Probably a lot of expensive work."

Margaret looked at Bea. "What do you think?"

Bea reached to take Tess and Margaret's hands. "I think we should do it. Even though like the song says, I think we might have to ford quite a few streams."

"The last thing you need is more water damage," Luke said.

Tess flashed him a glare before throwing her arms around Bea. "I know we can save it."

~

After Bea locked the door to the theater behind them, Tess stood with her, Margaret, and Luke on the sidewalk. Luke took Tess's hand and gave it a squeeze. "I should get going. Good luck with the owner."

Although she wanted to throw her arms around him for a much-needed hug, she refrained. "Good luck with the wall."

He turned and walked off in the direction of Oak Street. Tess returned her attention to Margaret and Bea, pushed her bag up higher on her shoulder, and cleared her throat. "Okay, so I guess we've decided to make the offer. What do we say?"

Bea said, "We have a booklet of information that Jan compiled about the history of the theater. They don't have a plan for it and we do. We've compiled an offer that's based on what they paid for it, real estate values in Alpine Grove, and sales of other theaters in other parts of the country that were later restored."

"In round dollars, what does that mean?" Tess asked.

"The nonprofit will offer two hundred thousand dollars to buy the Grove," Bea replied.

Tess slapped her hand on her chest. "How are we ever going to get that kind of money?"

"We'll get a mortgage," Margaret said. "We plan to offer a twenty percent down payment, so we need to raise forty thousand dollars. And, of course, money for the restoration work."

Tess patted her chest, willing her heart to stop racing. It was more money than she'd ever seen in her life. "I'm suddenly finding this a lot more scary. Terrifying even. I had no idea it would cost so much."

Bea pointed down the street. "The building with the ad agency sold a year or two ago for a half a million dollars and it needed a lot of work."

"In *Alpine Grove*?" Tess was incredulous. She'd walked by these buildings her entire life and never thought about how much they would cost to buy. They were just there.

"There's quite a bit of money to be made in commercial real estate," Margaret said. "That's why investors swoop in and buy property with good frontage. Then they look for ways to profit from it."

"Over the years, I've watched this community step up and do amazing things," Bea said. "Most recently was the dog adoption group. They started with only one woman who saw a problem and had an idea."

Margaret said, "And we're *three* women. So that makes us unstoppable."

Tess laughed. "Two smart savvy entrepreneurs and a failed actress. To paraphrase *Sesame Street*, one of these women is not like the others."

"Oh, Tess, don't be so hard on yourself," Bea said.

That was almost exactly what Tess had said to Luke. Maybe she should take her own advice. "I'll do the best I can. Let's go make this guy an offer he can't refuse."

The meeting was in Gleasonville, so Tess hopped in the Hyundai and followed Bea and Margaret out of town. During the drive, she thought about the theater and her free-flowing emotions. Bea wasn't the only one who'd cried. While

Tess was singing, tears had been streaming down her cheeks. Maybe Bea was right and the community would step up. They'd need to promote the heck out of the project though.

Maybe Tess could go to the local paper and get them on board. She knew the publisher well because they got a lot of printing done for inserts and other marketing materials that weren't printed on newsprint. The local paper always did a big toy fundraiser over the holidays because Ward, the publisher, had a particular soft spot in his heart for kids. Maybe they could set up a kids' theater troupe or drama classes.

Her mind turned to Luke and the fact that he'd been doing this drive every day twice a day. What a pain. No wonder he'd taken advantage of the opportunity to sleep late. He was probably relieved the job at the dog kennel was over. But then Tess would see him a lot less, which was depressing. Just when they were starting to get to know each other better, he'd be off at work digging up things in Gleasonville while she remained in Alpine Grove selling printing for all eternity.

Tess tried not to dwell on what might happen with Luke. Long distance relationships never worked, and her love life would undoubtedly return to the sad frozen wasteland it had been before. Luke was interesting, kind, and unbelievably sexy, which made him a rarity among the men of Alpine Grove. She'd learned from years of experience that finding a man in such a small town wasn't easy. They were either married, involved, or guys she was unwilling to spend more than fifteen minutes with, much less date.

After a small confab in front of the office building, Bea, Margaret and Tess went inside. The lobby sported typical corporate decor with standard muted gray carpet and sleek, shiny metal and black furnishings. Above the long reception counter, the words Pollard, Wickham, and Hughes, Inc. were proudly displayed on the wall.

Tess looked down at her skirt and hurriedly brushed some dust from the Grove Theater off the fabric. She scanned her mind for a suitable role to portray and remembered she'd done some low-budget corporate training films about leadership. Time to play Ms. Executive.

The ever-so-efficient secretary ushered the three women into an office and declared that Mr. Hughes would be in shortly. Tess set her bag on the floor and had a chance to take a few deep breaths before a lean man in a suit walked in and announced that he was Aaron Hughes. With the dark suit and striped tie, he was the image of the consummate successful businessman, complete with wavy salt and pepper hair and shrewd, deep-set eyes.

Everyone shook hands, introduced themselves, and sat down. Tess said, "Mr. Hughes, thank you for taking time to meet with us."

He smiled. "Call me Aaron."

Tess leaned forward and folded her hands on the table. "We have documentation about everything you could possibly want to know about the history and value of the Grove Theater."

"It sounds like you've done your homework. Obviously, I did too before I purchased the building."

"I'm sure you did. But there's something you don't know." Tess unfolded her hands and spread her arms wide. "Something you *can't* know because you don't live in Alpine Grove."

With a skeptical look, he leaned back in the chair and crossed his arms. "I have spent plenty of time there. It's a cute little town."

"But you don't live there. You aren't part of the community, so you don't know how much the Grove means to the people who live there." Tess paused and set her hands in her lap. "I grew up in Alpine Grove and performed at the Grove many times. It's a major part of why I wanted to go to Hollywood and become an actress. To you, it's just an old building, but the Grove is where I learned to love the arts, theater, and performing."

Bea added, "Tess is a wonderful singer. She was in many musical productions at the theater."

"That's nice," Aaron said.

Tess glanced at Bea and continued. "My talent, or lack of it, isn't important. What is important is that the children and adults living in Alpine Grove need the arts. We need that creative outlet. Arts help us understand who we are as people and give us empathy for others. What happens when we lose all the songs, the music, the dancing? When we lose literature and plays? What are we left with?"

Aaron said, "I'm not going to argue the value of the arts. But you realize this place has been boarded up for a decade, right? Everyone seemed to manage okay."

"It's been a loss to the community. And we realize it now that the Grove is in danger of being destroyed. It's a historic landmark, and it would be a tragedy for it to be torn down."

Margaret slid a spiral-bound document across the desk. "When we talked the other day, you said to make you an offer. We're here to do that now."

Bea sat up straight and pointed at the document. "The bottom line is that we'd like to take the Grove off your hands."

Aaron flipped open the booklet and turned a couple of pages. He looked up. "I appreciate that you've laid your cards on the table. Here are mine. The building is a white elephant. We haven't come up with a viable commercial option for the space. And tearing it down would have ramifications for future investments in Alpine Grove."

"You certainly wouldn't be popular," Tess said. "It's a small town and people would talk."

"Will you sell the Grove to us?" Bea said. "Our offer is detailed in those pages, but the bottom line is that we're offering you two hundred thousand. It's a fair deal."

"You're prepared to do this now?" Aaron said.

"Yes. Margaret and I have talked to a bank. If we need to, we'll co-sign on a loan, then transfer it to the nonprofit we're forming, which will own the Grove."

Margaret added, "We have houses with lots of equity we can pull out."

Tess felt a knot form in her stomach. These women were talking about second mortgages on their *houses*. They could go into debt or even lose their homes if this didn't work. "I'm in too." It was a feeble offer since her assets consisted of one crappy car and four cats.

Bea reached to clasp the women's hands on either side of her. "We're all in this together. Please say yes."

Aaron flipped through the pages idly. "Fine. But I need the down payment in three months."

Tess stifled a gasp. Three months? Was this guy on drugs? How were they going to raise forty grand in three months?

Bea reached across the desk. "It's a deal."

Aaron said, "If you don't come up with the money, I'll look at other options."

"Don't worry. You'll get it," Margaret said.

Tess wanted to scream, "Are you insane?" but mustered up her inner actress and said in a confident voice, "We are committed to saving this important historic and cultural landmark. You have nothing to worry about."

When everyone shook hands and said their goodbyes, Tess was relieved that her hands had stopped trembling. They left the building and stood outside in a small group, much like they had stood in front of the Grove hours earlier.

Tess smiled weakly. "We did it."

"You were wonderful, Tess." Bea clasped her hands in hers. "I knew it would make all the difference to have someone with real passion at that meeting."

Margaret added, "I agree. I'm so glad you were there. I always turn into a shy little girl in situations like that."

Tess looked at her aghast. "But you talked about the money. That's the hard part."

"No, honey. The hard part is getting someone to listen to the offer at all." Margaret smiled. "You were brilliant."

"Maybe, but now we have to raise forty thousand dollars in ninety days," Tess said. "I think I need to go lie down."

Bea patted her on the shoulder. "You do that. And then, tomorrow, we'll get to work."

~

When Tess walked into the house, Luke was in the kitchen. He strolled into the living room, holding a sandwich and trailed by Barney who wasn't taking his eyes off the food prize.

Tess tossed her bag on the sofa and threw herself into Luke's arms. He took a step backward, then recovered, wrapping his arms around her. "Hey, what happened? Did they say no?"

Tess leaned back to look up into his face. "They said yes. But we have to raise the down payment. I spent the whole drive home getting more and more freaked out. Margaret and Bea could lose their houses."

"What do you mean lose their houses? I'm not sure what to say. I thought this is what you wanted."

"How about saying the Grove isn't going to fall down and this isn't a fool's errand. You were pretty negative about the state of the place."

"I didn't have time to look at it thoroughly." He stepped back from Tess and held the sandwich up away from Barney's inquisitive nose. "You could see just by looking around in there that the theater's not in great shape. It's old and building codes have changed a lot in the last seventy years. Not to mention ADA compliance."

"What's that?

"Americans with Disabilities Act. Public buildings have to be accessible. No one was thinking about that in 1927."

"Is what we're trying to do completely stupid? Margaret and Bea are risking so much. I said I'd help, but I don't have my house at stake. If someone repossessed my crummy Hyundai, I'd probably say thank you."

"Being a renter has some advantages," Luke said with a smile. "I'm sure you'll find other ways to help. You had a bunch of ideas. Like what about inviting that friend to do a show?"

"Where? The theater is a mess. Will you help work on it?"

"I have to deal with this house, and I have to go back to work. They're building a new shopping mall south of Gleasonville. Another big box store is moving in and I have to go look at the site tomorrow. The whole area is turning into one big strip mall."

"I know. It's horrible. I hate it when I have to drive through there. The traffic gets worse all the time."

"Some people call it progress." He shrugged. "As long as Gleasonville keeps sprawling south, I'll keep having work."

"It sounds like you'll be busy."

"Yeah, I've got a bunch of stuff to do that I've ignored the last few days. Tomorrow, I need to get back to it." He gestured toward the wood where the French doors had been replaced with large sheets of plywood. "I cleaned up all the stuff I was working on in here and the back yard. Barney and I need to head home now."

"This is your home too."

He smiled. "Technically, it's *your* home."

"But you may have noticed I'm willing to share." Tess put her arms around him again and leaned her cheek on his chest. "Very willing. Is it too sappy to say I'm going to miss you?"

Luke moved to kiss her. "I hope not because I'm going to miss you too. I'll be back on Saturday."

"Having you here has been great. All kinds of wow. Would it be possible to convince you to return Friday night?" Tess reached up to put her arms around his neck. "It's going to be a lonely week."

"True." Luke gave her another one of those serious kisses that made her legs get all wobbly and said, "See you Friday night."

After Luke left and her hormones settled back down, Tess finally dealt with making dinner. She also let the cats out for more exploration time. The house seemed extra quiet without Barney clattering around or Luke hammering on something. Having the Fab Four cavorting around might help.

Before they parted ways in Gleasonville, Margaret had handed Tess a bunch of papers that were copies of notes she and Bea had taken during their meetings and conversations. She also gave Tess a copy of the offer package they'd shared with Aaron Hughes. Bea said there would be another meeting Tuesday night at 7:30 to tell everyone what was going on.

While she ate her frozen dinner, Tess began going through everything. It looked like Margaret had read every fundraising book in the bookstore and the librarian, Jan, had done the same thing with books in the library. Everything pointed to the fact that the community needed to be involved.

Someone with nice handwriting, probably Margaret, had noted that with a town of 5,000 people, if you averaged fifty dollars for every person, that was two-hundred and fifty thousand dollars. Tess chewed thoughtfully. She'd never thought of it like that. What if there were a way to make people feel personally involved in the reconstruction? Maybe they could be persuaded to help. Luke had gotten her to help paint the house, after all. Okay, it didn't hurt that he was the world's sexiest landlord. But that wasn't why she was painting. After hearing Luke talk about it, she wanted to see the house return to being a pretty home again.

It had been a long day, and Tess retired to her room to finish reading through her piles of papers about the Grove. John curled up and settled into purring before falling asleep in a large orange tabby heap. Ringo leaped up on the bed and snuggled up to her other side. Clearly, it had been another rough day of napping for the Fab Four while she was driving all over the county.

Cats and papers flew everywhere when Tess jolted awake at the sound of the phone ringing. She rolled over, flailed for the phone on the nightstand, and mumbled hello.

"Tess?" Luke said. "Are you okay?"

"I'm fine, but I think John may be a little addled. Sorry Johnny-boy." Tess shook her head, trying to wrap her brain around being awake. "So hey, what have you been up to in the last few hours?"

"Not much. Driving. Thinking."

"Did you think about *me*?" Tess asked with a smile.

"I did. I couldn't tell if you were angry about what I said about the Grove before I left."

"Believe me, when I'm angry, you'll know. I think I was more depressed than angry. There are so many unknowns." Tess leaned to pick up some papers from the floor. "For the record, I know it's not your fault. But I was still upset."

"Okay, I get it."

"I've been racking my brain trying to figure out how to get people involved. Make them feel like a part of the restoration. Do you think people would be willing to help?"

"If nothing else, they could help clean it up. I mean there's still popcorn on the floor from the last time they showed a movie. Ten-year-old trash is pretty gross." He paused. "Speaking of gross, I didn't say anything, but it would be great if you could clean up the house a little this week. Maybe do your laundry?"

Choosing to ignore the comment about her housekeeping or lack of it, Tess said, "I'd say Willy trash gives ten-year-old theater trash a run for its money. I was thinking that no one has seen the inside of the Grove in years. Maybe that would be inspiring. Or depressing. I'll see what everyone thinks at the meeting tomorrow. More than anything we need money. But to get donations, we need a way for people to feel like they're involved in the renovation."

"When I was in college, there was a walkway that had engraved bricks with names of alumni who had made donations."

"Alumni bought bricks?"

"The brick had their name on it for posterity and I guess they liked that, even though people were walking on it."

"One of the magazine advertisers engraves headstones. Maybe he could do bricks too. And there's that tile artist in town. She could make tiles for people who don't want their name stepped on."

"That sounds like a good idea."

"I hate math, but Margaret pointed out that if all five thousand residents of Alpine Grove donated fifty dollars, that would be two hundred and fifty thousand dollars."

"Even if you got a percentage, you'd have enough to pay the down payment." He paused. "Like eight hundred people."

"Did you just figure that out in your head?"

"I have a calculator on my desk."

"That makes me feel better. Okay, what if we sell eight hundred bricks at fifty bucks each? Nah. That sounds like a lot. So maybe we sell four hundred bricks and do a show too. And maybe an auction. And mailers begging for money. Do you think we can do all that in three months?"

"I don't know, but I think you're about to find out."

Tess groaned. "This is going to be so much work. I wish you were here."

"Me too. That was another thing I thought about."

"I'm glad it's not just me. I know trying to save the Grove is going to make me crazy. I miss talking to you and having your huge shoulders to cry on."

"My shoulders are available long-distance too. What time does the meeting end tomorrow?"

"Eight thirty, I think."

"Okay. I'll call you at nine."

"It's a date. So how do you feel about phone sex?"

Luke chuckled. "I doubt it's as good as the real thing."

"Probably not, but it's better than nothing."

~

The next day, Tess did the whole work rigmarole, making calls and going to appointments. When she was meeting people, she discovered that what she wanted to talk to them about was the Grove, not advertising. But the meeting announcing the big offer hadn't happened yet, so she couldn't say anything to anyone. On the other hand, once their little group had a plan in place, Tess was in a unique position to help spread the word about saving the theater.

Tess hadn't thought about it before, but all the running around she had to do for her job could be helpful to the cause. In the process of selling printing and advertising, she talked to almost every business owner in town. Or tried to anyway. The idea of talking to people about saving the Grove was a lot more inspiring than discussing the latest employee forms someone needed to get reprinted for the umpteenth time.

The meeting at the gift store went by in a blur. Everyone was excited that the owner had accepted the offer and asked lots of questions. Bea, Margaret, and Tess all tried to reassure everyone that the Grove was not going to suddenly collapse into a pile of rubble the next day, but that it did need some extensive restoration work. It was a delicate balance, and Tess was starting to see why Luke had been so circumspect in his evaluation. People were pinning their hopes on the theater restoration going well and not turning into a total money pit.

By the time she got home, Tess was mentally and emotionally exhausted. She was a people person, but having so many people throwing information around was rough. On the other hand, they'd hammered out a plan that wasn't too far off what she and Luke had discussed the night before. Margaret loved the idea of selling bricks and committees were already forming for the various fundraising activities.

Not surprisingly, Tess had been nominated to set up a show to raise money. Where they might perform the show was a difficult problem to solve. Someone pointed out that they might be able to rent the Grove for a couple of nights, but ugly insurance questions needed to be answered first. Fortunately, Tess had to go chat with all the insurance companies in town about advertising, so asking would be easy.

Right as Tess was pulling on her favorite comfy sweatpants, the phone rang. Shoving George aside, she plopped down on the bed to answer it. At the sound of Luke's voice, she smiled. "I have to say you're certainly punctual."

"I try. How was the meeting?"

"It was great, but I'm worn out from thinking about it. And guess what, I'm in charge of putting on a *show.*"

"From the tone of your voice, I'm thinking this is a stage reference, isn't it?"

"Oh, come on. Judy Garland and Mickey Rooney made a whole lot of movies that were all about putting on a show. Apparently, it was the solution to everything in the thirties and forties."

"Maybe it will work for the Grove too."

"We can only hope." Tess reached over to pet George who had returned to the bed. "How was your day? Did you dig up lots of great things?"

He laughed. "If only. I was in meetings. I had to dress up and drink bad coffee at conference tables. It was a pretty lousy day all around."

"You had to sit in meetings? How come? That's usually my jurisdiction." Tess gestured flamboyantly even though he couldn't see it and said in a high-pitched voice, "Thank you for this scrumptious cup of six-hour-old burnt coffee. Wouldn't you love to advertise? I can make your business soar. Local advertising helps you reach new customers."

"I think you're better at sales than I am. I had to sit around and pretend to be excited about a strip mall. Now I've got to do a bid. And I found out there are all these companies from out of state who want in on the work too. Maybe I should try that whole local angle."

"It could work. Or you could just forget about bidding and find work up here."

"Speaking of Alpine Grove, Joe called me and begged me to come up there and fix his grader again. I don't know what he does to that poor old machine, but somehow he trashed Old Yeller's hydraulics again."

"Who is Joe?"

"A guy at the road department. I was filling in for him that day we met. When he needs a day off, he calls me. Or when he breaks the grader. Which is regularly."

Tess scritched George's ear and smiled at the cat's huge yawn. "You have an extremely wide range of skills."

"Joe is stupid when it comes to maintenance. You can't just run these machines without taking care of them," Luke said with a sigh. "Let's just say, this isn't the first time he's called me about problems with Old Yeller."

"You sound depressed."

"Just tired. I don't wanna talk about it. What kind of show are you going to put on to raise all that money?"

"I was thinking about a play, but I haven't decided."

"More Shakespeare? You're good at it."

"Maybe, but I'm not sure the Bard would draw a big crowd in Alpine Grove. I'm putting out a call for auditions. Maybe a bunch of talented people will be interested, but Shakespeare is hard. Remembering lines is difficult enough without doing it in Elizabethan English. A lot of words aren't quite the same as they were in the fourteenth century."

"Yeah, but they sound sexy when you say them."

Tess giggled. "Is this your roundabout way of hinting at phone sex?"

"That Shakespearean English you threw at Willy was pretty hot."

"We two hath met while plying the dirt. And lo, the Hyundai wast brought straight from the fusty ditch."

Luke laughed. "Wherefore are thou? Why in a ditch, kind sir."

"That was excellent. You should be in my show."

"No way."

"I wish you'd been at the meeting. There were so many questions about construction and restoration that we couldn't answer."

"You need to get a building inspector to look at the place."

"Becca said the closest one is in Gleasonville. So are you, and you're cheaper."

"And not a building inspector. I don't even know who the suppliers are that you deal with for that kind of restoration work."

"But you could find out."

"I've gotta work, Tess. We talked about this before."

"There's work here. You just dug up a septic system, and there's a broken road grader that needs you too."

"Someone else can fix Old Yeller for a change."

"You're going to spend all this time doing a bid for a job you don't want to do. Take a few weeks off. Just think about it. You could fix this house. Help with the Grove. Spend time with me."

"You want me to spend time with you?"

"Of *course* I do. Think of a sexy song title."

"What?"

"A romantic song. Pick one."

"All right. In honor of the kitty Beatles, how about 'I Want to Hold Your Hand'?"

"Nice selection." Tess sang, "And prithee sayeth to me thee'll alloweth me holdeth thy hand anon. Alloweth me holdeth thy hand. I wanteth to holdeth thy hand."

"Okay singing Shakespeare is *really* hot." Luke chuckled. "How about 'Love Me Do'?"

"Loveth, loveth me doth. Thee knoweth I loveth thee. I'll at each moment be true. So prithee loveth me doth. Heigh-ho, loveth me doth."

"Aww, that's kinda sweet. And yet still hot."

"So will you think about spending some more time in your hometown? Serenading you in person could be a lot more fun than over the phone."

"I don't doubt that, and I promise I'll think about it. To be honest, this whole strip mall job is part of what's depressing me. I think I mentioned that excavation isn't particularly exciting to begin with, but this job is especially dull. And then when it's done, it's gonna be filled with a bunch of franchises like every other strip mall everywhere."

"So, it sounds like what you're saying is that helping to build another ugly strip mall is a project with no soul."

"What do you mean soul? It's a job."

"Not every job has soul. Fixing this house and turning it back into a pretty home is a project with soul. You did it before and when you told me about it, I could see what it meant to you. Restoring the Grove to its former glory has soul. Alpine Grove itself has soul. Strip malls have no soul."

"I'm starting to understand why you're such a good salesperson."

"Is it working?"

"It might be."

Tess smiled and patted George's back gently. "Good."

~

The next day, Tess blocked out some time to embark on her plan of talking to the publisher of the local newspaper. She'd known Ward Tucker for years and enjoyed talking about the ins and outs of publishing with him. There were similarities between magazine and newspaper publishing, and they'd spent many enjoyable hours sharing stories about the nuances of deadlines, graphics, and fickle advertisers.

During the conversation, Ward complained that one of his columnists had left town and Tess saw her opening. She suggested that Ward could use the space to show the progress of the Grove fundraisers.

Ward initially was dubious, but leaned back in his chair. "I proposed to my wife after we went to a show at the Grove. We were standing on the sidewalk in the rain and I popped the question. I think it was when you were in that production of *Annie*."

Tess pressed her palms together. "That show was so much fun. I think I was seven or eight."

"Let's not dwell on age, you little whipper-snapper." Ward folded his hands on his ample stomach. "When Ruth told me about the efforts to buy and restore the Grove, she said, 'It's inspiring' and that she thinks I should help."

"I think you should listen to your wife." Tess grinned. "She's a wise woman. We'll be keeping close track on the donations, and I'm sure I can get someone to send you a daily write up of the ways people can support the effort. I'll make some calls and let you know tomorrow. If you give us the space, we'll give you the up-to-the-minute news on our progress." Tess made a mental note to ask Bea if there were any volunteers who liked to write.

Ward leaned forward and stretched his hand out across the desk. "Okay, you've got yourself eight column inches. Use them wisely."

Tess shook his hand heartily. "We absolutely will. Thanks, Ward."

Later in the day, Tess managed to talk Geoff into donating some free printing. Tess had been around the printing world long enough to know about the concept of "gang runs." If Geoff was running a job on the press on large sheets of paper, he could sometimes squeeze another job on the same sheet and cut them up.

Geoff was grumpy about it, but finally relented because the printing Tess wanted to do would be on paper that otherwise would be cut off as waste and recycled. So the cost to the company was negligible. Tess promised that they'd have artwork in time for the next big print run. She added a note in her day planner about printing next to the note about finding a writer for the newspaper. The flyers for the brick fundraiser could be printed on the same sheet as the accountant's brochure job she'd lined up earlier that day.

After she got home, she called Bea and told her about the various meetings with business owners. Bea said she knew just the person to handle writing and design issues, and by the time Tess hung up, she was glowing with her day's accomplishments.

Later that night, Luke called and Tess regaled him with the stories of her day's adventures. Finally, she stopped talking because he seemed oddly quiet. She twisted the phone cord around her finger. "Sorry to go on and on. It's been an action-packed day for me. Are you okay?"

"I'm all right. I just came back from a long run, so I'm kinda tired."

"You don't sound all right. The last time you mentioned running was when you wanted to kill Willy. Are you pissed off about something?"

"Today, I went out to a job site. I thought it was all lined up, but when I got there, the guy said they couldn't pay me, so never mind. I'm like, what the...? So you just want me to go *home*? And he said yeah."

"So you just left?"

"What else was I supposed to do? I took my trailer, dropped everything back at the warehouse, and went home. Then my brother called to rag on how I'm not doing a good job keeping an eye on my dad."

"Is it your job to keep an eye on him?"

"It's always my job. And always has been. Robby was off being Mr. Brilliant doing internships, and I was stuck working for Dad, listening to him whine about financial problems. Mom worked in the office, so when I wasn't working construction, at school, or at practice, I was babysitting Becky."

"I was always the one being babysat."

"Consider yourself lucky. It stinks to be the responsible one. Anyway, it's been a rotten day. Barney and I are gonna hit the hay early."

"If you don't have that excavation job, maybe you can come up to Alpine Grove and fix the grader."

Luke chuckled. "Still selling that idea, huh?"

"Why not? Is there a reason you *don't* want to come up here? I thought last weekend was pretty great. Didn't you?"

"I did, but here's the thing. I'm not an easy person to live with." Luke paused. "The longer we're in that house together, the more likely it is that we'll drive each other nuts."

"Last weekend, we didn't drive each other nuts. We had lots of great sex, and you made my cats a kitty tree, which was adorable. What's not to like?"

"I tried really, really hard not to be jerk. I didn't say anything, but, Tess, you're a slob."

"I believe my mother may have mentioned that about three hundred times when I was growing up, so thanks, but it's not a big news flash. I work all day and it's not like I'm going to scrub a house that's full of holes, weird art, and primer. Nothing I do will make it look good right now."

"I suppose, but doing laundry and dishes once in a while would be nice. Like I said, I don't want to get into it, so only seeing each other on weekends might be better."

"But you sound so miserable. Cheering you up long-distance doesn't seem to work."

"You're wrong about that. Talking to you has been the best part of my day."

"Well, hey, the offer's still open if you change your mind. Since it's your house, you have the key."

"That's true. I'll try to be in a better mood when I call you."

"I've got a Grove meeting, so I'll be home late. I could sing again if you think it would help."

"It might. I'll talk to you tomorrow."

Tess hung up the phone and rested her palm on the receiver. Luke had seemed so steady and even-tempered, it was odd for him to sound so depressed. The phone rang, and Tess jerked her hand away in surprise. When Tess answered, Claire said, "So what happened with your cats?"

Tess looked around the bedroom where the four felines were snoring in various configurations. "Nothing. The Fab Four are right here. Why?"

"I called you, and you said you had some cat problem. Then you never called me back."

"Oh yeah." Tess made a round-eyed shocked face at John who yawned in response. "Sorry. I forgot."

"What's going on with you? You're being weird."

"I'm *not* being weird. It's just been a busy few days. I got involved with a group of people who are trying to save the Grove from being torn down. Lots of meetings. You know how volunteer stuff can be."

"No, I don't know because you never called me back." Claire paused. "Wait. Is Luke around? Is that why you're being weird?"

"He's not here. But I just talked to him."

"*Why*? Are you consorting with that slime? Tell me you're not."

Tess decided to come clean with Luke's story about what had actually happened when Claire thought he was cheating. Maybe she was breaking a confidence, but clearly, he was never going to tell Claire himself. "I need to tell you something."

"What?"

"Just listen for a second." Tess explained Luke's side of the story of putting together the bookshelf with the girl formerly known as the skank. Tess also pointed out that he'd had no idea Claire was in the bathroom, or why Claire had driven his truck into the lake.

When Tess was done, Claire was silent for a moment. "Well, I wish I'd known this a long time ago."

"He said he tried to tell you, and you just ended up screaming at each other."

"I remember that part."

Tess said, "Luke is a little hard to read. Like I said, I just talked to him and he sounds so depressed. I guess it's a bunch of family and work stuff."

Claire sighed. "In high school, he was always trying to help out, but his family never seemed to appreciate it. I felt bad for him. It's probably why he partied so hard. I think he needed to let off some steam."

"He's a nice person."

"Oh, noooo. You're sleeping with him, aren't you?" Claire said. "I *knew* it."

"Well, not right now. He's in Gleasonville busy being depressed, remember?"

"I'm sure you'll figure out a way to convince him to return."

"I hope so."

"Oh. My. God. My entire world is tilting on it's axis. This isn't just about sex, is it? You're seriously into Luke Bennett, aren't you? Of all people in the world, you decide to be interested in *him?*"

"Yeah, 'fraid so."

~

The rest of the conversation with Claire consisted of her persistent attempts to worm details out of Tess. Now that Claire had no real reason to hate Luke, she was dying of curiosity to find out what she'd missed out on in high school.

Tess finally said, "Claire, that's personal. I told you. It was good and we had fun. That's all you need to know. If you want to talk about sex, go talk to your husband. Spencer might appreciate it."

"Fat lot of good that would do. I'm sure he's cheating on me when he goes into the city."

"You always say that."

"Well, I'm sure he is."

"It's after midnight there. Go to bed. Maybe give Spencer a big surprise by sleeping with him."

After Tess hung up, she read for a while but remained wide awake, which was annoying because she had so much to do the next day. Nothing like getting caught up in Claire's daily drama to foster a case of insomnia. As the clock ticked forward, Tess did mental math, counting down how few hours of sleep she was going to get.

When she woke up the next morning, Tess was predictably tired. It was likely to be another power-down-the-coffee day. Plus, she'd put the word out that people could audition for the show, whatever it might be, at her office after work. A few people had expressed interest in stopping by that evening, so she'd have to stay late.

The auditions weren't going to be like a true audition because she was going to let people perform more or less whatever they wanted. If they didn't have anything ready, she'd provide a scene and ask people to read lines.

Unlike her recent failures, there would be no memorization, improvisation, or nasty surprises. Although Tess wasn't volunteering the information, the fact was, pretty much anyone who could read lines without sounding like a robot was likely to get a part. Tess hadn't selected a play, so they could talk about that decision too. In the meantime, they could do the equivalent of a table read and go from there.

The idea of being in charge of a production was exciting, and Tess looked forward to meeting a bunch of fun creative people after work. It seemed like everyone knew someone who wanted to be in a show, so she'd be staying late for auditions almost every night. With the Grove being closed for so many years, maybe there was a pent-up urge to perform again among the locals.

After work, Tess welcomed four women to the office and they gathered in the conference room. They went around the table introducing themselves in turn, until Maren, a woman with blonde hair cut in a pixie haircut, said, "I thought this would be private. I don't want to audition in front of *people*."

Tess frowned. "A key aspect of performing is being in front of an audience. If you have a problem with that, this might not be the best way for you to help the Grove."

Maren squeezed her eyes shut and launched into a bout of hysterical sobbing. She put her palms over her face, and Tess wasn't sure if she was acting or truly crying. She got up and went over to the woman, "Maren? Are you portraying sadness? If so, you can stop now. I think we've got it."

"I don't want to audition in front of people. How could you do this to me?" She stood up. "I can't believe you'd make me do this. I'm leaving."

Everyone around the table watched silently as Maren stormed out of the room. Tess turned her palms toward the sky. "I, uh, don't know what happened there. You do all realize that performing means speaking in front of an audience, right?"

The three remaining women nodded somberly, and Tess continued, "Maybe it would be good if we just read part of a scene. Are the rest of you okay with that?"

A woman named Judith said, "I've done Shakespeare. I'm sure I can handle that."

Tess smiled in relief and clasped her hands together. "That's wonderful. I've played Juliet, Lady Macbeth, Ophelia, Portia, Bianca, and a couple of others. I adore Shakespeare. It's always exciting to find a kindred spirit. Oh I also was Katherine in *As you Like It*. 'If I be waspish, best beware of my sting.' Love it!"

Judith frowned. "I played a Roman in *Julius Cesar*. It was a long time ago."

"Friends, Romans, countrymen, lend me your ears," Tess exclaimed.

"It was a long time ago. I don't remember my line," Judith said.

Tess made an effort to rein in Crazy Tess before she scared off more people. "Of course. So would you all like to read some lines from *The Sound of Music*? I thought that would be fun since almost everyone has seen the movie so the story is familiar."

A woman named Debbie raised her hand. “How much time is this going to take? I need to get home and feed my husband. If I haven’t started dinner by six, I’ll never hear the end of it.”

“Okay, then let’s get going.” Tess handed out a sheet of paper. “It’s the scene where Maria meets the Captain and the children. It’s pretty straightforward. Judith, you be the Captain, Debbie, you be Maria and Leslie, you can play the voices of the children.”

After going through the scene twice, Tess wanted to cry in frustration. She didn’t want to be mean, but it was like the women were made of petrified wood. She’d worried about people sounding robotic, but robots were more interesting. If every audition was this bad, what was she going to do? It wasn’t like she could reject everyone. The whole town would hate her. Maybe tomorrow would be better.

Tess made a show of looking at her watch. “Well, look at the time, I know Debbie needs to get home, so I’ll be in touch with more information soon. If you have any suggestions for plays you think would be a particularly good draw in Alpine Grove, please feel free to let me know. Oh, and tell your friends that I’ll willing to stay after work if they want to try out. The more the merrier.”

Tess closed the door, locked it, and waved through the glass before lowering the Venetian blinds and closing them. She leaned her forehead on the metal door frame. Where were all the people she’d performed with when she was young? They couldn’t *all* be dead, could they? She sat down at her desk and made a list, which wasn’t very long. A number of the people, like Bea, were already over-committed doing other things. She wouldn't have time to be in the show with everything else she was doing.

Even though the drive home was short, it gave Tess too much time to think. What had she gotten herself into? Time for some comfort food and kitty love. She went to unlock the door and realized it wasn't locked.

When she walked into the living room, Barney leaped up and barked twice before he realized who it was and began wagging.

Luke was sprawled out on the sofa and raised his hand in greeting. "Hi there. Working late?"

Tess maneuvered around Barney and threw herself on top of Luke. "I'm *so* glad to see you."

He put his arms around her and gave her a kiss. "I'm glad to see you too. And I like your enthusiasm."

"I've had the *worst* day, and I was planning to console myself with pizza. Want some?"

"I never turn down pizza. What happened?"

She sat in his lap and related the story of the crier, Debbie Downer with the dictatorial spouse, and the Shakespearean extra. "Another woman named Leslie was there, but she didn't say much. None of them had any emotion in their reading. They were like zombies. It was a totally easy scene from *The Sound of Music* too. I don't know what I'm going to do."

"Not everyone is cut out for acting, and those women aren't the only four people in Alpine Grove. You said you're inviting people to audition all week. Maybe tomorrow will be better."

"I hope so." Tess stood up, still holding his hand. "I need to preheat the oven for the pizza and run up to my bedroom to change. Don't go anywhere."

"I'm not leaving. Need any help in the bedroom?"

Tess grinned. "I wouldn't say no to some help."

Chapter 10

Something Good

The next day, Tess held more auditions after work. Much to her dismay, the performances were just as bad if not worse than the ones the day before. At least it was Friday. She was so done with this week. It was difficult not to be discouraged by the whole thing. If she couldn't find anyone to be in the show, they couldn't do the show. And that meant there would be no lovely money from ticket sales to save the Grove. Was she looking at yet another failure in a long string of failures? Maybe when it came to acting, Tess had whatever the opposite of the Midas touch was. Instead of turning to gold, everything she touched turned to coal.

All she wanted to do was go home and snuggle up with Luke for a while and tell him her woes. But when she got to the house, Luke and Barney weren't there. Luke hadn't mentioned going anywhere except to the road department to see what was wrong with Old Yeller, the mechanically challenged grader. Was it possible he'd actually returned to Gleasonville?

Tess walked to the pass through and pressed the button on the answering machine. There were messages from Bea and Margaret about fundraisers for the Grove, and then a female voice she didn't recognize said, "I'm sorry. I think I might have the wrong number. I'm trying to reach Luke

Bennett. Is he there? Okay, never mind. I must have the wrong number. Sorry."

The next message was a hang up, and Tess stared at the machine as if it could reveal deep dark long-distance secrets. Luke had mentioned that if he were going to stay in Alpine Grove during the week, he'd need to forward his calls to her number because he had a bunch of bids out on jobs. Maybe the woman was a secretary. But maybe not. So who was she?

In any case, Tess needed to remember to change the outgoing message. But what was it supposed to say? If you're calling about the Grove, leave a message for Tess. If you're calling about excavation, leave a message for Luke. And if you're some girlfriend of Luke's that Tess doesn't know about, please leave a message for both of us, so we can have a huge fight.

Tess sighed. In her head, Crazy Tess was running around in circles waving her arms like a maniac, having a field day with the girlfriend concept. Yeesh, she needed to get a grip. She erased the messages and went upstairs to change. The Fab Four were pleased to be released from their confinement and ventured out into the hallway, ignoring her presence. Tess called after them. "It's great to see you too."

The door slammed, and the Fab Four came scuttling back into the bedroom. Tess laughed. "Sure, now you love me. Look at all my brave attack cats, defending me from marauders." She dumped some food in the kitty bowls and closed the door behind her. "Bon appetit. I'll let you back out in a few minutes after I say hi to the marauder."

She went downstairs and walked into the kitchen. Luke was standing at the sink washing his hands. Tess came up behind him and looked at his face, which was smeared with dirt and oil. "What did you do? Crawl around *inside* the grader?"

"Practically. I swear, Joe is going to get himself fired. I tried to help, but he may have killed poor Old Yeller this time."

"It's not going to be like the movie is it? Because just thinking about it makes me tear up."

"It's a grader, Tess. A machine."

"I know, but you call it *Old Yeller.*" Tess spread her arms wide. "And everyone knows what happens to Old Yeller in the end. Rabies. Death. It's horrible."

Luke dried his hands on a towel and then placed them on her shoulders. He leaned over to give her a kiss. "I did what I could. I need to take a shower."

"You really do." Tess poked his arm as he walked by. "Need any help?"

"I wouldn't say no to some help."

Tess laughed as she chased after him up the stairs. Friday night was suddenly looking like it might be a lot more fun.

The next morning, after not waking up early at all, Luke said, "We've got to get out of bed. I'm supposed to be here to work on this house, you know."

Tess ran her fingers back through his hair from his temples. "Do you always *have* to do what you're supposed to do? I don't care when you finish the wall. As long as you finish it before the snow flies, it's fine."

Luke smiled. "It's April, and I'm pretty sure I can handle a seven or eight month deadline. I thought you just wanted to stay here temporarily until you found something else."

"I've decided that there are advantages to living in an actual house versus an apartment. No shared walls. A back yard. More space for my stuff. And oh yeah. One more. Sexy landlord."

He pulled her closer. "Yeah, you're by far the hottest tenant I've had here."

"As far as I know, my competition is Willy and Stetson, so I'll try not to let all this flattery go to my head."

Finally, hunger and the need for breakfast became an issue, so they went downstairs. At some point, early in the morning while Tess was asleep, Luke had let Barney out into the back yard. Now the dog was eager to come inside and have his breakfast too.

Tess spent a lot of time on the phone while Luke worked on the wall. Spring weather could be fickle, but for the moment the rain had held off, so he was motivated to get as much done as possible. Later, Tess went into the office to hold some more auditions since some people could only meet on the weekends. The good thing about having the same job for so long and working odd hours was being entrusted with a key to the building.

The last rounds of auditions had been demoralizing, but Tess tried to remain upbeat as she handed out the scripts. She greeted Annabelle and her husband, Jon, who had owned the H12 motel for as long as Tess could remember. Tess had a vague recollection that they might have performed in a play years ago, and she'd put them on her list of people to contact. Bea knew the couple fairly well and apparently had made some inroads in convincing them to try out. The other person was a lanky man with striking gray eyes who introduced himself as Zack Flanagan. Tess had never met him before, but he seemed pleasant enough.

They read through the script, and no one was overtly terrible. All of them were definitely better than the petrified wood people anyway.

Zack set down the sheet of paper on the table. "So are you gonna do *The Sound of Music*?"

"We haven't decided on a play yet. I wanted to find out how many people might be interested first. And solicit ideas for shows. A couple of people have suggested Shakespeare, but I think the lines might be too difficult."

"Yeah, half the time I don't know what they're saying. I like musicals better."

"I'm not sure we can find enough singers to do a musical," Tess said. "Not to mention eight kids. Alpine Grove is a small town."

"I have a little singing experience," Zack said. "Not like professional or anything. Although sometimes I got paid if people were feeling generous."

Tess raised her eyebrows. "You performed for money? Were you on stage? Or in a band?"

"It wasn't anything that organized. Mostly I got pocket change, but it was good at the time," Zack said. "You want me to sing something?"

Tess nodded eagerly, and he launched into an a cappella rendition of "Edelweiss" from *The Sound of Music*. Somehow the dramatic tenor didn't match Zack's appearance and her jaw dropped as his phenomenal voice reverberated through the large room. Tess had performed with some talented musical theater professionals, but Zack would give any of them a run for their money. She joined in and he smiled at her as they harmonized together.

When the song was done, everyone clapped, including Tess. She exclaimed, "That was amazing. I'll figure out some way for you to be in whatever show we do."

Zack grinned. "Cool. I've been taking a little break from work, and my girlfriend says I need to find more things to do to amuse myself. I kinda get bored easily."

Tess handed out information about the next meeting. "I hope you'll all come. *Please*. We need your help."

"Sure. I'm in," Zack said.

Annabelle and Jon agreed to help as much as they could too. Jon said, "Even if we aren't selected to perform, we can help with sets, lighting, and that type of thing."

After saying their goodbyes, Tess locked up and went home. After days of despair, hearing Zack sing had given her a small glimmer of hope that this show might actually happen.

~

Back at the house, Tess went outside and looked up at the scaffolding where Luke was hammering on something. She called up to him, "Where did these posts come from?"

He peered down at her. "I set them while you were at your office."

"Now that the French doors are gone, you could be doing anything back here and I'd never know."

"Yeah I miss having the light coming into the dining room through the glass doors." Luke clambered down the scaffolding and took off his work gloves. "For all you know, I could be building an ark out here, instead of a wall."

"True." She put her arms around his neck and gave him a kiss. "Want lunch?"

"Sure." He walked around the side of the house and held the gate open for Tess and Barney. "Were the auditions better today?"

She practically jumped up and down. "Yes! A thousand times yes. Have you ever met a guy named Zack Flanagan?"

"Nope."

"Me neither, but his singing voice is unbelievable."

Luke held the front door open, and Barney shot around Tess toward the kitchen. "I thought you weren't doing a musical."

"I don't know now. I mean, if I found a few more people like him, it would be fantastic. He was sort of vague about it, but I guess he hasn't performed professionally."

"What do you mean vague?" Luke raised his eyebrows. "Who is this guy?"

Tess grinned. "Oooh, are you jealous?"

"Should I be? You're the one who fell in love with your costar."

"Eww, let's not talk about him. For the record, Zack volunteered the fact that he has a girlfriend. Plus, truth be told, the guy struck me as sort of weird. He always sounds like he's half joking. It's hard to explain. Maybe it's his accent. I don't know. But when he sings, he's like a different person."

Luke laughed. "Unless he sings constantly, it sounds like you aren't gonna fall head over heels for the guy. How do you feel about a sandwich?"

"Sounds good to me." Tess looked down at the drooling dog at her feet. "I think Barney feels good about a sandwich too."

While they ate lunch, Tess shared more details about the audition, and Luke teased her a little more about her new "costar." Tess set down her sandwich. "That reminds me, you had a message."

"Did you write it down?"

"Well, no, but whoever she was didn't leave her name or number. I didn't realize you transferred your phone here."

"I said I was going to if I was here during the week."

"You did it for one day?"

"Well, I might be staying longer than that, if it's okay with you."

Tess leaped out of her chair and threw her arms around him and kissed his neck. "Of *course* it's okay. Very, very okay."

"I was working on that bid for the strip mall. Well, it was more like I was sitting at my desk procrastinating. Anyway, it gave me a lot of time to think. I decided you were right. Why am I doing a bid for a job I don't want?"

Tess laughed and clapped her hands. "Oh my God, you said I was *right.*"

He took her hand and pulled her into his lap. "You have the most wonderful laugh. When I hear it, all I want to do is make you happy, so I can hear you laugh again."

"I think that's the sweetest thing anyone has ever said to me."

He grinned. "I doubt that. People are always going on and on about how talented you are."

"It's not the same. How a person laughs is personal. It's part of who I am, not a performance. So thank you." She kissed him. "And I adore the fact that you listened. You're a great listener."

"We'll see how you feel about me when I ask you to pick up your clothes off the floor." He pointed at the sink. "Or wash the dishes once in a while. I think we need to work out a system for cleanup activities before an army of roaches move in."

"First, eww, to roaches. Gross. If you think the sink is turning into a roach habitat, that does not make me want to get anywhere near it. Second, the clothes on the floor were partly your fault as I recall. You seemed more interested in taking them off me than picking them up off the floor."

He laughed. "Yeah, I'll give you that. I might have been a little preoccupied with other things."

"I noticed." Tess rested her head on his shoulder. "You have a nice laugh too, you know."

"Thanks." He pushed her hair back from her face. "I'll help you with the dishes. And if we find roaches, I promise I'll squish them."

Tess batted her eyelashes, clutched her hands together, and pressed them to her heart. "My hero."

The next day before heading off to audition a few more people for her proposed show, Tess worked to clean up the bedroom by chucking her dirty clothes from the floor into the closet. She still had no idea what type of show to do. The Sunday group of people seemed capable of reading better than the petrified tree folks, but not as well as Annabelle and Jon. And when asked about singing, everyone looked utterly horrified at the idea.

When Tess returned to the house, Luke was up on the scaffolding in the back yard again. More wood had been added to the posts, so it was starting to look less like a bunch of sticks and more like a structure. He seemed to be methodically adding cross braces to create the beginnings of a wall. Luke certainly was efficient and had no fear of hard work. All that hard work made Tess want to go take a nap.

Later when the front door opened, Tess sat up and looked around, bewildered. Luke smiled at her. "I guess you were tired."

"An unanticipated side-effect of having you stay here is that I'm getting less sleep. I'm not complaining, mind you, but I don't know how you can spend all day lifting heavy lumber after last night."

"Years of practice. I don't even think about it." He sat next to her on the sofa. "How were today's tryouts?"

"Sort of eh. Nothing special. Nothing awful. I'm at a loss for what to do. Being in charge is hard. I have to make a decision before too long, and I know a lot of people won't like what I decide."

"Welcome to management. That's why I went back to being a sole proprietor. Supervising other people has some downsides."

"I like telling people what to do." Tess sighed. "But I can't stand it when people are angry at me."

"Eventually, you'll have to decide on a show."

"I'm hoping I'll have an epiphany. The skies will open up, and there will be a sign from the heavens."

"That might be rain."

She shoved his arm. "You know what I mean."

"I do. But it *is* supposed to rain, so I need to get back out there and clean up my stuff."

"Wait. I need to ask you something. I was talking to Bea, and we were hoping you'd take a look at the Grove again. She asked the owner if he'd be willing to give us the key so you can spend more time and thoroughly examine the place. You can spend all day there if you want. The owner is going to be in Alpine Grove tomorrow and said he'd stop by the gift shop. You can pick up the key from Bea."

"Tomorrow?"

"Yes. Will you? I told her I'd ask nicely." She gave him a kiss. "This is me asking you *really* nicely about a project with soul."

He glanced at the windows. "It's supposed to rain tomorrow anyway, so I guess I could. Maybe I'll be able to figure out where the leaks are that caused the damage. But I won't be able to work on painting here if I spend the day at the Grove."

"I can stand living with Willy art for a little while longer. Please say yes. I'll sing you some Shakespeare if it will help."

He chuckled. "Maybe later. I don't have anything else going on, so I can go over there. But right now, I need to clean up the yard before your epiphany happens and rusts my tools."

Tess reached for him before he could get up and pulled him back so she could give him a kiss. "Thank you. This means a lot to me."

"I know. That's why I'm doing it."

~

The promised rain arrived with a vengeance, making Monday more manic than usual for Tess. Heavy rain fell all day and everything was shrouded in a grey, misty, gloomy fog that smothered the sun. Tess ran through the relentless downpour across slippery sidewalks from her car to her various appointments throughout the day. It was like the weather gods were making up for all the pretty spring weather of the last couple of weeks. Even the flowers looked droopy and depressed by the harsh, drenching rain.

By the time Tess returned to the office that afternoon, she was soaked, achy, and cranky. She called the person who was supposed to audition after work, asked to reschedule, and drove home.

At the traffic light, there was a pause in the rain and a ray of sunlight beamed through the ominous clouds. Gazing through her windshield at the sky, she smiled. The view was like her imagined epiphany. Maybe it was a sign that everything would be okay with the show after all. But by the time she got out of her car ten minutes later, an icy wind whipped by and the lone ray of sunlight had disappeared. She hustled up the sidewalk to the house and scuttled inside.

Barney ran up to her, panting heavily. She bent down to stroke his head. “Did you go for a run with your dad during the ten minutes it wasn’t raining?”

Luke walked into the living room from the kitchen. “No, he’s worried about the weather.”

“Well, I don’t blame him. The weather stinks. When I got out of my car, I swear the temperature had dropped twenty degrees.”

"A cold front must be moving in. That's not good news for Barney."

"How come?"

"Thunderstorms."

As if to emphasize the point, a massive booming noise roiled around them, followed by a flash of lightning. Barney flattened himself to the floor and tried to wedge himself under the sofa.

Tess sat down and reached down to touch his back. "You're way too big to fit under there, Barney."

"He hates storms. It's worse than the nail gun."

Tess looked up at Luke. "The poor thing is shaking. He's terrified."

"I know. The vet said that it isn't just the noise. Part of it is that dogs sense stuff we don't like the change in barometric pressure and smell of ozone from lightning strikes."

"What can we do?"

"The vet said we shouldn't make a big deal about it and keep him somewhere safe where he can't hurt himself. At my apartment, he usually hides in my bathroom. One thing I read said it might be because there's less static in there."

Tess said in a happy voice, "C'mon Barney, let's go upstairs and visit the tile."

Barney raised his head but didn't move. Luke bent down and scooped up the large dog, cradling the shepherd mix in his arms. "Let's go, buddy. It'll be over soon and there's a nice big bathtub upstairs."

Tess followed him. "Now I feel bad that he's been spending so much time downstairs because of the cats. He doesn't know there's a bathroom up there."

"Well, he's about to find out. He'll be fine once the storm is over." Luke placed Barney in the tub, and the dog uttered a long sigh. "See, I told you it's better."

A huge crashing boom reverberated through the house and the lights went out. Tess groaned and slid down onto the tile next to the bathtub. "Just when I thought my day couldn't get any worse. At least the Fab Four don't care about storms. They just roll over and snooze."

"The power will probably come back on in a few minutes. And even if it doesn't, I've got lots of candles." Luke sat next to her and reached over the side of the tub to put his hand on Barney's back. "He's not shaking as bad. The metal plumbing might be acting as a ground."

Tess leaned against Luke. "When I was little, I used to like storms, but now they remind me of scary scenes in plays. I expect something awful to happen. The terrible storm as a foreshadowing of unfortunate events happens a lot in theater."

Luke moved so he could look at her. "Telling you this during a storm might not be a great idea, but you're not going to like what I found at the Grove. The roof is pretty much shot. All this rain we're getting isn't going to help."

Tess sat up straight. The tile was uncomfortable. "What do you mean *shot*?"

"It's not keeping moisture out. The rain was dripping inside the building."

"What can we do?"

"First off, I'd say get a really big tarp. Have you raised any money yet?"

"Margaret is keeping track, and the donations are being listed in the paper every day. It's only been a week and we don't even own the theater."

"You might want to protect your future investment by covering it with a tarp."

"Do you think the owner would mind? But why *would* he mind? It's his roof leaking. We'd just be helping out." Tess stood up and looked down at Luke. "Do you have a tarp? We need to go over there right now."

"To cover a roof like that you'd need one of those huge silver tarps like you see on stacks of hay bales." He reached for her hand. "We can't do anything right now."

She shook her hand away. "How can you be so calm? We have to *do* something."

"That theater has been rained and snowed on since 1927. One more night isn't going to make a difference."

Tess exhaled deeply and settled back to the floor. "All right. Fine. I'll just sit here. I hate to ask, but how much does a roof cost?"

"For that place, I'm guessing a minimum of ten or twenty grand. I'm hoping the water hasn't damaged the ceiling too bad. Those decorative beams are made of wood that would be pretty tough to replace."

The phone rang in the bedroom, and Tess got up to answer it. As she predicted, the Fab Four were unaffected by all the flashing lights and noise outside. Cats didn't buy into foreshadowing either, so they all looked relaxed, sleeping their way through the nasty weather. John jumped up on the bed to say hi when Tess sat next to the nightstand and picked up the receiver.

Tess stroked his fur and realized she recognized the voice. It was the person on the machine who was again asking for Luke. John rolled over and Tess rubbed his tummy. She said, "Yes, Luke is here. Just a minute. I'll go get him."

She went back to the bathroom and sat with Barney while Luke went to talk to the mystery woman. He was gone for a while, which gave Crazy Tess lots of time to make up some elaborate stories about the past, present, and future of the torrid affair Luke was having with the woman on the phone.

When Luke returned, he sat down next to her. "Barney seems to have settled down. I think the storm is letting up."

"So who was on the phone? She sounded like the woman who called before."

"It was Stephanie."

Tess widened her eyes and waved her hands in a circular motion to indicate that she'd like it if he'd elaborate. "And who is Stephanie?"

"Old girlfriend."

"I *knew* it!"

"Knew what?"

"She sounded like a girlfriend. How old is she?"

"I don't think Steph would appreciate me sharing her age."

"You know what I mean. How ex is she? Is she an ex? She is an *ex*, isn't she? I mean, you wouldn't be here if she weren't an ex, right?"

"Calm down, Tess. You're stressing out Barney."

Tess peered over the side of the bathtub. Barney was panting again and looking like maybe he should be worried about the humans now. "Sorry, Barney. This isn't about you."

"Steph and I lived together a while ago. She called to see if I had still had something she was looking for."

"What?"

"A coffee table. We bought it together." Luke shrugged. "When we split up, she said I could have it. I didn't have a place to put it, so I stored it in the warehouse with my equipment. But technically I do have it."

"And she called because she wants it back?"

"Yeah, she and her cat are moving to a bigger place. She wants me to bring it over there."

"Wait. Is this the Maine Coon cat that Barney knows?"

"Yeah, he's huge, and his name is Charles. Like Prince Charles, I guess."

The bathroom light suddenly came on and Tess blinked as her eyes adjusted. "Let there be light. I feel illuminated in more than one way."

"You're not annoyed that Stephanie called, are you?"

"No," Tess said in a squeaky voice.

"Then what?"

"She's why you didn't want to stay here, isn't it?" Tess frowned. "Unless it was me. Was it me?"

"It wasn't you. I like being with you. Well, when you're not upsetting my dog, that is. By the way, the bedroom is ripe. When was the last time you did something about the litter box?" He reached over and patted Barney's head. "Storm's over, Barn. You survived."

"Don't change the subject. How come you broke up?" Tess asked.

"What difference does it make? Everyone has a history. I know you do with the scummy director guy."

"But I didn't live with him. Or anyone else. I've never been in that type of serious relationship. Have you been married too?"

"Nope. I suppose the thing with Stephanie was serious. Until it wasn't. Look, I don't want to talk about this and sitting on this tile is hurting my butt." Luke stood up. "C'mon, Barn, the lights are on and it's time for dinner."

Barney stood up, shook himself, and leaped out of the tub. He galloped down the stairs with a great clattering of claws. Luke held out his hand to Tess. "Let's have some dinner, okay?"

Tess took his hand and let him pull her up, but part of her was worried that Luke might remember why he'd been with the mysterious Stephanie. Like when he saw her to hand off furniture. Maybe she wanted him back. Maybe he wanted her back.

This wouldn't be the first time a man had found another woman—or every woman in the greater Hollywood vicinity—more appealing than she was.

Living in this house right now was a convenient arrangement for both her and Luke. But she should have known better than to think it might be something more.

~

After dinner, Tess was in the living room watching TV with Luke when the phone rang. She got up and received the bad news from Leigh Miles's agent that the celebrity wasn't available to do a show in Alpine Grove.

Tess hung up the phone and stomped back to the sofa.

Luke muted the TV and gave her an appraising glance. "I'm guessing from the look on your face that you didn't just win the lottery."

"Far from it. Apparently even D-list cult celebrities are far too busy to act in my as-yet-to-be-determined show. When I talked to Leigh, she said it sounded like fun and she'd check her schedule. But she didn't even have the guts to call me back herself. She made her agent do it."

"Who was this person again?"

"Leigh Miles. She was in *The Prism Protectors*. It was a science fiction TV show, and she played Harriet Plumb."

Luke shook his head. "This was on TV? I don't remember it."

"Oh, come on. Back in the eighties, half the guys in high school had a poster of Leigh on their bedroom wall because her boobs looked like they were going to fall out of her jumpsuit. The show was incredibly stupid, but people watched it anyway." Tess stood up, fluffed up her hair with her hands, and affected an English accent. "T minus 45 and counting. We need more fuel. Oh *bugger*! They're getting a bit antsy at Mission Control that we won't have enough fuel to make it to Pluto. But Biff Meadows has to get there with the laser torch. The future of the entire galaxy is at stake."

Luke rolled over on the sofa laughing. "Oh jeez. That's classic. I remember it now. I had no idea you could do impressions."

In her normal voice, Tess said, "It's just acting. Imitating Leigh is easy because it's so over the top and her accent was *so* bad. She's from Brooklyn, and she couldn't quite cover up the nasal New York element." Tess switched back to the lame quasi-British accent. "I'm chuffed! Biff has defeated the ogre, and the tribe of furry aliens has returned to their home world. Order has been restored to the galaxy. Let's go to the pub and have a pint."

Luke laughed again and then looked thoughtful. "I've never met anyone who can improvise like you can. After the hot Shakespeare and the impressions, I'm curious if any of the roles you played were comedies. You're great at it."

"Nothing I did was a comedy per se. Some of the musicals I did were funny. I mean *Annie Get Your Gun* has some funny moments. But I never tried out for sit-coms or anything like that. Most of the time, I couldn't even get parts in commercials or as an extra." Tess waved her arms. "Don't remind me. After the last trip, I've been trying not to think about acting or Hollywood. The last time I let Crazy Tess out from under her rock, I blew the audition and lost my agent."

"Crazy Tess? Is this someone I should know?"

Tess shook her head. "I can't believe I'm telling you about this. Crazy Tess is my name for the weird part of my personality I try not to show to the world. When Crazy Tess comes out to play, it's like my mouth starts speaking before my brain catches up. I think of her as separate from me because I never know when Crazy Tess is going to leap out and say something dumb. Crazy Tess is part of the reason I have so much trouble getting acting roles."

"I didn't mean to bring up the bad auditions, but maybe you're being too hard on Crazy Tess. Maybe she's just your funny side trying to come out."

"Yeah, right."

I'm serious. You're really good. Do another impression."

"Well, while we're on the topic of my failures, here's my impression of sticks of petrified wood reading a scene from

The Sound of Music." Tess recited the page that she'd now heard about twenty-five times.

Luke laughed. "I'm not sure how you managed to make petrified wood funny, but you did. You could do comedy skits like they had on the *Carol Burnett Show*. Remember that?"

Tess sat down next to him. "That show has been off the air for years. Too bad vaudeville is dead too."

Luke chuckled. "Well, the Grove was originally a vaudeville house. You're just seventy years too late, that's all."

Tess looked at him and her eyes widened. "That's brilliant."

"What?"

"I wrote off the idea of a talent show because, as I now know all too well, almost no one in Alpine Grove has any talent. But what if it were like vaudeville or burlesque, where the performers aren't supposed to be good. They're supposed to be *funny.*" Tess stretched her arms wide. "If people were willing to not take themselves too seriously, the show could be hysterical."

"What do you mean?"

"Imagine Annabelle and Jon doing a skit that features some of the, um, interesting things they've seen at the H12 motel."

Luke grinned. "I sense small-town scandals. Or you could do fake local news. Like they do on *Saturday Night Live.*"

"Exactly! I could do a bawdy song with sort of suggestive lyrics. Or suggestive movements." Tess returned his smile. "And that guy Zack would probably do pretty much anything. Talk about not taking himself seriously."

"Do you think the rest of the group would be up for this?" Luke asked.

"I don't know, but I'll bring it up at the meeting tomorrow night. Bea said I have to make a decision on the show, so they can start promoting it."

"The worst thing they can say is no, and then you're back to selecting a play."

"Deadlines help inspire my creativity. It's the only way I've ever managed to memorize lines. Fear is a big motivator." Tess grinned. "I bet I can convince them that this could make a boatload of money. Think about how fast gossip travels in this town. You hear that there's gonna be a skit with your neighbor dressed in drag and you've gotta see it."

Luke patted her hand. "I think you're on to something here. In Alpine Grove, word of mouth marketing is everything."

Tess got up. "I need to figure out an appropriate song to help convince them."

"Can I watch you rehearse? Your use of the term *suggestive* intrigues me."

"I thought it might. I have some intriguing ideas for costumes you might appreciate as well."

"Okay. This could be fun."

Chapter 11

A Long Way to Go

The next day at the meeting, Tess was thrilled to hear that the brick fundraiser was off to a great start. Money was already flowing into the bank account of the newly formed nonprofit. Even though it would take months to get tax-exempt status from the IRS, it didn't seem to be slowing down donations. Luke had opted to avoid the meeting but had already reported his findings to Bea who shared them with the group. Tess also had to bring up the unfortunate immediate expense of a tarp, but everyone seemed to agree that even if they didn't own the building yet, it would be a good idea to keep any more rain out of the Grove.

Bea introduced Kat, the owner of the dog boarding kennel. She'd been tasked with writing up the lists of donations and emailing them to the paper. Kat held up a sheet of paper. "If you've got ideas for topics I can talk about in my space, please write them down. Listing the donors is great, but sometimes I have more room, so I'm looking for memories you have of the Grove, stories, *anything*."

Tess said, "I can tell you a bunch of stories. Give me a call."

Kat assured her she would and sat down next to Tracy Sullivan. Tess was amused to see Bea's daughter there. Apparently, Bea finally wore her down and convinced her to help.

After all the committees had reported on their activities, Bea turned to Tess. “Have you decided on what you’re going to perform for the fundraising show?”

Tess said, “I’ve done a lot of auditions, and we have a wide range of talent. I’ve been wrestling with how best to take advantage of all the enthusiasm. After a lot of thought, I’m not sure doing a play is the best option. Rather than focusing on just one thing like a drama or a musical, I think we should do more of a revue.”

Margaret furrowed her brow. “What do you mean? Is that another type of play?”

“I mean a revue like a variety show. I was talking with someone who pointed out that the Grove was originally designed to be a vaudeville house. What if we play that up?”

Bea smiled. “Like the Ziegfeld Follies, you mean?”

“Variety shows and vaudeville were funny with skits and funny songs. There was dancing and elaborate costumes with feathers.” Tess grinned. “We could have a good time with it.”

Jan, the librarian piped up, “Vaudeville has roots in traveling shows and burlesque acts. At the time, it was huge and people loved it.”

“What I’m thinking is that we can push the local angle too. Maybe a skit with local news. Songs with funny lyrics about life in Alpine Grove. The funnier, the better. We can make it kind of risqué and bawdy with sex, drugs, and rock and roll. Really let it all hang out. The idea is to get people talking and laughing. The more chatter we can get going, the more people will show up.”

Tracy said, “Is Maria here? Kat’s bachelorette party was bawdy. It even had phallic party favors. I can’t think of the right word to describe it, but people definitely talked about it. And everyone who was there laughed a lot."

A woman with large, curly brunette hair waved her hand. "Excuse me, but the word you're looking for here is *fabulous*."

Tracy grinned and returned the wave. "Hey, Maria, I think you and Tess need to chat, since she wasn't exposed, so to speak, to the party."

"Exposure was a key element of that event because, as you know, I am the party planner extraordinaire."

Kat said, "I agree that it was memorable. My hangover lasted well beyond the party."

Maria pointed at Tess. "You. Me. Later. We need to talk. It's clear that you need my help."

Judith, the Shakespearean extra from an early audition, stood up and glared at Tess. "What are you trying to turn this fundraiser into? Is it going to be some type of x-rated strip tease show?"

"No, that's not what I mean," Tess said. "Remember old TV shows like *Sonny and Cher* or *Carol Burnett*? Our show could be like that with singing, dancing, and comedy skits, but more edgy. We could gear it toward an adult audience, but stay within the boundaries of what's legal. I have a little song that I prepared to give you an idea of what I've been thinking."

Maria shouted, "Sing it, girl!"

Tess said, "Normally, shows like this have an MC, so I invented a character named Duchess Fifi diVine, who can open the show with a little warning and a song."

Tess stood up and pretended to swoop a feather boa over her shoulder. In her best burlesque purr, she drawled, "All right, everyone, I want you to know that this show may include some bad words. And if you can't handle the naming of body parts that one-hundred percent of you have or certain kinds of colorful language, then you might want to take notice of the exit doors at the back of the theater and use them. Yes, I'm taking to you over there in the lime green cardigan. If you have delicate sensibilities, you'd better get out now because things are about to get a whole lot worse, honey."

Tess launched into a rendition of "Let's Get Physical" by Olivia Newton-John, which most people remembered in connection with aerobics classes in the eighties. The song had received tons of radio airplay back then and wasn't filled with bad language, but the motions Tess had thought up to accompany the lyrics were somewhat obscene according to Luke who had laughed his way through her performance when she'd given him a private viewing the night before.

When Tess was done, Maria jumped up and down and clapped. "That's outstanding. I'm never going to look at Olivia the same way again. If this doesn't get people talking, they're dead and buried. This is going to be *fantastic*. Little ole Alpine Grove might never recover."

Judith had moved to the back of the room, apparently too horrified to be within a hundred feet of Tess. She said in a shrill voice, "I cannot be a part of something like this… this…*smut*. If you perform this show, I will stage a boycott."

Zack stood up and said, "Hey, I just had an idea for a song I could sing. Have you ever seen *The Rocky Horror Picture Show*? I'd need the right costume, but remember the song that Dr. Frank-N-Furter sings when the dopey couple arrives at the scary castle? It's kinda catchy."

Tess laughed and gave him a sweeping two-handed gesture for him to proceed. Zack launched into an especially indecent version of "Sweet Transvestite," which did Tim Curry proud.

As the last word "Transylvania…" echoed through the gift store, the bells on the door of the gift store jangled merrily. It appeared that Judith had seen and heard quite enough.

Everyone applauded and Zack took a bow. "This could be a blast. I'm filled with antici...pation."

Tess stood up and waved her hands. "I have a few thoughts for skits and acts we can do, but we need more. Anyone who has tried out or wants to try out should attend a meeting tomorrow night after work, so we can brainstorm ideas."

"What are we going to call the show?" Bea asked. "It needs a name so we can start promoting it."

Tess said, "Someone suggested calling it the Grove Groove, and I kind of like it."

Everyone applauded again and Maria hooted, "Yeah, baby. We're gonna get our Groove on."

~

Kat stood in the front of the gift store, gazing out the plate glass window while Maria talked to Tess about her act. Kat had parked in the parking lot at Maria's apartment building. It was close to everything in Alpine Grove, and they had walked to the meeting.

To Kat, the entire idea of standing up in front of people and performing was utterly horrifying. Although Maria had somehow convinced Kat to sing karaoke at her bachelorette party, no amount of alcohol could convince Kat to participate in this show.

Maria patted her on the shoulder. "Okay, girlfriend, I have an approved act, and Tess thinks it will rock the house. Let's hit the sidewalk. I gotta see your new wheels."

"You're going to sing in the show?" Kat gave Maria a worried glance. Although her friend loved to sing, she couldn't carry a tune. "Are you sure that's a good idea?"

"Tess thinks it's better if I lip sync. I confess, I can't sing as well as she does. Or that guy Zack. Who woulda guessed that skinny weirdo dude would have such a set of pipes."

"Not me." Kat shrugged. "I only met him a couple times when he came out with Sara to board her dog, Holly."

"I don't understand how those two work as a couple. They seem incompatible, but it's not like they had a choice. They're just two more people that got besotted with each other because of your love connections. You have a gift. And I don't understand why as your best friend, I'm not getting the benefits of that gift."

"I don't have a *gift*. I have a boarding kennel." Kat grinned. "I could always lend you a dog."

Maria shook her head so vigorously her curly hair flapped into her face. "I've met your dogs and they're rude. Cats are more refined."

"Your loss."

"It's a love conspiracy. I knew that buying your old hunk of crap car would kill my image. My love life went into the toilet after I sold Greta. I looked cute in a sexy, red Miata. There's no hope of ever looking even a little sexy driving your old beat-up Toyota."

"But you were able to drive it in the snow."

"Winter was long and cold. Remind me why I moved to this godforsaken town? My lady parts are gonna atrophy at this rate."

"You got a job. And you missed me."

"I suppose. My unfortunate period of extreme destitution did require taking drastic action." Maria looked up at her apartment building. "Things were looking dire back then. I do like having a roof over my head, even when it's covered with snow."

Kat pointed at a green Toyota RAV4. "That's it."

"You got another Toyota? I think you're in a rut." Maria put her hands on her hips. "At least it's not as ugly as the one you sold me. Not to mention newer. Isn't this the same car your dog walker has?"

"It's the same model. I liked Mia's and she was able to drive it in the winter, so I checked it out and bought it. Well, technically Joel and I bought it together."

Maria peered in the window. "It's *new*. I thought you said the engineer was too cheap to let you buy something that was manufactured within this decade."

"I think he'd prefer the term frugal."

"Gimme a break, girlfriend. This is *me* you're talking to. You were pissed off. You called him a penny-pinching tightwad and then said he was so tight, he squeaks." Maria gestured toward the door. "So lemme see the inside of this baby."

Kat unlocked the car and opened the door. "I was just venting. We talked about it and compromised. The car is used, but only a year old, so it's got a great warranty."

"Hey, there's no cup holder in this thing. What kind of crap car has no cup holder?"

"There's a spot in the center console."

Maria reached to poke at the preset buttons on the radio. "The stereo sucks too. A cassette player? You've gotta be kidding."

"I'll listen to the radio. On the dirt roads around here, CDs would just skip. It's all-wheel drive and the back seats fold down so I can take dogs to the vet."

Maria put both hands on the steering wheel and made some revving noises. "Your priorities are all kinds of screwed up, but it's a decent car. Where'd you get it?"

"At a dealer in Gleasonville. I found the car I wanted, but it took two trips down there." Kat got in the passenger side. "It turns out Joel is an annoying negotiator. Car salesmen don't know what to do with him."

Maria paused and turned to Kat. "Waitaminute. You never say he's annoying. *I* say he's annoying. I mean, I can't understand how you put up with that geek factor. You're not getting divorced already, are you? You can't do that when you just bought this fine automobile."

"We're staying married. Do you want to drive it?" Kat handed Maria the keys.

"You're sure you're not getting divorced?"

"Very. I meant the dealers found Joel's negotiating tactics annoying. We went to every dealer in Gleasonville and he brought this fancy engineering calculator with him. So he's sitting there calculating payments and interest rates. I thought a couple of those poor sales guys might lose it with all the math."

"He did the whole Mr. Spock thing, didn't he?" Maria turned the key so she could turn on the radio.

"Totally. No emotion at all. Just numbers." Kat tapped the dashboard. "Then I saw this one and I really, really wanted it. Because it was used, it was cheaper. I even like the color."

"So you bought it. Aww. That's like automotive love at first sight." Maria put the car in gear and backed out of the parking spot.

"Actually, we left the dealership."

"What? Did you miss out on the whole going and talking to the sales manager thing? I like when they do that."

"The sales guy was named Tony, and he was wearing these tight leather pants, so he looked like Sandy at the end of *Grease*."

"You mean when she got all slutty?"

"Yes, except with smaller hair. He was practically jumping up and down when we got into Joel's truck to leave. The sales manager came outside and was trying to calm him down when we left."

"So you're saying the slutty guy didn't sell you this car?"

"No, he did. Eventually."

"Where did you go?"

"Home. Joel had researched the Blue Book value of the car, so he knew it was overpriced. It was all typed up in a spreadsheet. When they wouldn't agree to a fair price, we bailed."

"Spreadsheets give me the shakes." Maria shifted gears.

"I know. Me too. But when we got home, there was a message on the answering machine offering a lower price."

"Did you buy it then?"

"I was ready to run down there, but Joel called them back and made a counter-offer."

"And?"

"They refused, claiming they were losing money."

"Well, since I'm driving this thing around, I know you bought it." Maria turned on the radio, jumped in her seat when it blasted out Van Halen, and turned it down. "Guess the stereo works. So what happened?"

"They called back the next day and agreed to Joel's price, so we went and picked it up."

"Remind me not to ever play poker with the engineer." Maria cruised back into the lot and slipped the car back into its parking space. "Now that you've got decent wheels, we should take a road trip."

"Where?"

"*Anywhere*. The world is ours to roam freely. We can hit the road anytime."

"Except you have a job. And so do I."

"Way to be a buzz kill, girlfriend. You know how being responsible brings me down." Maria handed the keys to Kat. "Want some dinner? I've got fried baloney sandwiches on Wonder Bread on deck. With some delectable Tastykakes for dessert."

"No Twinkies?"

"I'm branching out."

~

The next day after work, Tess had a meeting with the performers, which went remarkably well. People brainstormed ideas and then signed up to be in skits like the news show, goofy lip-synced dance numbers, and other borderline absurd acts. Tess and Zack were both going to sing accompanied by troupes of back up singers and dancers. Against all odds, it was starting to look like a great line up. The fact that there was a lot of laughing during the rehearsals was a good sign. If the audience had as much fun as the performers did, they'd have one heck of a fundraiser.

One issue that remained was that there was no large space where they could do final rehearsals. Bea, Margaret, and Tess decided they couldn't put off another meeting with the owner about renting the Grove for a few days so they could clean it up, do a dress rehearsal, and, of course, hold the show itself.

Because of the absence of theater space, Tess set up individual rehearsals with the people involved in each of the acts after work at her office. There wasn't much room, but they managed to work around the desks and printing paraphernalia. Every evening for the foreseeable future, Tess would be helping someone with a performance. Her day planner, which had always been crowded with appointments, was turning into *War and Peace*. In many cases, helping people rehearse was less about acting and more about counseling the performers. For some people, the idea of being on stage was terrifying, so Tess spent quite a bit of time trying to convince them that standing in front of an audience wasn't the worst thing invented since death.

When she wasn't helping others, Tess also spent time working on her own act at home. She knew she would sing, but she hadn't quite found the right song yet. In addition to her song, Tess also needed to come up with a bunch of funny transitional material to introduce each act during the show. She spent a lot of time practicing her lines, and Luke commented that she was reverting into the mumbler he remembered from high school.

The rest of the week passed in a blur of work and rehearsals. By the time she got home, Tess was exhausted. At night, she ate dinner and passed out next to Luke on the sofa while watching TV.

Bea set up the big meeting with the owner of the Grove for the following Monday to try to negotiate the rental of the theater for the show. If he said no, they were going to have to do the show outside in a park or a field somewhere. That option was a potential disaster given the unpredictable nature of late spring weather. It could be seventy degrees and sunny or forty degrees with torrential rain. Tess figured Murphy's Law assured that torrential rain was the most likely scenario. Aaron Hughes had to say yes. He just *had* to.

On Saturday, when Tess returned from yet another rehearsal, Luke was in the front yard placing his tools into the bed of his truck. When Barney stood up in the passenger seat and wagged at her, Tess stopped short. It looked like Luke was packing to leave. She walked over to his truck and pointed at the big red metal toolbox in the bed. "What are you doing?"

"Loading up stuff."

She readjusted her bag on her shoulder. This was unexpected. "Don't you need tools to work on the house?"

"Friday, I got a message that one of my bids was accepted. When I called them back, I found out I've got a job in Gleasonville that starts Monday. I just got back from returning the scaffolding, so now I'm loading up my stuff."

"When did you take down the scaffolding?" Tess hadn't been in the back yard in the last few days, so she hadn't noticed.

"I took it apart the other day while you were at work. The new structure is dried in, so I can leave it for a while. The next step will be taking apart the existing wall, rehanging the French doors, putting on siding and repainting everything inside and outside. But there's no rush. I need to go home, check out my equipment, and get organized, so I'm ready to get to work on Monday."

"So you said you're leaving the wall project for a while. How long is *a while* exactly?"

"Depends. I've got a job, so I need to get home."

"When were you going to tell me?" Tess threw up her arms in exasperation. "Or were you just going to drive away while I wasn't looking?"

"I'm telling you now. I've gotta work, and I need to get back to my own space anyway."

"This is your space."

"Legally, yes, but the smell of dirty cat box is getting to me."

"I cleaned it!"

"When?"

Tess thought back. "Um, well, recently, I think. If it gets too bad, the Fab Four get cranky, so it can't have been *that* long."

"Maybe they're fine, but it's been too long for me. I'm tired of cleaning up after you or pointing out messes that you don't notice. I draw the line at dealing with the kitty litter. I mean I like the kitty Beatles, but they're *your* cats."

"I never asked you to clean up. And you know I've been busy."

"I do know. You've got a lot of stuff to do before the show. And I've got this job." He gestured toward the truck. "I've got a little more stuff to load up, then Barney and I are hitting it. I want to get back to my place before dark."

Tess followed him to the house and inside. "So can we talk about this for a minute?"

"This what?"

"Us. Our relationship or whatever you want to call it. Does the fact you're leaving mean you're dumping me? Because that's what it feels like." Tess threw her bag onto the sofa with more force than necessary. "I mean it's not like that's uncharted territory, but I can't tell what you're thinking at *all*. If you're dumping me, I'd like to know."

"This whatever with us is fine."

"*Fine*? That's all you can say when you made the decision to leave without even talking to me?"

"The job just came through yesterday. You came home and fell asleep before I got around to saying anything. It might be good for us to both have some time to think about what we want anyway."

"I *am* thinking. When I'm talking, I'm thinking."

Luke raised his eyebrows. "How does Crazy Tess fit into that?"

"Sometimes I need to talk to figure out what I'm thinking. And Crazy Tess might get there first sometimes, I guess. Or says something I don't think, so I know it's wrong. You just never know with her." Tess waved her arms wildly in a frantic erasing motion. "It's complicated. I just can't believe you're suddenly packing up your truck without any warning."

Luke sat on the sofa and looked up at her. "If you'd had warning, what would you have said?"

Tess sat next to him and clasped her hands between her knees. "That I like having you here, and I thought you liked being here."

"There are some definite upsides, but like I said, being the live-in maid is getting old."

"The *maid*? What's that about? So now you go and decide that fun sex doesn't make up for the fact I'm a slob anymore? Who are you? Felix Unger?" Tess stopped at the horrified expression on his face. "I'm sorry. That was a terrible thing to say. I didn't mean it."

Luke stood up. "I'm not enjoying this thinking by talking thing, so I'm gonna grab the rest of my stuff from the bedroom. I'll see you around."

"Wait! Where do we stand?" Tess wrapped her arms around her midsection. Crazy Tess had screwed up bad this time.

"I don't know. Like I said, it might be good to spend some time away from each other." Luke turned and jogged up the stairs.

Tess sank down onto the sofa again. What *did* she want? Hurting his feelings definitely was not what she'd intended. But if he was such a neat freak that he couldn't handle living with her, then okay, maybe it was better that they just give up now before they got any more attached.

Luke came back downstairs with a duffel bag. He stopped, crouched down in front of her, and wiped a tear off her cheek with his fingertip. "Hey, don't look so sad."

"Is this about your girlfriend with the coffee table? You decided to go back to her, didn't you?"

"She's not my girlfriend." He leaned forward to give her a kiss. "You are, if you want to be."

Tess smiled weakly. "I'm going to miss you."

"I'll miss you too. Give me a call if you get bored."

~

Tess went through Sunday in a daze. She said all the right things at the rehearsal, but it was like part of her brain was running the terrible things she'd said to Luke on a loop. Maybe this was a new way for Crazy Tess to make her miserable and ruin her life.

Now that Barney was out of the house, the Fab Four had free run of the place twenty-four hours a day although they didn't necessarily take advantage of it. Sleeping away the afternoon on the bed still seemed to hold a lot of appeal, and when Tess returned home from the rehearsal, all four cats were crashed out in their favorite spots. Tess also decided that from now on, she'd make a point of keeping the kitty litter clean. Luke hadn't been wrong. It had gotten a little gross in there. Oops.

Sunday evening was lonely and depressing, but Tess resisted calling Luke. He was the one who needed time to think, so he could call her. It wasn't like she was suddenly going to become Ms. Neatnik all of a sudden, making the bed with perfect hospital corners and folding towels just so. Suddenly getting all blissful and joyous about folding laundry would never happen. Instead, she'd wander around mumbling her lines like she always had. Leopards didn't change their spots. Unfortunately, all the righteous indignation about accepting her true nature and being in the right didn't make her any less sad.

Monday, she had to haul down to Gleasonville to meet with Aaron Hughes about the theater with Bea and Margaret.

Although she had Luke's phone number, she had no idea where he lived, which was annoying. She would have loved the chance to snoop around his apartment building to see what it was like.

Just as they had before, she met Bea and Margaret in front of the big, swanky office building that housed the offices of Pollard, Wickham, and Hughes, Inc. Tess mentally coached herself to adopt her Successful Executive persona again. It worked last time, so she figured she should run with it again.

The secretary led them to an office where Aaron Hughes sat behind his massive shiny wooden desk with a phone receiver pressed to his ear. He gave them a small smile in greeting and gestured for them to sit down.

He ended his call and said, "Hello, ladies. It's nice to see you again."

Bea said, "I know you're busy, and as you know we've been fundraising like crazy to make the down payment. It's looking good, but our next fundraiser is a show. We're here to ask if we can rent the theater for a few days."

"We'd like a week, so we can clean it up and do a dress rehearsal. And then the show itself," Margaret added.

"I'm not sure I can allow that," Aaron said with a frown.

"Why not?" Tess said.

"There are liability concerns." Aaron folded his hands on the desktop and steepled his index fingers. "As you know, the place is in terrible condition. People shouldn't be in there."

"We believe that we can do some of the urgent repairs and get event liability insurance," Bea said. "One of our board members is an insurance agent."

Tess didn't volunteer the fact that the board member also was Bea's husband. Aaron didn't need to know that, just like

Luke didn't need to know that she was about to volunteer him to help with the urgent repairs. Even if he refused, they'd find someone. Probably. She flashed a serene I'm-being-reasonable smile. "We have some people on deck to come in to clean and do some quick repairs so it's safe."

"It's only a week." Bea slid a piece of paper across the desk. "Here's the rental agreement. I can write you a check right now."

Aaron scanned through the document. "I'll give you two days."

"Two days? Are you kidding?" Tess blurted out.

"The more time, the more risk. You said you need a clean-up day, and then the rehearsal and the show." He set down the paper. "Two days is all I can do."

Bea took the paper, pulled a pen out of a holder and started writing. "I'm just adjusting the amounts." She slid it back across the desk with the pen. "We've already signed it. Here you go."

Aaron looked down at the paper as if it had a communicable disease. Finally he picked up the pen and signed it. "If something happens, my lawyers will tear this to shreds, you know."

Tess said with far more confidence than she felt, "Nothing will happen. This show is going to be amazing. You'll have your down payment ahead of schedule."

Bea, Margaret, and Tess were quiet when they left the building. Bea said to Tess, "Do you think the show will work?"

"I do. I'm a little more worried about the theater. Can we come up with approximately two thousand people to clean it up and make it safe for use in one day?"

"I guess we'll find out," Margaret said.

For most of the drive home, Tess quietly freaked out about how she'd managed to screw up the show and what she had with Luke in a matter of days. How could Bea have so calmly signed the rental agreement? And Tess had put her name on it too. Was she totally insane? How were they supposed to clean up a place that had been boarded up for years in only twenty-four hours?

By the time she got back to Alpine Grove, Tess was beside herself. She hadn't scheduled any rehearsals that evening because of the trip to Gleasonville, but as soon as she got back to her office, she canceled a sales appointment that afternoon. She just couldn't face it.

All she wanted to do was go home and get into her jammies. Tonight was going to be all about eating ice cream to the point that she made herself sick. A big bout of crying and snuggling with cats while watching bad reruns on TV were also likely to be on the agenda. Maybe a glass of wine. And then maybe catching up on some much needed sleep too. It felt like she'd been running full-tilt forever.

Later that evening, the phone rang during a particularly stupid episode of *Mork and Mindy.* It was so bad that Tess had poured herself a second glass of wine. She grabbed the glass from the coffee table and threw the afghan off herself, dislodging John and Ringo from their warm spots. Both cats stretched and gave her the evil eye as she staggered over to answer the phone.

She couldn't decide if she was happy or depressed to find Luke on the other end of the line. She mumbled, "How are you?"

"I'm fine. Bea called me to let me know about the rental agreement. She wanted to find out if I could help with some last-minute repairs."

Tess tilted the glass back to suck down the last of her wine. "Yeah, today I signed my life away agreeing to get sued if someone falls or does something stupid while cleaning up or performing in a derelict theater. Oh, and on the way to Gleasonville again, I remembered why you don't like that drive. It sucks."

"Are you okay?" Luke paused. "You sound a little upset."

Tess flopped into a bar stool and rested her forehead on the cool counter, looking down at her feet. "I've messed up everything. Bea and Margaret…and all these people are counting on me. I don't think I can pull this off."

"Why not?"

"It's going to take a labor force of thousands to make the Grove fit for any human occupancy. And we have twenty-four hours. Then the dress rehearsal. Then the show. There's just no way. When are we supposed to sleep?"

"You'll work it out."

"Yeah, like I worked out things with you. I'm batting a thousand here. I just want to go to bed. And maybe throw up first."

"Tess, hold on for a second."

"What? I'm feeling kind of barfy here."

"I've been thinking."

"Great."

"We need to start playing on the same team here."

Tess lifted her head. "What team? Is this you telling me you're gay or something? That's just perfect. The absolute pinnacle of a supremely crappy day. I wish I could say it was the first time, but I can't. Why do men suddenly confront their sexuality after dating *me?* I mean sure, everyone knows that there are a few gay men in musical theater, but not you *too*. Could my love life possibly be any more pitiful?"

"What? *No*. I was talking about *sports*, not sex. You're missing the point."

"What point? You'd better make it quick because the porcelain throne is looking more appealing all the time. Ice cream and wine are a bad combo."

"I believe you. What I mean is we need to compromise. I miss being with you. Here in my boring, clean apartment, I realized how tired I am of being by myself. It's only been a couple days, and it's like the light has gone out of my life."

"Was there a storm? Poor Barney. That dog can't get a break."

"Not the electricity. I mean the light is you."

"Huh? I'm a light?"

"Once this job is done, I want to come back there. I'll hire a maid or something. Preferably one who likes cats."

Tess sat up straight. "Wait. I get it. You're saying the light is me *metaphorically*. That's so sweet. Are you serious about this?"

"Completely. And I'll help you with the theater. I might be able to talk a couple guys I know into helping. When is this twenty-four hours you've got to clean and fix the Grove?"

"We're renting the theater Friday and Saturday."

"So clean-up day is this Friday?"

"Yes, so it's ready for the dress rehearsal on Saturday at ten. The show is that night."

"Okay. Got it. Technically, we've got a little more than twenty-four hours. I'll take Friday off and drive up Thursday after work. Is that okay with you?"

"*Okay*? It's not okay. It's fantastic." Tess clapped her hands together. "Oh my God, you're my hero. I think I love you."

"Good. I feel the same way."

"What?" Tess immediately sobered up. "What did you say?"

"I think I love you."

"Wow. And by wow, I mean a whole different kind of wow. I think Crazy Tess might be right this time because my heart says it's true. I love you too."

Chapter 12

Let's Put on a Show

At the full group meeting the following Wednesday night at the gift store, Tess made an impassioned plea for everyone to practice, practice, practice, so they'd be ready for the dress rehearsal. And if they could help clean the Grove on Friday that would be dandy too. People looked a little shell shocked, but a few promised to help clean.

Thursday night, Tess had no rehearsals, but she was standing around in the living room practicing her own lines when, right on schedule, Luke walked through the front door. She threw her notes onto the couch and threw herself into his arms. Barney strolled by, heading for the kitchen.

Luke kissed her and dropped his duffel bag on the floor. "I need to bring in my tools, but first Barney needs his dinner."

Tess turned to look at Barney, who was sitting in the kitchen doorway looking stern. "I guess so. Did you bring wood and other mysterious construction and repair goodies?"

"I've got some leftover materials here, and the guys are driving up with more tomorrow morning." Luke smiled. "They'll be here pretty early. Which means for you, *very* early. Bea said Aaron was dropping the key off with her at eight, and the plan is for us to be waiting at the door of the theater to get in."

Tess put her arms around his neck, gave him another kiss, and bounced on her tiptoes. "Hurry up and feed your dog and unpack because I need to show you my latest costume ideas. I'm pretty sure you're going to like what I've come up with now."

He nuzzled her neck. "I'm sure I will."

The next morning, the alarm clock went off at six, and the earsplitting noise almost gave Tess a heart attack. With the exception of her trips to Los Angeles, she was a big believer in arising when you woke up naturally and that alarm clocks were wicked devices. Luke grabbed her hand and dragged her out of bed. "Rise and shine. We've got work to do."

Tess fed the cats and stumbled downstairs, following the scent of coffee. Luke looked disgustingly awake, and Tess clutched her hands around her mug. Cleaning was not among her top ten or top ten thousand things to do, so she wasn't looking forward to the day's activities. But after a shower and another cup of coffee, she was mildly more awake and resigned to her fate. Only with a serious caffeine infusion could she face the horror of cleaning twelve-year-old dust, desiccated gum, and soda off the floor of the Grove. With any luck, when they turned on the electricity, the whole place wouldn't explode like a seventy-year-old grenade.

Barney barked furiously at a knock on the door. Tess gestured with her mug. "Who is harassing us at seven thirty in the morning? Good dog, Barney. You tell 'em. Make them go away."

Luke placed his hand on her shoulder as he walked by, shushed Barney, and continued to the door. He opened it and an enormous burly man with gray hair and a red baseball cap slapped Luke on the upper arm and said, "Get moving you lazy dirt dog. The boys are all here. Let's get to it."

Tess stood up and walked into the living room. Outside the window were ten or twelve pickup trucks chock full of men in the cabs and lumber hanging out the back. She looked at Luke. "How many guys are out there?"

"I'm not sure everyone is here yet," Luke said as he leaned to peer out the window. "Tess, meet Hal. Hal, meet Tess. Hal and I have known each other since I was a little kid."

Hal said, "Luke said you played *Annie* at the Grove. God, I loved that show. Even made me sniffle a little too. Look at you all grown up. It's like Alpine Grove old-home week here." He turned to Luke. "So, hey, slug, let's move it. We've got some FNGs here that don't know their heads from, yeah, never mind. Nice to meet you, Tess. We'll see you over at the Grove."

"The truck's loaded. I just need to grab my toolbox." Luke pointed at Tess. "Could you put Barney's leash on him? He's gonna be pretty excited to see some of these guys."

Hal walked back to the row of trucks and leaned in the window of an old brown Chevy to talk to the driver.

Tess said, "What's an FNG?"

"New guy."

"What does the F stand for?"

Luke went to the pass through and scribbled a note that he pinned on the door. He grinned at Tess. "I think you can guess, but how about if we just say it stands for 'fascinating.' I'll pin this on the door, in case there are any FNG stragglers."

Tess wasn't sure how fascinating these guys were, but as she walked outside with Barney, Tess tried to calculate how many were in the trucks. Maybe thirty or forty? This was far more than the "couple of guys" she'd expected.

Luke, Barney, and Tess got into the truck, and she reached over Barney to tug on Luke's work shirt. "How many people did you call?"

"In construction, it's almost like there's a phone tree because everyone knows everyone else. So suppose someone gets a job or even hears about it through the rumor mills. That guy knows who to call for electrical, plumbing, excavation and so forth. It's a fairly close-knit community. Some of these guys know me from Dad's company and some from Gleasonville. I've known Hal and some of the other guys for years, but they called people they knew too."

"Is this going to cost us millions of dollars in labor?"

"They're volunteering, but we have to buy them beer and pizza. And some of them might end up sleeping in the living room and downstairs bedroom. The fact there's only one bathroom could be nasty though."

Tess laughed. "Good thing you're hiring a maid. I know pizza and beer are good, but even free food isn't *that* motivating. How on earth did you convince so many people to do this?"

"I said it was for a good cause. But I also described the show and what I'd seen of your act. I pointed out that seeing you in your costumes is something they might not want to miss."

Tess turned to look at the convoy of pickups. "That guy in the truck behind us is gorgeous. Is he one of the FNGs?"

Luke checked the rear view mirror. "That's Trevor, and yeah, he's a pup. I'm sure Hal talked him into this because

Trevor's his youngest kid. Probably wants to keep him out of trouble."

"Do you think Trevor would be willing to be *in* the show?" Tess smiled lasciviously. "Like maybe with his shirt off?"

Luke laughed. "Is Crazy Tess having another idea?"

"Oh, come on. Can't you see it? Hot half-naked construction workers soliciting donations in toolboxes and five-gallon paint buckets? It's totally in keeping with the theme of this show. If we can find twelve hot FNGs, maybe we can do a calendar fundraiser too. Do you think Trevor would be willing to take off his shirt and prance around the stage?"

"Trevor's maybe nineteen or twenty, so I think if you're in costume when you ask him, you'll have no problem convincing him to participate. He might drool on your outfit though."

Once they got to the theater, Bea unlocked the door to let in the crowd of workers standing on the sidewalk. She raised her eyebrows at Tess who shrugged a silent *I had no idea* in response.

After everyone was inside, Luke showed the construction crew around, explained the scope of the problems, and started telling them what to do. Tess had never seen him work with anyone else, and it was sort of surprising to discover that he was an incredible taskmaster. Who knew? At home, working by himself, he was quiet and methodical, but when given a work crew, he sure knew how to keep them busy. Some were assigned to repairs and some to cleaning.

Tess helped with the cleaning program, which gave her an opportunity to talk to Trevor about her idea. He was agreeable and even unbuttoned his work shirt so she could check out his stomach muscles. Tess grinned and said in her Duchess Fifi diVine voice, "Oh yes. With those abs, you'll do quite nicely. Quite nicely indeed."

When everyone took a break for lunch, Tess sat in the theater seats next to Luke who was eating one of the sandwiches that had been delivered by the deli near the H12 motel. The owner of the deli, Betsy, was in one of the skits in the show and had volunteered to provide lunch for the cleanup and repair crew.

Tess took a bite and leaned back in the seat, looking at the ceiling. "How's the roof doing? Those huge beautiful beams aren't going to fall off and kill the audience tomorrow, are they?"

"The roof needs help, but the tarp will keep everyone dry for the time being. The beams are basically just decoration. I've got a crew up there working on the structural stuff so I think you're safe from a cave-in."

Tess sat forward. "I never asked before, but were you a general contractor? Is that what you did for your dad?"

"Sort of."

"What does that mean?"

"Well, after his stroke, I ran the company, not the jobs. It was different. All bookkeeping, billing, and payroll. Before that, I did work as a general contractor, although no one ever called me that. Dad was always the boss. But he wasn't around a lot, so I did what needed to be done. You could say I had the job, but not the title."

"I've never met your father. What's he like?"

"The life of every party. Everyone loved him at work." Luke shrugged. "But he wasn't necessarily the guy you'd want in charge of a job site. He wasn't much for details. And there were accidents that I think shouldn't have happened. But when you're fourteen, who's gonna listen to you or even believe you?"

Tess put her hand on Luke's. "I guess I knew it before because of the work you did on the house, but you really know what you're doing. I don't know how I can ever thank you enough for all this."

"Once the show is over and you're not so busy, maybe I could help Crazy Tess think up a few creative ideas."

Tess giggled. "Why yes, I think maybe you could."

~

It was a long day of working, but by the time everyone left the Grove, the theater was in significantly better shape than it had been. It wasn't restored, but it was no longer scary either. Luke said that the electricity and plumbing were functional, and they'd made a lot of repairs to shore up or block access to areas that were falling apart.

The best news to Tess was that the stage was fine. She'd taken a few moments to walk around backstage while people were working on getting the curtains to work again. When she stood in the middle of the large wooden stage, she closed her eyes and let the memories wash over her. The Grove would return to its former glory. She could feel it.

After eating an astonishing quantity of pizza and drinking many cases of beer, the cleanup party ended and various workers from Gleasonville went back to Oak Street to crash on the living room floor. Barney was in heaven having so many people around to pet him, play with him, and slip him food. By the time the show was over, Tess knew there would be absolutely nothing to eat at all in the house. It was like being invaded by a starving plague of enormous locusts.

Luke and Tess retired to the bedroom where the Fab Four were loudly expressing their discontent about the late dinner. Luke flopped face down, spread-eagled on the bed with his feet hanging off the end.

By the time she was done feeding the cats, he'd fallen fast asleep. She nudged him, and he rolled over. Tess grinned. "I think this is the first time I've ever seen you so tired. You might want to take off your shoes though."

He propped himself up on an elbow and gazed down at his feet. "We worked our tails off. Tomorrow, I've gotta get over there early to work with the sound crew and make sure the electricity doesn't fry in the middle of the show."

Tess twined her fingers through the curls at the back of his neck. "It will be worth it. I promise."

"It already is. This is the most fun I've had working in years." He pulled her down to him and wrapped her in his arms. "Thanks for giving me the opportunity to work on a job with soul."

"Why don't you keep doing it?"

"Doing what?"

"Being a contractor. Not just excavation. You're really, really good at getting stuff done. I had no idea. But you are."

"There was some bad blood when I shut down Dad's company. Employees were pissed."

"Given the turnout today, I think a lot of people must have gotten over it."

Luke looked into her eyes. "Hal said more or less the same thing."

"I love it when I'm right." Tess grinned. "You don't have to build skyscrapers. Can't you just hire subcontractors when you need them by calling around with the phone tree you told me about? You could restore old houses like this one. Or be a building inspector. Do kitchen remodels. Or something else. Whatever you want. You have incredible skills."

"I suppose I could do something different."

"Think about it." Tess stroked the stubble on his chin. "But first, take off your shoes and get some sleep. We've got a big day tomorrow."

The next morning, Luke slipped out of bed at some point when Tess was still asleep. She heard noise from the many people downstairs getting ready to head back to the Grove and approximately seven thousand trips up and down the stairs as they visited the bathroom. Tess pulled the covers over her head because there was no way she'd let any man other than Luke see her this early in the morning. The cats clustered around her since they probably felt the same way. There was far, far too much testosterone in the house.

At the sound of the bedroom door opening and closing, Tess pulled the sheet down and gratefully took the mug of coffee Luke handed her. He sat down on the bed next to her. "We're taking off now, so I'll see you at the rehearsal. If we're lucky, the microphones will work."

"I'm sure between you and Fred, you'll be able to fire up all the music and lights we need. Have you heard any of his roadie stories yet? Being the sound guy for that band sounded, uh, interesting."

Luke laughed. "Yeah, he's shared a few tales from the tour bus. One of Hal's buddies is an electrician too. We'll get it figured out. People are bringing by all the backdrops and props too, so when you get there, you need to tell us where to put everything."

"I will." She set her mug on the nightstand and put her arms around his neck. "I'll be all dressed up and ready to rock the house."

"I know you will."

Tess spent the morning gathering her costumes and makeup together to take down to the Grove. She had no intention of putting on full stage makeup until the show, but she did need to get her costume changes laid out in groups so she could go backstage and do quick changes between acts.

When she got to the Grove, she moved into full-on producer mode and barely had a moment to think. Then at ten o'clock, she put on her stage director hat and gathered all the performers in the first couple of rows to give them a pep talk.

She spread her arms wide toward the back of the theater. "I want you all to look at what the people of our little town have accomplished. For the first time in a decade, there's going to be music and fun and laughter here. You all should be so incredibly proud of everything you've done to make this happen. I know we haven't all been able to perform together until today, but that's okay. Now that the big day has arrived, all you have to do is remember everything we went over in rehearsals individually. This morning is all about getting the lighting and sound right for your act."

She pointed at Fred who was running wires across the stage. "That man you all know as a mild-mannered bar owner and bartender has mad sound engineering skills, and he's going to help get you wired up with microphones. We'll run through all the acts, and then you all have a few hours to decompress before the big event."

Tess clasped her hands together. "The main thing I want you to remember is that this is all about having fun. There aren't any drama critics in the audience. This is about raising money and making people laugh. Most of you haven't seen the other acts, but I have and they're fantastic. You're going to love it. And don't worry about getting everything perfect. If you screw up, you won't be the only one. I'm sure I'm going to screw up. But it's okay. The trick is to just keep going, no matter what happens. Like they say, the show must go on. And the last thing I want to say is thank you from the bottom of my heart. For putting your time and your energies into saving this theater. I know you all are going to bring down the house—hopefully not literally. Give me five minutes to get into my costume, and we'll get this show on the road."

Everyone applauded and Tess took a bow. "Let's do this thing."

The dress rehearsal ended up being hysterical and Tess laughed so hard she was practically crying and struggling to spit out her lines.

When Fred was trying to find a place to attach the microphone onto Maria's skin-tight outfit, Maria said, "Just do it. You're not going to see anything you haven't seen before."

Tess giggled at their banter. It was obvious that Fred and Maria knew each other rather well. Although Tess had seen all of the acts at rehearsals, people had set aside their inhibitions and let the creative, weird sides of their personalities out. Crazy Tess was definitely among friends, and she couldn't remember the last time she'd had so much fun before a show.

At the end of the rehearsal, everyone hugged and said the traditional *break a leg* before going home. Tess told everyone to tell their friends to come. The show was actually close to being sold out. The campaign to boycott the show had consisted of one letter to the editor in the newspaper, which apparently had been ignored and drowned out by all the great word-of-mouth marketing from performers and volunteers. If the show did sell out and they filled all five hundred and fifty seats in the Grove, they'd be well on their way to making the down payment.

After everyone left, Tess sat on the edge of the old wooden stage with her legs dangling down. She gazed out at the theater in front of her. The worn red seats were still ripped, and the walls had peeling paint and chipped plaster, but it would come back. Tess felt like she'd come back too.

She stood up, stretched out her arms toward the nonexistent audience, and warbled, "There's no business like show business," a song she'd performed in *Annie Get Your Gun* right before the theater had shut down. Her voice increased in intensity, and finally she was singing the song with a level of gusto even the ghost of Ethel Merman might have appreciated.

After Tess finished the song, she heard a single set of hands clapping behind her. Luke put his fingers in his mouth and gave her a wolf whistle that made her laugh. "I thought you'd be gone by now. Aren't you tired?"

He came over and wrapped her in a hug. "I'm never too tired to listen to you sing. I wish my dad could come to the show. He'd love it."

She put her arms around his neck. "I hope I get to meet him sometime."

"I'll take you for a visit. Even though my dad and I don't always see eye-to-eye, I bet you'd get along great with him, particularly if you sing."

"I sing when I'm happy and it looks like I might be doing more of it."

He removed her hands from his neck and held them his. "So I was thinking about something."

"Uh, oh."

"I'm thinking I might not want to go back to Gleasonville for a while."

"How long is a while?"

"Maybe never. I talked to Hal and some of the guys again, and they claim there's a lot of work up here if I don't limit myself to excavation."

"Interesting. What are you saying?"

"I'd like to work in Alpine Grove, learn more about rehab and restoration, and stay at the house. With you. If that's okay. Well, assuming we can find that cat lover to clean the house."

Tess pulled him to her, put her arms around his waist, and rested her cheek on his chest. "It's better than okay. I'm sure we'll find someone. The Fab Four are adorable."

He tilted her chin up so he could look into her eyes. "Ready to get outta here?"

She grinned. "Sure. I need to eat something and mumble my lines a few more times before the show."

"Okay, Mumbles. Let's go home."

~

Tess and Luke walked into the theater, which was bustling with activity in preparation for the show. He pulled her to him, wrapped his arms around her and gave her a smoldering kiss. "I have to go check on electrical stuff. Break a leg."

"Thanks. Go make sure the theater doesn't burn down."

She gave his hand a final squeeze and turned to go up the steps to the stage when she ran into Maria.

Tess smiled. "Are you ready?"

"I was born ready," Maria said as she put her fist on her hip. "But I have a question for you. I'm guessing you have a dog, don't you?"

"No, I don't. You saw my act at the dress rehearsal, didn't you? It's not a lie. When you have four cats, you're officially a cat lady."

"So you didn't board a dog at Kat's kennel and meet that unbelievably fine-looking man?"

"Luke and I went to high school together, but we hadn't seen each other for years until I met him on the road when I was delivering printing to Kat. He also did some work out at her house a little while ago."

"Hmm. Interesting."

"Is there something wrong?"

"So, seriously? You *really* don't have a dog?"

"No, but Luke does."

Maria pointed an accusing index finger at her. "A-*ha*! I knew it."

"Knew what?"

"It's part of a long tragic story related to my own status as a cat lady and the sad state of my love life." Maria's eyes widened and she grinned. "But this gives me hope. I just need to find a man with a dog."

Tess smiled weakly. Maria was a little eccentric. "Well, good luck. I need to get my makeup on. Shall we head backstage?"

Maria clapped Tess on the back. "Right there with ya, girl."

Backstage was bustling with people, and everyone was practically buzzing with nervous excitement. As Tess put on her heavy stage makeup, she reveled in the unique energy of people about to perform on stage.

Finally, it was show time and Tess walked out to the podium at the side of the stage and picked up the MC's microphone. She was decked out in her full Duchess Fifi diVine outfit, which included a skimpy leather top, pink ruffly skirt, black fishnet stockings, a huge pink feather boa, and an extremely tacky rhinestone crown.

The crowd started clapping, whistling, and yelling as Tess vamped across the stage waiting for them to settle enough for her to be heard. She started off with the lecture about how this would be an adults-only performance and that it was for charity. The show was all in good fun and part of the larger mission to save the theater.

She turned and waved at Trevor to indicate he should prance across the stage and put the sign for the first act onto the easel. The act was titled "Only You," and Maria strutted on stage with an economy-size box of Twinkies, turning to check out Trevor's rear view. She fanned her chest with her hands, and at the round of applause, she bowed, and pulled a Twinkie from the box. She held it up in front of her, cradling it lovingly in her hands.

The music began and she lip-synched "Only You (And You Alone)," a song originally made famous in the fifties by the Platters, none of whom were likely to have seen a Twinkie, much less crooned to them. But Maria did a convincing job of suggestively portraying how much Twinkies could thrill her.

When she was done, applause rang out in the theater, and she threw the rest of the Twinkies out into the audience who snatched them up with enthusiasm. While stagehands set up a couple of props, Trevor trotted out with a new sign for the next act, which was called "No Tell Motel."

Jon and Annabelle stood behind a makeshift counter with a gigantic basket sitting on it that said, "Take one or more than one."

A couple looking to rent a room had a conversation with Jon and Annabelle while Zack, dressed like the Hamburglar, slithered in and grabbed a silver foil package out of the basket. He flamboyantly showed his condom prize off to the audience and ran away. Several more people went through the same routine, and then Kat walked by with the giant brown dog Linus, just as Jon and Annabelle were explaining how the motel didn't allow pets.

After the skit was over, Tess came back out and did a short monologue about George Carlin's list of bad words. After reciting the monologue and the versatility of a certain "f" word that can be a noun, verb, adjective, and adverb, she paused. "There's another "f" word that has a lot of uses, my darlings. And that's word is…*flamingo.*

The audience laughed, and Tess continued, "Oh sure, you think it's funny now, but I dare you to yell the word flamingos. Try it. You'll feel better."

The whole audience yelled "flamingos" in unison as Tess crossed the stage, waving her feather boa in front of her. "See! I told you. The word *flamingos* throws people off. They don't know what to do with it. So suppose you're in a bar and a guy hits on you. Yell *flamingos*. He won't know what to do with it, maybe think you're nuts, and the bartender will give him a dirty look. Or if you're in a revolving door and you're embarrassed because you were checking out a guy's butt so you missed the exit, just yell 'flamingos' really loud and go around again. Or when you're at the grocery store and the clerk asks, paper or plastic, yell 'flamingos.'"

"And with that, I give you the next act, which is about a different kind of animal." Tess returned to the podium and waved to Trevor who strolled across with a new sign for the easel, which said, "AGAA."

Kat walked on to the stage with Linus and told the huge hairy dog to sit. She said, "Good dog," and he wagged his tail. She said, "Stay," gave him a treat, and left the stage, passing by four women dressed like the Village People. The women stood on either side of the dog and sang about adopting dogs from the AGAA to the tune of "YMCA." Linus looked on and wagged during the chorus when they encouraged people to "Adopt your dogs from the A-G-A-A."

When they were done, the women bowed and exited the stage with Linus. Next was another skit related to the glacial speed of the Alpine Grove post office. The problem was that the postal employees were actually aliens bent on driving people slowly insane by forcing them to stand in line.

When the skit was done, the house lights were turned on for intermission. While people stood up, stretched, and chatted, the merry band of shirtless FNG construction workers walked around collecting money in their paint buckets.

After the stage was set up again, the show resumed. Tess did her version of "Let's Get Physical," and Zack performed his song from *The Rocky Horror Picture Show*. Both of their acts were even more well-received with musical accompaniment than they had when they'd performed a capella in the gift store. The racy costumes also inspired a great deal of hooting and hollering from the audience.

The publisher of the newspaper, Ward Tucker, did a skit with Bea, reading the local news as announcers for a fictitious station called KAGL, which proclaimed it was all local gossip, all day, every day, about everybody.

Margaret and Jan did a skit called "Encounters with Moby Dick," reading passages from books that could be interpreted differently by modern audiences, particularly given the inflections.

The next act featured Joe from the road department, playing a guitar and harmonica medley called "A Farmer's Love Affair." Behind him, Tracy was dressed up as Little Bo Peep and a parade of others were dressed as cows and sheep dancing with her.

The stage was darkened while they cleared the props, and Tess came back out, standing in the middle of the stage with her head bowed holding a microphone in both hands. When the lights came up, people laughed because she was dressed in a pink baby doll nightie and huge fuzzy slippers with cat faces on them.

She lifted up a foot to show off a slipper and said sadly, "Don't laugh. When you have four cats, sometimes you end up talking to your slippers." Then she crooned a song about pussy cats that, depending on the interpretation of the phrasing, could be perfectly innocuous or exceptionally filthy.

The audience was roaring and when she was done, she said, "We cat ladies are misunderstood." Maria voice whooped from the audience, "Speak it, girlfriend."

Tess left the stage, and a group of large grizzled men in tights, pink tutus, white tank tops, and boxer shorts tromped onto the stage. Trevor put a sign on the easel that said, "Hunker Up to the Barre." The men skipped, twirled, and leaped around the stage to Tchaikovsky's *Nutcracker Suite*. People in the audience started cheering when they stood in a row arm-in-arm and kicked like the Rockettes.

After the large men scampered off the stage, Tess came back out in her Duchess Fifi outfit again for the last number. She opened her arms to the audience and said, "Thank you all for being here and helping us save this historic theater. Now I want you all to stand up and dance. It's time to get into the Grove."

The music swelled, and Tess launched into a rendition of Madonna's "Into the Groove" from the movie *Desperately Seeking Susan*, replacing the words *the groove* with *the Grove*. People jumped into the aisles and started dancing and singing along as the construction workers collected more money in their paint buckets.

As the last lyrics faded away, Tess waved all of the performers onto the stage. They held hands and bowed repeatedly as the audience screamed for more.

After the final bow, everyone hugged and danced on stage as the audience continued to applaud. Tess looked out at the front row where Luke was standing, clapping madly with everyone else. She blew him a kiss, and he grinned and gave her a wolf whistle in response.

Tears were running down her face, destroying her makeup, but Tess didn't care. The show was a success, and the entire night had been like a magical dream come true.

Chapter 13

Favorite Things

The next morning, Tess and Luke slept in late. Tess was looking forward to a lazy Sunday to completely decompress from all the stress and adrenaline of the last few weeks. The phone next to the bed had rung far earlier in the morning than either of them were willing to deal with, and Luke reached over and unplugged it. When he went downstairs to let Barney out, Tess just rolled over and went back to sleep.

Much later, Luke poked at her back. "Are you ever going to wake up?"

She rolled over and stretched her arms out to wrap him in a hug. "Maybe. I'm hungry."

"And you want coffee."

"That too."

"For that, you have to get out of bed, you know. The phone has been ringing downstairs. You might want to check your messages."

"Leaving you and this warm cocoon isn't appealing at all."

Luke kissed the tip of her nose. "I think your fans want to talk to you."

When he moved to get up, Tess grabbed his hand. "Wait. You said I have *fans*."

"I did. Lots of them. You had that audience eating out of your hand."

"I've never had fans before." Tess sat up. "I had an agent who grudgingly put up with me. A few directors who tolerated me even though they thought I was weird. Hollywood producers and casting directors who sneered at my lack of credits."

"I thought you vowed never to set foot in Hollywood again."

"I did because I was giving up performing."

Luke put his arms around her. "I believe I pointed out quite a while ago that you don't need to be in Hollywood to be an actress."

"I know and that was sweet. But I didn't believe you. I felt like I needed Hollywood's permission."

"Permission to do what?"

"Perform." Tess shook her head. "I'm not explaining this very well, but I felt like needed some type of validation from directors or producers. If I only could get enough screen credits, then I'd be a real actress. But it doesn't matter what they think. What matters is what the audience thinks."

Luke grinned. "And as last night showed, the audience loved you. Well, except Trevor, who's not in love. He's in lust because he's horny. I swear he almost tripped over his feet putting that first card on the easel."

Tess laughed. "He managed to pull it together without hurting himself anyway."

After they went downstairs and Tess had coffee, she pressed the Play button on the answering machine. The first message was from Bea who said, "I'm sorry it's so early, but I was too excited to wait any longer. Margaret came over to the house last night, and we counted up the receipts. Holy moly, the show earned more than we could ever have hoped for. Call me as soon as you can."

The next message was from Zack, who said that a bunch of people had told him that they missed the show and wanted to see it. A couple of other people she didn't know well, but sold advertising to also left messages saying they'd heard about the show and wondered if there would be another performance.

Luke leaned on the counter and sipped his coffee. "So, do you think you can do it again?"

"Of course I can. But we need the down payment first."

"From what Bea said, you might be close to having it now." He set down the mug. "Put an article in the paper that says, buy a brick, and we'll give you another show."

"You're pretty good at this whole marketing and fundraising thing."

"It's human nature. The people who missed out are pissed about it. Everyone's talking about the show, and they didn't get to see it."

"I'll call Bea. I bet I could convince the performers to give it another go. Even if a few people drop out, I had other people ask to be involved after I had the lineup. So I have understudies."

"Sounds like you've got it all figured out."

Tess walked into the kitchen and wrapped her arms around Luke for a hug. "Thanks for being here."

"I live here."

She looked up at his face. "And that makes me happy."

"Me too."

Chapter 14

Epilogue

Several weeks later, Luke, Tess, and Barney got into the truck to head out to the Wag On Inn boarding kennel. Tess was in the middle next to Luke, and Barney rode shotgun, poking his nose out the window.

Luke drove north of town to the back roads that led to the kennel, and they passed the spot where Tess had dumped her car into the ditch on the side of the road.

Tess put her hand on Luke's on the steering wheel. "I forgot to ask. Did Old Yeller survive?"

"Yeah, Joe told me that they had to overhaul the engine, but the patient made a full recovery."

"That's a relief. I hate sad endings."

Luke turned down the long driveway that led to the kennel, and Tess gazed at the enormous cedar trees that lined the winding gravel drive. They parked in front of the kennels where a group of people and dogs were standing. Kat, Joel, and Zack were there, along with an extremely tall woman with long straight dark hair. Tess now knew she was Zack's girlfriend, Sara, who taught at the local elementary school.

Tess grabbed Barney's leash, and they both got out of the passenger side of the truck. She grinned at Zack, "How's my favorite sweet transvestite?"

"Glad I don't have to wear that outfit too often because it chafes in places I don't want to discuss." Zack looked down and tugged on his jeans.

Sara rolled her eyes and smiled at Tess. "It's nice to see you again. We're off to visit my parents, but my dog Holly and their cat don't get along."

Kat walked over and ruffled Barney's ears, "Welcome back. I bet you and Holly will like each other." Barney wagged his tail and lapped up all the attention.

Tess handed Kat a folder. "This is all his information from the vet. The main thing is that he's afraid of thunderstorms. If we forgot anything, Tracy from the vet clinic has a key to the house because she'll be stopping by to take care of the cats."

Kat nodded. "Luke told me about Barney's storm phobia. If we have a storm, I'll bring Barney inside the house so he can curl up in the bathtub."

Luke said, "He's really good in the house."

"I'm sure he is, but now that the kennels are done, we've been trying to keep the boarding dogs out here. It doesn't always work out though. Some of the little dogs are spoiled and kind of lose their minds, so they end up in the house with me. When I let them be 'special dogs,' they get to hang out in my office." Kat shrugged. "Joel isn't too excited about that, but I think he's getting used to it. I do charge more for the special dog service, and he likes that part since we got the new car."

Tess said, "Lucky you. I hate my car, but I can't afford a new one. Worst purchase ever. I was so set on a *new* car, and I wish I'd put more thought into it instead of walking onto the lot and just buying the first thing I saw."

Kat smiled. "I'm glad it's not just me because that's what I would have done. Joel created spreadsheets and there was math. Lots of math. It was horrible, but worth it in the end."

"Spreadsheets?" Tess said.

"Don't ask," Kat said. "When does your flight leave?"

Luke looked at his watch. "Yeah, we should get going. It's a red-eye, but who knows what L.A. traffic is going to be like."

"At least on the other end, New York is the city that never sleeps, so it doesn't matter when we get in," Tess said.

"We'll be back for the big Grove extravaganza when the theater officially changes hands," Luke added.

"The closing is on June 1. I'm so proud of us for beating the deadline. Poor ole Aaron didn't know what to say when Bea called and said we had the money." Tess giggled. "When the guy saw the second performance of the Grove Groove, he probably realized he could actually make money with that old building after all."

"Hey, a deal's a deal," Luke said. "But there's still a ton of work to do to fix it up and restore it. That roof can't stay tarped forever. I'm hoping to find out more about plaster repair at this trade show. A bunch of renovation and restoration outfits will be exhibiting."

"There are more old houses out East I guess." Tess gestured toward Zack as she said to Kat, "Zack knows about this, but we're starting a theater troupe. Our first show will be *Oklahoma.* If you're interested, you should try out."

Kat frowned. "Uh, no thanks. Walking Linus onto the stage is about all I can handle. The idea of actually speaking while on stage makes me want to crawl into a hole and never come out. Kind of like Barney in the bathtub."

"After the Grove Groove, I had a bunch of people call me who wanted to be involved in future shows. I had no idea." Tess shrugged. "I mean I knew that there was a group years ago, but now there's a whole different set of people that have moved to Alpine Grove and like to perform. Singers, actors, dancers. It's amazing."

Kat repeated that it would be some time just this side of never that she'd willingly get on stage, so Tess let it go. They all said their goodbyes, and Luke and Tess got into the truck.

As they wound down the driveway back toward the road, Tess leaned on Luke's shoulder. "I can't believe I finally am going to New York. This is going to be an amazing trip. I can't wait to give my regards to Broadway."

"I'm guessing Crazy Tess might have a few choice words too."

"I'm sure she will."

Thanks for Reading

Thank you for dedicating some of your reading time to *The Hound of Music*. I hope you enjoyed the adventures with Tess and Luke. I'll be writing more books that will feature Kat, Joel and various other residents of Alpine Grove who bring dogs to the boarding kennel, so keep your eye out for the next book in the series.

If you would like to be notified by e-mail when I release a new book, you can sign up for my New Releases e-mail list at SusanDaffron.com.

I know that not everyone likes to write book reviews, but if you are willing to write a sentence or two about what you thought of *The Hound of Music*, I encourage you to post a review at your favorite book vendor site or share a message with your social networking friends.

If you would like to share your thoughts about the book with me privately, you can reach me through the contact page on the SusanDaffron.com web site.

I look forward to hearing from you!

~ Susan C. Daffron

Acknowledgements

Writing a novel is never easy and I'd like to thank my husband James Byrd for his support and encouragement throughout the publishing process.

I'd also like to thank my alpha and beta readers for their eagle-eyed reading and great feedback:

- James Byrd
- Nancy Brashear

The Hound of Music is very loosely based on the story of how the community stepped up and saved the historic Panida Theater in Sandpoint, Idaho. Three women, Susan Bates-Harbuck, Jane Evans and Laurel Wagers, who were affectionately called the "Panida Moms" worked to save the theater from demolition in 1985.

As far as I know, back in the eighties, they didn't have a show like the Grove Groove, but another Sandpoint nonprofit, the Angels Over Sandpoint has been putting on the Sandpoint Follies since 2002. Performed at the Panida, the organizers warn people that it's "rated R for racy, risque, and ridiculous," but it has raised boatloads of money for the Angels and sells out within days every year.

I was a truly terrible backup singer in the Follies one year, but it was a tremendous amount of fun. Special thanks go out to Kate McAllister, aka Sandpoint's very own "Queen Kate," who has performed and been the MC of the Follies for years. Over lunch, on a gloriously sunny day, she regaled me with lots of hilarious stories about the show.

About the Author

Susan Daffron is the author of the Jennings & O'Shea series and the Alpine Grove romantic comedies, a series of novels that feature residents of the small town of Alpine Grove and their various quirky dogs and cats. She is also an award-winning author of many nonfiction books, including several about pets and animal rescue. She lives in a small town in northern Idaho and shares her life with her husband and three really cute dogs.

www.ingramcontent.com/pod-product-compliance
Lightning Source LLC
Chambersburg PA
CBHW020347120726
47904CB00002B/487

* 9 7 8 1 6 1 0 3 8 0 5 7 7 *